HARBOR IN THE TEMPEST

ARIANA ROSE

This is a work of fiction. Names, characters, organizations, places, events, and incidents are either products of the author's imagination or are used fictitiously. Any resemblance to actual events, locales, or persons living or dead are entirely coincidental.

© 2024 Ariana Rose

No part of this book may be reproduced, or stored in a retrieval system, or transmitted in any form or by any means electronic, mechanical, photocopying, recording, or otherwise, without express written permission of the publisher.
This book is licensed for your personal enjoyment only. This book may not be re-sold or given away to other people.

Playlist

Vertigo – U2

Let Me Take You There – Max Styler Feat. Laura White

With Or Without You – U2

Desire -U2

Strangers In The Night – Frank Sinatra

I Still Haven't Found What I'm Looking For – U2

Don't Know Why – Norah Jones

Don't Go - Nat King Cole

Beautiful Day – U2

Adagio For Strings – Samuel Barber

I Believe In You – Michael Bublé

One – U2

The Little Things You Give Away – U2

All I Want Is You – U2

Sometimes You Can't Make It On Your Own – U2

Gravity – Sara Bareilles

For the women who chase their dreams,

and the men who love them

more for it

Love IS infinite

Chapter One

Elijah

An August weekend in New York City, two more weeks before Labor Day. I should be in the Hamptons with the rest of my family, but I just can't seem to find the motivation to go. It's not that I couldn't drag my ass out there. I just have no desire to be on. I've been putting on a brave face, as my grandmother would say, so much lately that I don't know what it's like to turn it off.

Whoever said time heals all wounds should have their heads examined and told to fuck off. Time doesn't heal anything. All time does is give you more time to think. Think about what went wrong, all the signs you should have seen, and every way you could have done things differently. None of those things are what I *want* to have in my head. This is why I do two other things to feed a distraction.

The first is being a workaholic. I work so much, and I work so long. My family thinks it's nothing new. This is what I do. This is what *we* do. When I refer to we, it's my grandfather, my father, and me. I'm the third generation in our marketing dynasty, as my grandfather jokingly refers to it. Pops, as I call him. Andrew Sawyer founded AnSa International with his own two hands and a shit ton of blood, sweat, and tears.

He was born after my great-grandfather returned from World War II. His family had it hard. My great-grandfather sometimes worked three jobs so my grandfather could go to college. Pops had that entrepreneurial spirit at an early age. He always had some idea or angle to make something work. Gran always said he could talk anyone into anything and make them believe anything was possible. Not only did he talk the talk, he walked the walk.

By the time Vietnam rolled around, Pops had married my gran, Evelyn, and had my father. He was in grad school, which also saved him from the draft. He doesn't talk about that time much. Many of his friends were lost over there. I think that's what led him to gearing our company toward nonprofits. It was his silent way of giving back in their honor.

My dad, Jackson, followed right behind him. To hear Gran tell it, Dad came out being my pops's mini-me. He wanted to be just like him. Follow his path and share in his dream.

That leaves me, Elijah Jackson Sawyer, the third generation. I feel like I took the long way around. I fought against the family norm for a while until I found my way. I went to Boston College instead of NYU so I wouldn't be treated like a legacy. I could be just me. The only place I felt comfortable with the legacy was the fraternity, Alpha Psi. Pops was an Alpha; Dad was too. Being an Alpha gave me an instant brotherhood I could count on for life. Even now, those relationships are still important. Crucial even.

After BC, I got my master's at NYU, my father's alma mater. Dad was right. NYU was part of the best time of my life. Not only was it because I was beginning to enter the business fold Pops created, I merged my life with Tori.

Victoria Jensen and I met in our junior year at BC. It was a Halloween party that went way wrong. Some asshole thought it would be funny to let off a few smoke bombs inside our frat house. That asshole was later determined to be my best friend, Wes Taylor. Needless to say, when the smoke alarms started blaring, the fire department showed up, and the party was over. Tori broke a heel coming down the stairs to get out. I broke her fall at the bottom. That was the first time she looked at me as her knight in shining armor, as she called me.

One date turned into two, which eventually turned into living together. The day we graduated, we drove to her parents' Alexandria, Virginia, home to get the last of her things. I sat in her parents' living room, while she was packing her last box, and asked their permission for Victoria's hand. For all the nerves I had, permission was easily granted. Tori's mother even gave me her mother's two-carat, European-cut diamond to propose with. I fidgeted the whole ride back to New York. Even though she denied it, I think she knew.

We walked into our apartment on Central Park West and, after flopping down on the bed, we rolled to watch the lights come up over the park and shine through her ring. Her answer was yes. I thought I honestly was living in a dream. We instantly were grown-ups.

We were the perfect complements to each other. Her dream job was to work anywhere around Vera Wang. There were so many fashion magazines on our coffee table I thought the glass would break. Her creative spirit kept my logical side in check. We were married on June 13, 2009. My parents' summer home in the Hamptons was the perfect backdrop. Tori looked like a beautiful princess as she walked toward me. Her ball gown absolutely sparkled in the sun. The only things that shone brighter were her eyes and her smile. I always thought her smile could change the world.

I was wrong.

The first five years of our marriage were like our honeymoon in St. Lucia. The city rose like the mountains around it. We conquered every peak together. The waters were still and calm like us until, or unless, we created a playful splash, which was how we made love. Even now her laugh still rings loudly in my ears. The way her legs would slide up and down mine. The little gasp before she came in my arms.

When her smile left is when our world changed. I know the moment it happened. Tori had gotten a job as an assistant to one of the top stylists on the Eastern Seaboard. It was around award season as I said the words that I was ready to be a father. Her *words* said she was all-in, but her actions said otherwise.

She began working late, later than I did. She seemed to have her period all the time or she was too tired otherwise. We went from having sex every day, sometimes twice a day, to next to never. It should have been a red flag. I ignored it. I had to ignore it. If I looked at it too hard, it might break us apart.

Now I stare at the bed we shared, I don't see the laughter or Tori wrapped around me. I see something else. When you catch your wife fucking her boss in your bed, it never leaves your consciousness, no matter what.

I was frozen. He turned his head back toward me as he was driving his cock into her. Instead of doing the right thing and leaving, he rolled off and stayed on my pillow at her side, while she confessed she never wanted children and we'd grown apart in what we wanted a long time ago.

I had no words for what I saw or heard. I walked out and sat at the dining table with my head in my hands as he finally got dressed and left. She kept saying the same bullshit monologue over and over again. It sounded so fucking scripted. I finally put my hand up to get her to stop. The next words were, "I don't love you like my husband anymore" and "I'm leaving".

She packed two bags inside of ten minutes and was gone. The rest of her things disappeared the next day while I was at work, and her keys were left on the kitchen counter.

That was two years ago. I haven't changed a thing other than the bedding since she left. I left the walls just the way Victoria decorated them. She was better at it than I ever could have been. I could have changed it, but that would have erased the one last thing I had of her besides the ring on my finger.

So, because of my commitment to my work, people think I sleep in my office. They aren't totally wrong. Sometimes I do, but it's getting easier to go back to my apartment most nights. Wes still wants to slash the art pieces Tori bought as well as take a hammer to the tile backsplash in the kitchen. He thinks that going the male version of *Waiting to Exhale* is going to solve something. It's not.

I started going to the gym every day, twice a day. I didn't know how to get rid of everything I was feeling. In some of my night reading, when I couldn't sleep, the American poet, Edna St. Vincent Millay, seemed to speak to me. She was quoted as saying, "Where you used to be, there is a hole in the world, which I find myself constantly walking around in the daytime, and falling in at night. I miss you like hell." That right fucking there was it. I spent the first two weeks of my new gym routine punching a goddamn heavy bag. That only rattled my arms. I needed something that rattled my whole body. That leads me to the number two thing I do when I don't want to think. I run.

My father jokes I should qualify for the Boston Marathon by now. He's probably right, but that's not why I need to do it. I need to because the ache of my legs takes away the ache I feel in my chest still. The burn in my lungs eclipses the memories burned into my brain.

Six point one miles is the distance of the full loop around Central Park. I've become well acquainted with every tree, bush, and inch of pavement. I've also found breaks from the running when it just gets too physically hard or doesn't work to get rid of the feelings.

Today it was raining. The water falling from the sky were large cool drops. They felt so good. The only true bummer of the deal was missing my weekly chess game with a man I met on my first run after Tori left. I nearly ran David down behind my tears. I don't cry often. It's not something I normally do. In order to make it up to him, I offered to play a game.

His grandson had just passed away, so I feel it was divine intervention that we found each other. I could talk to him without bias, pretense, or judgment. I could also give him the companionship he needed. That's something that was both selfish and selfless in the same breath. Without David, on this day, I chose my indoor sanctuary. I stop today's loop at the Central Park Zoo. Some choose to watch the big cats or even the majestic bears. I chose the Polar Circle and my favorite animal, the penguins.

Penguins mate for life. That's how it should be. That's how I want to be.

For my eighth anniversary with Tori, I adopted one of the Gentoo penguins for her. Unfortunately, she left the week before I could give the certificate to her. I named him after the U2 front man. So, I go and sit with Bono on my own. I can always spot him quickly, even without looking for the little band around his foot. He's a connection I can have. He's still a constant. Once in a while, he'll waddle up to the glass and just hang there. I'd like to think my little buddy knows who I am.

I'm running for all the reasons I usually do today and one more. Wes Taylor only takes the word no for so long before it becomes irrelevant what you say. He's tried to get me to go out for the last six months. Nothing crazy, at least nothing crazy by his standards. He insists I need to simply wade into the meeting other people cesspool, even if I don't drink.

I could always hold him off with a work function or a good nondescript prior engagement. However, tonight, he said there was a surprise waiting for me, so my normal *no* or *not tonight* could fuck right off. He's even going to pick me up so I can't back out.

When he lets himself in with his key at nine thirty, I've got U2 on and up, nursing a beer as I pregame on my couch. "Jesus Christ, will you fire up?" Wes tosses my jacket at me. "I won't push the clear potential we'll see tonight at you, just don't be a Debbie Downer, would ya please?"

"Look, I'm going along with this because of your shitty insistence. Don't push it by forcing me to like it."

Our circle of friends has had *Top Gun* style call signs since I can't remember when. It would be easier to say how long we haven't had them. We've either taken a persona or had one given to us. For better or worse, Wes and I are Maverick and Goose. He's the cocky shit, and I'm the cleanup wingman specialist. They couldn't have been better suited for anyone else.

Crowds, especially when I feel like this, are not my friend, even when we go someplace I know like the back of my hand. Rooftop 93 has been a hangout for us for years. We've celebrated birthdays here. We've celebrated work milestones. Now, tonight, I suppose Wes sees this as another milestone of sorts.

The last of the happy hour crowds mingle with that of the crowds coming in post-show, concert, or simply after an early movie time.

Laughter from every corner of the bar hits me like knives behind my eyes. I slide the pads of my fingers along the undersides of my glasses before I grab my IPA and head for the outdoor patio.

The sun has moved deep behind the skyscraper lined skyline leaving the deep rich blues of an impending night sky a comfort to the headache that seems to find me this time of day like clockwork. Small bites of several conversations invade my ears from behind as I look off in the distance toward my apartment.

I could hear what seemed to be a first date. When I turn around with my drink in hand, a college age pairing is huddled on one of the benches along the cocktail rail. She looks like she's hanging on his every word with a smile or a touch of her fingers across his arm.

Just behind them is a group of young male professionals, well, younger than me at least. They're settling into a healthy debate on who is a better goalie all time, Patrick Roy or Marc-Andre Fleury. I look down into my beer and shake my head. "Flower. Every day, all day," I whisper to the suds in my glass.

"Are you shitting me? Have I taught you nothing?"

As I look to my left, the cocky figure of my friend, Sam Roark, in our group he's call sign Iceman, leans against the rail next to me. "You've taught me anything?" I ask.

"At least humor me by getting it right. How the hell are ya, Goose?"

I offer Sam my hand, but we go in for the hug anyway. "I'm good. I'm here anyway."

"Fuck. Sometimes here is all a person can do."

"What are you doing in New York? I thought you were sticking pretty close to home."

"Home is a great thing my friend. It hadn't felt like home in years. I can thank Lucy for that."

"I think you can thank yourself for a lot of it too."

"Yep. Three and a half years. I was an idiot for not getting here sooner."

"Congrats. Seriously. It doesn't bother you being around it?"

"Nah. Not when I have everything in the world to stay sober for."

Sam Roark was adopted into the friend group about ten years ago. Wes has always introduced me to many of his clients. Sam seemed to fit more than others. His carefree attitude and our mutual love for hockey were instant connectors. It didn't matter where he was playing, Tacoma or Seattle, we've supported him from the East Coast. And when he hit rock bottom, he needed us to help keep him grounded and support him even more. Now it looks like he might have been brought in as a closer to help Wes get me back in the game.

"So did Wes fly you in as a part of his save Eli campaign?"

"Look, he's your brother for all intents and purposes. Even if he's a tool."

"I heard that," Wes hollers across the crowd, barely skipping a beat in the conversation he's having with a beautiful blonde server.

"Why do you think I said it?" Sam fires back. "Make yourself useful and get me a coke. Get this one another of whatever he's having. We all know he wallows in beer and not the hard stuff."

"Fuck off." I lightly shove him before heading for the bench along the rail that's just opened up.

The not so gentle grip on my shoulder shows me that Sam followed my lead. "Wes worries about you."

"He doesn't need to. I'm fine."

"Yeah. I can see that. I remember how many times I told my parents I'm fine, or coaches, or teammates, or even Lucy. I was never fine."

"Well that's you. I'm fine. I *am* fine."

"Look, I have no business being a therapist. Hell, I'm the last one you should take advice from."

"Good," I bark, "then don't offer any."

He pauses for a moment as if he'd changed his mind. I was wrong. "Wes and I corner the market on asshole. It's not a good look on you. Too pretty."

I set my nearly empty glass on the floor between my feet before my right thumb and index finger do the dance they've been trained to do. They massage forward and back over the wedding band, which is still part of my daily existence.

Sam knocks the side of his closed fist over my knee a couple of times. "You don't have to apologize for what you're going through. No one can understand but you. However, I've done enough solo and group therapy to recognize what I'm seeing."

"What is that Dr. Roark?" I joke with a small smile.

"Fear. You're afraid to let go of what was and afraid of what could be. Let me guess you go to work, not just because you have to, but because it's safe. You stay locked up in your palace in the sky because then you don't have to face what might be without her even though you're without her no matter what.

"Listen, brother, fear is the enemy here, not what's beyond it."

"Jesus, Ice, have you been reading some of my philosophy books?"

"No. I know all too well about fear. Don't forget, Lucy left me too. The only difference is, I did it to myself. You didn't. I have a feeling you still think after over two years that if you'd done something different she'd still be here or, and I hope this is not the case, that she might still come back."

"I know she won't come back."

"Would you want her if she did?"

He asks the question so quickly I don't have time to come up with a sexy response. It only needs one word. "No."

"Exactly. No. Tori was not and is not good enough for you. I won't tell you all the reasons why, you already know. I won't call her all the names I want to now, it won't help. She took your past, don't let her take your future. Fear is the enemy. It's the only one that matters."

We sit next to each other for a few minutes in silence while the city and the crowds around us remain a constant buzz. Every time I've seen Sam since he got out of rehab four years ago, he seems stronger and more put together than I've ever known him to be. "I'm proud of you. I don't think I've ever told you that."

"Thanks. I'm proud of myself, too." Sam winks with a smile. "Now that the sap is out of the way, how about you let the Eli I know out for just a little while. I'm not saying make Wes the wingman for once, just have some conversation. I might even have a project for you."

"You want to talk shop? Shit. I thought we were going to get back into the Roy/Fleury battle."

"You'd lose that battle all day every day. I'd like to take my Foundation, well my family and I would like to take it, to the next level. I'd like to get your take on it and see what potential there is."

"With the new Iceman, I think the sky's the limit."

Ariana Rose

Chapter Two

Elijah

Sam gave me a lot to think about, nearly too much. After I left Wes and Sam to close it down, I didn't want to go home. For once, I don't want an endless night at the office either. I choose to leave the city and head to my parents' house on Long Island. They're supposed to be in the Hamptons, so I can raid the kitchen and portions of the liquor cabinet with the cat alone.

I punch in the code for the gate, and the slow slide of the metal is all I can hear out the window besides the crickets. I'm glad I left the noise of the city. I need a quieter environment to think about all the things the boys pointed out in their clear, and not always tactful, ways.

I put my car in park outside, behind the fourth stall, my usual spot. I sit still with the car running when the motion lights finally pick me up. Just to their right is the basketball hoop.

I played every day as a kid. I teased my dad for not taking it down after I left. My sister, Hayley never picked up a ball for even one single granny shot. Dad said he didn't mind leaving it. He also said we weren't done playing, the grandkids would use it. He wanted a four-generation game of H-O-R-S-E.

I want that too. Very much.

I'm glad our nearest neighbors are a good quarter mile away. Two o'clock in the morning basketball usually is frowned upon. I just want to live by myself in that dream for a minute or twenty. I can tell it's going to be well past four before I'm even settled enough to consider sleep.

Kicking off some of this funk with a bit of sweat doesn't seem like a bad idea. I pop the lid on the outdoor gear bin. All three balls are in there. We have my father's ball from when he was a kid. He refuses to retire it. He said it's like an old glove and has tons of miles still on it.

He's deep into tradition, as is my whole family. We have ways of doing anything and everything. I didn't appreciate it when I was younger, but then as Tori and I were going through all the wedding planning, I saw the personal value away from the business side. It was a warm blanket Pops and Gran handed to Mom and Dad, who handed it to Hayley and me. I guess I was looking forward to passing the tradition on to the next generation.

I hold my father's old basketball in my hand and dribble it a couple times. He's right, this does feel right even with all the miles it has. I dribble a couple times on the right, then shift to my left, then shoot. The vibration of the hoop echoes into the night with the crickets.

I slide my jacket off, laying it across the hood of my car, as I pull my keys and phone from my pocket. After setting them down, I open an extra button on my shirt, trying to go full-out. I'm dodging and dekeing like King James is chasing me. I'm hacking the hell out of my dress shoes, and I don't give a shit. I miss more shots than I make. I'm kind of enjoying the pounding I'm giving my body. I go for a layup to the left and try to grab the rim.

"Still can't go to your left, Eli."

I grab the ball and slap it. The shadows give way to my father. He's got his NYU half zip on with his flannel pajama pants and his hard-soled slippers. His hands extend to me to toss him the ball. "What are you doing here?" I ask.

"I live here." He smiles.

"I mean, I thought you were in the Hamptons. Shit. I'm sorry I woke you."

"Your mother has a charity function in the morning, so we opted out, and you didn't wake me. I was night owling it with my newest World War II depiction. I saw the light come on and went to check the security footage. This is late even for you, Son."

"I was out with Wes. I'm supposed to pass on a hello from Sam Roark too."

"Sam? That's a name I haven't heard in a long time. Where did you see him?"

"He was in town I think partially as part of a two man intervention for me and to ask for our professional help with his foundation. Wes forced me to go out with him tonight, so Sam met us after Wes finally got me out the door."

"You were out in the city with them but ended up here?" Dad gives the ball a couple of bounces, taking a couple steps forward. "Want to talk about it?"

He bounce passes the ball back to me like he who has the stick talks. Instead of saying what's on my mind, I set the ball down on the cement drive, sitting down on top of it. "Do I ever?"

"No, which is why I'm finally asking." My father comes slowly to my side, placing a soft hand on my shoulder, and crouches down. "I've never been through what you've been through. I can't imagine it. What I do know is your mother and I love you very much. We hate to see you in pain. We'd like to see you finally be able to get through to the other side."

I sigh. "I don't want you both worried."

"We're parents. It's what we do. Do you think your gran and pops have stopped with me?"

"No. I know that's not how they're built."

"Neither are we, Elijah."

"Am I that bad? I mean, I know how bad it is in here," I run my fingers through my hair in a subtle hint to my head, "but how bad does it look to you?"

"If we didn't love you and know your true nature, we likely wouldn't notice. You're excelling at the office. Eli, you were built for our business. I couldn't be prouder if I was able to be. That's never been the issue, even in the darkest days. Your mother and I would just like to see you open your heart back up again."

"Seems to be the theme of the evening."

"What do you mean?"

"Wes tried to hook me up with any number of women tonight. He seems to think a string of women in and out of my bed is going to fix everything. I'm not sure Sam agrees with him. What Sam did say is take the time I need, just not too much. He's become very philosophical as he's gotten sober. Sam said he would have been fine alone, but his reunion with Lucy made him better. He thinks I'm wasting time and that's not good."

"I've heard what they think. I know what I think. What do *you* think?"

"I left all the pseudo pressure to go get a round for us when Wes was, well, trying to get me laid. I ended up standing next to a woman at the bar. We had a nice conversation for a few minutes. She was an attorney for Blake and Bloom. She gave me her business card. Dad, she was beautiful, intelligent, well-spoken, and I had zero interest. I don't know. Maybe I'm just too broken."

"Eli, you're not too broken. Son, I know it's not going to be easy, but you're going to have to begin again. That will start when you allow the last piece of healing." He looks at my hands that hang between my knees. "Maybe it's time to take off your wedding ring."

I rest my head in my right hand as my left thumb rubs against my wedding band. "She was my penguin."

"No, Elijah. I know you don't see it right now, but your penguin is still out there. She will find you if you allow yourself to be open enough."

"I don't want our marriage, or my time with Tori, to be reduced to memories. If this ring is still on, it's still alive."

"No, Eli. That ended with her decision to walk away. Removing that ring won't make your time with her any less. You gave her all of you. That's all you could have done. Give yourself back to you."

I know they're right. Every single one of them. This ring on my finger and the way my apartment is fucking frozen in time are the only physical representations of what's left. "I don't want to throw it away like trash."

"You don't have to, and I'd never ever suggest that. Why don't you give it to me? I'll put it in my safe for, well, safekeeping. It will be here if you need the visual. I think you'll find after a while, you might even be able to let it go."

I flip my hand over and stare into the palm. My left thumb glides over it one last time. Over and back. Reaching in with my right index finger and thumb, I wind the ring back and forth, wiggling it over my knuckle until it frees. It's within millimeters of leaving the home it's had for over nine years.

My father's hand comes into view just under mine. He's holding it open, palm up. I let the gold and diamond ring drop, allowing it to fall into his hand. He gently closes it over the unbroken circle that became the circle of something very broken. Me.

"I'm proud of you."

The groove at the base of my finger is still visible. I slide my thumb over the skin that's just returned. "I feel naked without it."

"I think that's normal. I might have a solution to ease it. Come in the house."

"Nah, Dad. I should go."

"Elijah. It wasn't a suggestion. Stay here tonight. Your mother would relegate me to the couch if she knew I let you leave this late, especially after she finds out you'd been in the city with Wes. She loves him, but she's no fool regarding his... tendencies."

"You mean she knows he's a player and likes alcohol."

My father chuckles. "Yes, something like that. Grab your things. Bring the ball inside too."

"I'll be right behind you." I watch as he disappears into the shadows, where the motion lights don't catch, then I hear the door latch. After I rise off the ball, I give it another bounce or two before taking it in my hands. My phone and keys slide back in my pocket as I cloak my now bare hand with the jacket from my hood.

I don't want to watch my father lock the ring away. It would feel like the close of a casket. I'm well aware of how morbid that sounds in my head. I've had a lot of time to reread all of my philosophy books from undergrad to attempt to make logical sense of all this, because I can't look at the rest. I've spent hours seeking the origins of love, which led me to one of my current topics. Heartbreak.

I spent a year in the depths. I longed for and hated love in the same breath. I read about five variations of love. Kierkegaard looked at agape, or unconditional love, quite closely. This was the love I subscribed to.

This was the type of love that had always been my model. My parents and their parents before them. It was what I wanted, what I needed, maybe still do. It's unfortunately elusive and leads to very high highs but even lower lows.

Next in line is Jean-Paul Sartre. He wrote extensively on the subject. He delved into the need for both that "essential love" but paired with other love affairs. Tori seemed to have subscribed heavily to this theory, clearly. I couldn't spend too much time here or I'd never have left.

Nietzsche was bitter. His work entered my research about the time I was hitting my anger phase. Perfect timing! He called women "dangerous, creeping, subterranean little beast[s] of prey." I can't tell you how many times I slammed the covers of that book closed. I don't agree with his assessment of the fairer sex, but I did buy into the fact he felt one must be able to stand on their own two feet or they are incapable of love.

Long about this time is when I plugged in more at the office and subscribed to a lack of female company, unless it was family. The next read was a true favorite of mine, Aristotle. He was quite intrigued with the idea of love being based in friendship. I thought I had that with Tori. I supported her in every way I had available.

But it must be a two-way street. You should be each other's best friend. However, we're now also back to self-love. He said you're unable to love another without being a good self-lover first. If you can do well for yourself, you can do well for each other.

Lastly in my reading journey was the opinion of Judith Butler. She feels there should be a commitment, but one that is flexible and open to the ever-evolving human. For a long time, I blamed myself for not seeing that Tori's needs changed. She wasn't satisfied with just me. She needed more. Fine. Great. Just fucking tell me. You can't tell me the plan has changed without *telling* me the plan has changed. Fucking communicate!

All these looks at love kept coming back to the common denominator of me, myself, and I. So, I had to acknowledge the true heartbreak I was, and am, in in order to break free. I go back to Germany and Nietzsche. One of his enduring principles is that our suffering is what makes the pain so great, but the senselessness of it is what hurts the most.

Wes and Nietzsche would have been bar buddies. They have both offered the same sense and guidance. Victoria didn't leave because of me. She blamed me because she couldn't look at what she'd done. She changed and didn't tell me. She made the choice to step outside our marriage. She's still never owned her part, her *huge* part in our destruction.

She likely never will. It's not who she is anymore. In the same breaths I'm laying blame at Tori's feet, I need to take my own share. That's the other half of Nietzsche's introspection. I must look at my own issues and deal with them to hopefully be open to the next chapter in my life.

Dad turned the page for me. I just need to start writing.

Chapter Three

Elijah

The inside of my parents' home is mostly dark, as it should be at two thirty in the morning. There's the glow of the kitchen countertop lamp my mom always leaves on "just in case" for Hayley or me if we need it. I love that physical representation of "I'll leave the light on for you". It's love in the unconditional lane. I'm the luckiest son who ever existed.

The only other glow is coming from under the door of my father's office. The golden stream of light is creating a path for me. I hang my jacket over the stool at the breakfast bar as I walk past. Pushing father's door open farther, he's in his chair behind the desk.

That's the most comforting thing. I can't even count the number of times I've pushed that door open, and there he sat. Any time advice is needed, or consoling is the order of the day, there he'd be ready and waiting. I've always known there isn't anything I couldn't tell him. Our dynamic has changed with my age. We've gone from that place of parent/child to one of true friendship and mutual respect.

He's got a tumbler of amber sitting, breathing for me in front of my chair. His matching glass is in his hand. "I thought this might help you sleep. I know it does me."

"Thanks, Dad. I still feel bad."

"Don't. We haven't caught up much outside of the office lately."

"There hasn't been much to say."

"I doubt that very much. I have something for you, Eli."

I take a slow drag from my glass. My left hand makes no noise as my grip changes. The gap from where my ring once was shows off like a neon sign to me. The heat from the liquid burns from the back of my throat down into my chest. "What is it?"

"I consider it a passing of the torch. Your grandfather and I had a meeting before they left for the Hamptons yesterday."

"You did?"

"I have one question for you. Are you ready?"

"Dad, it's two forty-five in the morning and I've had a couple. English, please?"

"We'd like to announce to the board and staff as soon as we can, that Pops is moving to consultant, I'm taking his slot at the head of the board, and you will be our new president, effective Labor Day."

I lower the glass to rest on my thigh and stare blankly at my father. "I mean. Shit, Dad. Wow. I knew this would likely happen sooner or later." I run my hand up and through my hair. "Pops is okay, right?"

"Yes, he's fine. That's the point. He wants to hand it all over and transition to focusing more on your grandmother. I think she's been patient enough, don't you?"

I smile. "More than anyone I know. Mom's on board? This will change life for both of you as well."

"You're right. It will. You'll be key in that."

"I won't let you down, Dad."

He leans back, pondering what I just said. My father palms what appears to be a small box in his left hand before rising to come to my side. He settles his right hand on my shoulder. "You never have, Elijah. I feel like this is the right time to give you something I've been holding on to. You're the fourth Sawyer man to have been gifted this. I'm hoping it will remind you of family and give you an extra bit of strength for your next adventure."

I set my glass on the table to my left and open the blue velvet box as my father settles back on his desktop. The slow creak of the lid reveals my Sawyer crest ring. My great-grandfather gifted one to my grandfather, and he carried on the tradition with my father. It's usually given the day your first child is born.

"Dad. The ring? Really? I shouldn't have this yet."

"Yes, you should. I want it to be a symbol for you of the confidence I have in your talent, intelligence, and heart. I also want you to know I'm confident you'll have everything you desire in due time."

I pull the ring from its resting place and slide it on my left middle finger. The sterling silver ring emblazoned in blue with hints of black, gold, and red fits perfectly. "Cherches et tu trouveras," I repeat as I read the words engraved on my mind.

My father nods. "Seek and thou shalt find. Our motto. Although, I wonder, in this case I feel if you stop seeking, you'll find."

I down the last bit of my drink and palm the glass. The clear clink of my new ring replaces the one I'd hear with the old one. Now I know what he meant by a solution. As I rise out of my chair, my father joins me. He opens his arms, and I meet him in a comforting hug.

My father is clutch at saying just enough but not too much. "Thanks, Dad." His holding me a little tighter and longer than usual tells me he understands what I'm truly thanking him for.

As we step apart, he grips my shoulders. "Now off to bed. Your old man has had it."

"Yeah. I'm tired too. I'll shack up in the guest suite. Tell Mom so she doesn't freak out?"

"I will. Sleep in. She'll want to see you after her brunch."

"I'll stay into the afternoon. Good night, Dad." I shove my hands in my pockets and wander back toward the foyer, up the winding staircase to the second level. Closing the door quietly, I sit on the right side of the bed and fumble with the laces on my shoes. That tumbler with Dad sent me over the edge.

My shoes flop to the floor as I lie back on the bed. I stare up at the ceiling and try to soak in the quiet. I don't get a lot of that inside my head, and this bed is the softest thing I've ever lain on. I sigh so deeply I could sink through the mattress. The pillow next to me ends up getting wrapped in my arms as I turn to my side.

I'm too tired to screw with my clothes. Sleep is what I want and need. There's something about sleeping down the hall from your parents as an adult. You're drawn back into that sense of security they silently offer from the monsters under the bed or the dragons in the closet.

My dad offered me a shield tonight. He took the monster that's been plaguing me. I guess it's up to me to deal with the damn dragon.

Chapter Four

Elijah

Waking up a little hungover in the morning is always amplified by sunlight. It's a thing. I'm experiencing it right now. Each little ray of light is like a needle. If I were at home, the blackout shades would cover this quite nicely. I reach down and pull the blanket over my head.

Wait. Blanket? I open my eyes slightly to see the queen-sized weighted blanket from the foot of the bed pulled up across my chest. *Mom.* She even set a glass of water on the bedside table for me. I stuff my head back between the pillows and immediately fall back to sleep.

The next time I wake it's due to the bed bouncing on my left. "Time for lunch, Brother. Get your drunk butt up."

Fuck. Hayley.

"Hayles, Jesus. Could you give me a minute?"

"Mom's back and she wants to make you lunch. She sent me to get you."

"Bullshit," I grumble. "You offered. You knew I was going out with Wes last night and wanted to torture me." Hayley is my little sister. She is the definition of annoying, especially right now, but she's also someone I would take a bullet for without question.

She was the second person to see me after Tori left. Wes was the first. He called her. I hadn't moved in hours from the chair I sat in, waiting for Tori and her boss to leave, and it freaked Wes out. He knew if anyone would be able to reach me, it would be Hayley.

She's going to be a senior at NYU. She took a year off to travel after high school. Mom and Dad thought she'd never come back. I pulled her aside the day before she left. She promised me it would be one year off and then she would hit the ground running. She's never broken a promise to me.

She's much more self-aware than I was at that age. She knew she needed time. She knew she wanted to experience the world. She knew it would be better for her in the end. I've seen how right she was. Now I'm jealous I didn't do the same thing.

Hayley's going to slide into our art department as a junior designer after graduation. Her style is modern and fresh. She will be a key asset for her demographic moving forward. The fact I will now also be her boss is just icing on the cake.

She bounces one last time to settle against the headboard. "You're right," she giggles, "I did. Seriously though, you good?"

I push myself up so I'm sitting beside her, rubbing my hands over my face to try and clean out the cobwebs. "I'm all right. Wes insisted we hit Tao. I wasn't super into it, but going for a while was easier than listening to him whine because I said no again. Added bonus of going was Sam is in town."

"Sam? Really? Has he fucked up again yet? I will kick his ass myself if he makes Lucy cry again."

"Calm down. Jesus. Everyone's good. He's not the same guy you met. Anyway, the two of them were tag teaming me all night about moving on, finding a girl not for forever just for tonight type thing. Sam was more subtle about it. Wes was not."

She rolls her eyes. "Is he ever subtle with anything? How did you end up here though?"

"Yeah, he's like a sledgehammer, so no. End up here? Well, I was going to go home then my car just ended up in the driveway. Dad found me shooting hoops, and I wanted to stay actually. The city was too claustrophobic."

"I'm looking forward to going back to school and the city. I'll be closer so I can harass you more often."

"Remind me to change my locks and revoke your security access at the office."

She smacks my chest. "Shut up."

"Damn. Easy. Don't use your kickboxing kung fu on me."

"You're such a wuss." She reaches over and takes my hand. "Not gonna lie. I was happy your car was in the driveway when I got up."

"Thanks, Kiddo." I reach across my body and mess up her hair with my left hand.

"Ouch! What's with the brass knuckles?" She takes my hand and looks at it. "The Sawyer ring. When did you get it?"

"Last night. Dad thought it might ease the sting of taking my ring off finally."

"It looks good on you, Eli. You really took your wedding ring off?"

I shrug. "Yeah. I did."

"Don't shrug that off. It's a huge deal. I feel like it's been a weight on your soul. Weird if I say I'm proud of you?"

I gently brush her hair back and kiss her forehead. "No. I appreciate it. Now get lost. I'm going to shower quick and steal clothes from Dad."

"Yeah, don't need to see that. I'll let Mom know you'll be down in a few." She pats my hand before diving off the bed, closing the door behind her. The armoire in this room has Dad's workout gear in it, which is lucky for me. I grab a well-worn NYU T-shirt and some black joggers from the drawers before letting the hot water wash over me.

This shower is amazing. The constant rain down my back helps wash away some of the doubt from last night. Hayley is right. It is a big deal. It was weighing me down. I didn't realize how much until just now.

The pants I slide on are just a hair too short, but I don't care. I give my hair a once over with my towel before looping it over the bathroom door. As I wander the upstairs hall to the landing, I scratch through it to a fake style in some fashion. The smell of bacon and French toast smacks me in the face as I reach the end of the stairs in the foyer.

The kitchen is bustling as I lean against the doorframe and just watch. My mother should have been a chef. She's cursing at the pan on the stove under her breath. Then she bends to check the bacon in the oven. I don't know why she worries so much about her culinary skill. I have, and will, eat anything she puts in front of me.

Lily Gilbert Sawyer. She's the toughest and softest woman I've ever known. She commands all your attention, respect, and admiration. She came from money, but you'd never know it. She's spent her entire life giving back, whether it was to her friends, the community, or her family. She's always come last on the list.

She is the gold standard all women need to live up to for me. There needs to be a fire but a gentleness. A willingness to put others first, but not at the expense of family. Her family is her everything. Where I look to my father as a mentor in industry, my moral center lies in my mother. She's a true hero.

The breakfast bar is perfectly set with dark placemats on the white quartz. Water, juice, and coffee are at every place setting with a cloth napkin to match. I slide into my former usual spot at the counter and get my first issuance of caffeine for the day.

"Good morning, Mom, or afternoon I guess it is at this point."

"Did you sleep well, sweetheart?" she asks.

"I did, until Hayley came in as the bouncing alarm clock."

"Oh dear," she giggles. Her giggles can stop time and make the grumpiest human smile. Seeing her happy is one of my favorite things. I hate that I've not contributed, but subtracted, from her joy the last couple of years.

"I was a little more colorful internally than that, but it works." I reach up to kiss her cheek as she puts a full plate before me. "You didn't have to go all out, you know. I'm not picky."

"It's not often I get to cook for you anymore, so I wanted to take advantage."

"There are only two places set. Where's Dad?"

"He's still out playing nine with your grandfather. I'm sure the round went long because they had a late tee time. I'm glad you chose to stay here. I would have worried about you driving so late."

"I know, Mom. That's part of why I stayed."

"I think I can guess the other part." She slides into the seat to my left and sets her hand on mine. "Your new ring suits you."

"I hate that Dad had to break tradition because of my situation."

"Elijah, your father didn't have to do anything. That ring gift has always been based on a major life event. I'd say this qualifies. I would never wish ill on Victoria, however, I'm very glad her last hold on you is gone."

I set my fork down, laying my other hand over hers. "When I went to bed last night, I wasn't so sure. I woke up here and felt... better."

"That's what I like to hear. Knowing you've been in pain and powerless to help has been hard."

"You know I didn't want you to take any of this on personally, Mom."

"Just as you know I can't help it. My prayer for you is that you can move forward and remember the lessons you've learned."

"Once I figure out all the lessons, I'll let you know."

Chapter Five

Elijah

Late brunch with my mom was great. She, like my father, doesn't linger too long on the hard topics. They know I need to process and follow my own schedule. Wes interrupted our afternoon with a text barrage when he realized I didn't go home last night.

He was hopeful I'd taken a dip in the shallow end, but I doused that flame right away. I didn't know he'd been paying attention to the conversation I had with the attractive attorney. He was absolutely paying attention. I let him down gently by sharing that I'm leaving my wedding ring behind.

There was a fist pump GIF followed by a yes with several s's. It's a signature move of his, so I wasn't surprised his joy came like that. Mom hung my suit jacket, shirt, and dress pants from last night on a hanger, and I grabbed my slides from the pool house.

Before I leave, I find Mom and Hayley on the patio by the pool with an early afternoon cocktail pitcher between them.

"Can I trust you both with a pitcher of whatever between you without Dad here?"

Hayley rolls her eyes. "God, Eli. It's a weak margarita mix. I think we'll be fine. I'm helping Mom with a secret project, so that's our focus. This is just a bonus."

"Hayley Jo! Are you ever able to keep a secret?" my mother chides.

"You got double named so one, you're in deep shit, and two, it must be about me, so what gives?" I ask.

"Well," she glares a bit at Hayley, "since your sister partially let the cat out of the bag, I want to have a small gathering here at the house to celebrate the transitions at AnSa."

"Small gathering? Mom, do you even know how to do something small?" I tease.

"Elijah Jackson, I certainly do."

Hayley laughs. "Now who's in deep?"

I sit on the end of Hayley's chaise and pinch the back of her calf playfully. "You don't need to go to any trouble on my account, Mom. Seriously."

"It's not just about you, Eli. Your grandfather deserves recognition, and so does your father. It would be the department heads and their plus ones, a few family and friends. We can consider it an end of summer party, a bit into the fall school year. September, even at the end, is still so beautiful, and I thought it would be nice."

"It *is* nice, Mom," Hayley agrees. "Someone is just being anti-spotlight."

"I'm not being anti anything, smart ass. If this is what you want, Mom, and it's not too much trouble, thank you. It would be nice. Let me know if you need my help in any way. Just make sure there are plenty of eligible *nice* girls for Wes to talk to."

"No way, Mom! Do not set up a buffet for the man whore."

"Hayley, enough. A nice girl would do Wes some good," my mother scolds. "I'll do my best, dear."

I lean across and give my mother a kiss on her cheek. "I'm going to head back to the city. Tell Dad I'll check in with him tonight and see him at the office in the morning."

"I will, sweetheart. You're welcome to stay here more often if you like."

"I know. Thanks." I kiss the top of Hayley's head. "See ya later, Kiddo."

"Bye." She twists her fingers lightly around where my wedding ring used to be and winks.

"Be sure to..." my mother begins.

"Text when I get home. I know. I will."

After I pull out of the drive and onto the highway, I shut the radio off and power both the windows down. I rarely drive without music, but it feels good today. Instead, I just focus solely on what is just beyond the hood of my car and simply breathing. I need these seventy-five minutes to get ready to purge my apartment of "the former us" when I get home.

I walk in my front door with more determination on this subject than I ever have. The only thing is, I don't know where to start. I find myself staring at the walls of my apartment, frozen. I haven't got a clue how to make this place me.

A knock at my door snaps me out of my frustrated fog. I look out the peephole, and it's my neighbor, Lauren. She and her girlfriend of eight years live across the hall from me. They run an interior design studio together in Tribeca. She knew Tori too. We moved in within a month of each other.

I turn the deadbolt and open the door. "Hey."

"Hi, Eli. Sorry to bother you, but I'm making this chicken dish for dinner and ran out of butter. Can I steal some?"

"My fridge is your fridge. Top shelf on the right."

"Thanks. You're a lifesaver."

She runs past me into the kitchen in her tank, shorts, and blue fuzzy socks. Her red hair is wound in two sticks on the top of her head. Lauren stood by me through everything. She's like a bonus sister.

"I would've run down to the store, but I have to watch this like a hawk while it's baking."

"You know I don't care. It's fine." I can hear the refrigerator door close, then nothing. I turn toward the opening to the kitchen and Lauren is leaning against the wall staring at me. "What?"

"That's not what you wore out last night. I also know you didn't come home."

"Really? And how do you know that?"

"I had to run to the studio quickly this morning for some plans I'd left behind, and your car wasn't here."

"I ended up staying at my parents'. Last-minute thing."

"I see. Are you okay?"

"Yeah. I think so."

"You think so? Is it a, I need to go turn the chicken down I think so, or an I think I should take the chicken out I think so?"

"It's a do you have time to take on a side redecorating job I think so."

"Um, okay. Wow. Sure. For whom? Your mom?"

"Me. I want the slate wiped clean, Lauren. I just need help."

She smiles, slides over to me in her socks, and wraps me in a huge hug. "I've been waiting for you to ask. Stacey and I will bring some materials over tomorrow night, and we'll make some choices."

I can feel how truly happy she is, and it makes this next step even easier. "I'll feed you both. Chicken parm, okay? I know that makes chicken two nights in a row, but it's what I make best."

She shoves my shoulder a bit. "You had me at you'll feed me. I'll bring a white. See you at seven."

Ariana Rose

Chapter Six

Elijah

I don't usually sleep well on Sunday nights. It started with the habits I've formed over time, especially since being on my own. Sunday used to be our day. Tori and I would wake each other with leisurely sex that lasted well beyond lunch, then while she was showering, I'd make us a brunch so big we wouldn't eat the rest of the day.

We'd graze over that for an hour or so, then break off for a little solitude. I'd go for a double lap around the loop while she'd catch up on a couple hours of designing. We'd reconnect for dinner, if we needed it, and a movie that we'd sometimes watch and sometimes not.

This is the kind of repetition I never minded. I counted on it like the smell of the kitchen at my parents' house. Since she left, my new Sunday routine leaves a lot to be desired. The run is still an absolute staple. I'd never give that up. The homemade dinner and a movie have turned to takeout and my laptop at the kitchen table.

I've decided that being prepared on Monday gives me better focus. The downside to that, however, is my brain decides when, or if, I'm going to be able to shut down for the night. Tonight was different. The takeout and emails still happened, but even though I got up way later than usual, I crashed equally early.

My alarm goes off at five in the morning, and it feels like I've just gone to sleep. The light is on next to the bed, my messenger bag contents are cascading all over the left side of the mattress, and my laptop has tipped to its side. This is pure evidence of sleeping hard. I can't remember the last time this happened.

There are two emails I recall in the haze my brain is left with while I'm in the shower. The firm-wide email went out last night about the town hall today at eleven, announcing the upper management shift. The other was from my former academic advisor at NYU.

Professor Will Stone has elevated to one of my most trusted friends since I left campus. He consults for us from time to time on special projects as they arise, and in turn, I speak during his senior seminar every year. Will initially wanted me to come in to scare his students. After the first year, we've altered it to look at AnSa as an industry leader example. We have a lengthy question and answer session afterwards to address the needs of that particular class of students.

AnSa takes four interns from him each semester to give them the experience they need to take their first steps with the firm of their choice, whether in the nonprofit sector, in-house with a corporate giant, or part of a boutique firm with a smaller client roster. Each student is different. What they need is different. It's my way to give back and lend a hand.

My speaking date is next month already. Pops always says time goes by so fast. You blink and tomorrow is yesterday. I feel like that's a great way to describe our shuffle. I guess I was destined to be in the spot I am. I'm so grateful for the belief my father and grandfather have in me.

I don't want to take anything for granted, so when congratulations start coming my way during our board meeting, then in the town hall with our staff, it's humbling. There is genuine happiness, and if there is any doubt or concern, it isn't shown.

I will also leave Operations in a good direction. My right hand, Skye Vaughn, will walk into the vice president slot I'm vacating, and the chain won't be broken. This was the position for her from our initial interview five years ago. She's smart, tenacious, and will meet any challenge this role will toss at her with grace, kindness, and humility.

The knock at my door at the end of the day comes as no surprise to me. Board meeting days come with a check-in from my father at day's end. "Have a minute, Eli?"

"Here I was thinking you'd forgotten. Come in, Dad."

My father closes the door quietly. "I see the new title hasn't eliminated your sense of humor."

"Did you expect it to?"

"Never." Smiling as he sits, he asks, "How did you think today went?"

"Fine. I didn't hear anything to indicate otherwise. The Ops staff is thrilled I can't micromanage anymore." I laugh.

"Like you did that to begin with. They will move our offices mainly over the Labor Day weekend, and transition should be seamless for IT."

"I'm not worried for the most part."

"For the most part? Is there something I should know?"

"Nothing earth-shattering, Dad. I just have a request. Historically, the management of the interns is done in partnership with the VP of Operations and human resources. I'd like to continue to maintain the intern program with your permission."

"That's a tough load, Eli. You may have to travel more, and your meeting schedule will double. Are you certain you want to do that?"

"Dad, it's my favorite part. I like giving the kind of mentorship I had with Pops, you, and Will. I want to continue to pass it on. If it becomes too much, or I'm not an asset to the interns, I will gracefully hand the reins to Skye. Fair?"

"She's on board with this?"

"She is."

"Then I won't stand in your way. Just know I'll have to keep a background eye on things from a board perspective."

"I understand. I won't let you down."

"You never do, Son."

Two bottles of wine with a Monday dinner is a good idea, said no one ever. Lauren, Stacey, and I had the first one gone and the second uncorked before our meal even hit the table. I could have agreed to black walls for all I remembered by the time they laughed their way back across the hall.

What I do remember is I feel good about all the changes in here they suggested. I'm going all-out and replacing everything. New hardwood throughout. An area rug for the bedroom and for the living room. All the furniture will be switched out. Even Tori's backsplash masterpiece will go.

The one item that will stay and remain the focus is a contemporary painting by Dutch artist, Jessica Hendrickx, called *Angels and Demons*. For a long time, I looked at this painting as a symbol of darkness moving into light. Now, I look at it as one soul and everything contained in it.

It's hung in the bedroom since the week after Tori left. I bought it at a gallery opening we were supposed to attend together. It spoke to me, and after finding out what the title was, I was sold. On the nights I couldn't sleep, I'd stare at it, hoping to find an answer or comfort in it. I suppose in some screwed-up way it became a companion for me.

Lauren asked if she could move it to the living room and make it the center of the palette for that space. I agreed. I know she and Stacey will bring me back into the place. They said they could do it all in one weekend if I could bug out. They also decided they don't want me to help, and a finished surprise would be better in the long run.

I don't care so much as long as the memories fade, and I can get on with living. Wes would argue I made the choice to remain stuck. I could never convince him that sometimes what looks like simple sand and rock can quickly become mixed with one last component that will keep you stuck. Twisting that ring off my finger might do what he said it would. Set me free.

Ariana Rose

Chapter Seven

Elijah

Thursday before Labor Day, three thirty in the afternoon. That's when the questions come that I've been trying to avoid. "What are you doing for the holiday weekend? Are you going to the Hamptons?" I know my assistant only wants to know how to get a hold of me, but the anxiety these questions provoke must be written in red on my forehead.

She quickly says I can let her know anytime. I sit here thinking as she closes the door. *I'll let you know as soon as I sort it out.* The pros... Mom and Gran would love to have me there. It's all they've asked for the last two summers. I could allow Wes to drag me out to Southampton Social and finally shut up about it. I could be with my entire family all at once.

The cons... standing at the shoreline on the beach where I was married. Seeing those images play out over and over in my mind. I know in my head it's not worse than still living in the same apartment in New York, where I caught Tori in bed, but I can somehow reason that it is.

Fucking suck it up, Sawyer. I can hear Wes barking at me like he does. The words that stick, though, are those of my father and Sam. My father always encourages me to try. If it ends up not being right, at least no one can say you didn't put in the effort. Sam's take is simple. Fear is the enemy.

It's time to fully reenter the world.

I call Anna at her desk. First, I apologize for my reaction to her questions. Second, I tell her I'll be leaving after my last meeting tomorrow. I will be going with my family for the holiday, and lastly, I ask her to do something I normally wouldn't. I ask her to coordinate getting my motorcycle tuned and ready. I'll be taking it with me.

How Anna found a mechanic on such short notice I'll never know, but she's getting the biggest bouquet of flowers as well as a dinner for her and her husband for it. By the time I hit my parents' driveway to park my Tesla Model S for the weekend and send my bag with Hayley in her car, my 2018 Harley Heritage Classic with the Milwaukee-Eight 114 engine is blue, shining, and ready for riding.

Gran and Pops went up late yesterday and my parents left this morning. I swore Hayley and Anna to secrecy about going to the Hamptons for the weekend. If anything, I'll get to make Gran and Mom cry in a good way for once.

Even without riding it for a year, this bike purrs like a kitten... or roars like a lion, depending on who you ask. I secure my helmet and anchor my sunglasses as I wait for the gate to fully open. Once at the edge of the driveway, I angle left and get my bearings in the neighborhood.

This is not a skill you forget, but I want to make sure I feel settled before I open it up. By the time I make it to the 27 East, I'm ready. Nearly an hour atop this bike, full-out with the wind at my face, U2 is blaring via wireless to my ears. Even on random, it hits with the best of the best. "Vertigo." It drives with a beat that matches the roar beneath me.

I weave in and out of traffic as the minutes turn my brain off thinking of nothing but the music and the road. Once I get closer to the Hamptons, the traffic slows. It's a holiday weekend and the last one of summer. The bays will be packed.

My little over an hour trip takes more like two hours before I turn onto Three Mile Harbor Drive. My parents and grandparents built this house together in the mid-nineties. It settles across three and a half acres. We don't really have neighbors out here. We own the adjacent land as well. I remember coming here as a kid during construction. I couldn't believe the size of it.

I asked my dad why it was so big. He responded with a smile and a hand to my shoulder. He said this would be a family home for years to come. It was a place where we could all come to be together with children, grandchildren, and great-grandchildren. Legacy is a keyword to our family. That's their dream. Honestly, mine too.

I can hear the engine echo off the trees around me before I kill it in the driveway. I pull off my helmet and rest it behind me, after I slowly pry myself away from the seat. Your body is the one thing that loses its practice. I feel like I've done about a thousand squats when I settle both feet back on the ground.

There's no welcoming committee, so that can only mean I got here undetected. The front double door opens quietly. I can hear low chatter coming from the kitchen around the wall to my right. I'd forgotten how beautiful and warm this house is. The back of the house faces the pool and hot tub with a double height great room that features floor-to-ceiling windows. I can see my mother and grandmother curled up on the sofas in the morning with their coffees and books. Sitting silently but together.

Hayley rounds the corner and nearly plows me over with her water bottle and tennis racket in hand. I grab her shoulders lightly before she gives me away. She smiles even after I pinch the underside of her arm as I let her pass. I wait for the door to latch then move to the doorway. I lean against the entry and watch for a minute.

Mom and Gran have their backs to me. Mom is at her usual spot over the stove. It looks like she's boiling potatoes for her world-famous potato salad. Gran is at the sink washing and chopping a few random vegetables and fruits. I slowly unzip my leather jacket and lay it across one of the stools at the breakfast bar.

I listen to the exchange of their recipe differences on the potato salad. My mother is completely against mustard, and my grandmother, being more of a traditionalist, is all for it. "Need a third opinion?" I ask. They both startle, turn in unison, and squeal at the same time. "How are my girls?" They attack me with kisses to each side of my face. "Okay, okay," I laugh, "I take it you're happy to see me?"

"Happy doesn't begin to describe it, Elijah." My grandmother cups my cheek in her hand. Evelyn King Sawyer is the heart of this family. She's the first to a family function and the last to leave it. She's the most caring and giving woman. "I should want to smack you for keeping the secret though."

"You're not violent, Gran. Don't start now. Will I get to taste test, Mom?" I peer into her pot.

"That depends on how long you're staying," she says.

"I'm going to be here until midday on Monday." I lean back against the peninsula. "It was time to walk through the weeds so to speak. That, and my apartment is being renovated this weekend."

"Renovated?" Gran asks. "I thought it was beautiful as it was."

My mother comes over to my side. "First one step then another. Good for you, Eli."

"Did I miss something?" Gran asks.

"Evie," Mom says, "why don't you sit out in the sunroom with Eli for a bit? I can finish up here."

"Yeah, Gran. It's been a long time since we've been on a date. I'll bring us two glasses of rosé."

"The last time we had rosé out here, it wasn't the best news."

"Evie, this is," Mom adds. "The bar out there has some in the cooler."

I offer my arm to my grandmother. "Shall we?"

"I suppose I could make your grandfather jealous."

She wraps her petite hand around my elbow. I offer it a gentle pat as she leans into my arm while we walk. "I'm glad you never get too old to talk to me, Elijah."

"More often than not, you're where I go first."

"It's nice to hear that." I settle her on the couch before I grab our glasses of wine. "This sounds like it might be big."

"It's not as big as Pops finally being mostly retired."

"Don't say that too loud, dear. He's not fully accepted it or understands its meaning. Eli, if it's big to you, it will be big to me."

I hand her a glass to match mine, and we both take a sip before I continue, "I've had a few conversations with Wes, Dad, and a couple other friends. They've all been encouraging me for well over a year to take my wedding ring off. They felt it had been too long."

"I'm not going to be the one who will tell you what to do. The facts are, your divorce was final over eighteen months ago, and she left before that. You don't owe her to keep it on. I do understand your need to be ready."

"I know, Gran, and thanks. I ended up taking it off. Looks like I'm headed for a bunch of changes all at once, again." I shrug. "Seems to be the way things go for me."

"It's not just you, Elijah, it's everyone. I've learned over the years, in some cases, it's better that way. It may seem like turmoil at the time, but this too shall pass. It's a season turning over."

She's right. I know she's right. Feeling it is another. I hope that comes sooner rather than later.

The pride in my grandparents' faces at the dinner table could not be contained. My grandfather sits at the far head of the table with my grandmother to his right. My father sits to his left with my mother beside him. I take the seat next to my grandmother, at her request, with Hayley across from me. It is a formal picnic.

We sit with the sliding doors open to allow the breeze in and the sounds of the water rolling against the shore. I'm allowed to play grill master for the first time in my adult life. Count it as another in the line of positive changes placed before me. Fear is the enemy. *Sam Fucking Roark.* That's what I keep saying over in my head when the doubt creeps in. The longer I'm here, the more I laugh, the more I realize that's what it is. Everything else is an excuse.

Wes blows in like a storm around eight thirty as we're putting the food away and doing the dishes. He immediately begins flirting with Gran, which she loves. He gets a huge plate of food out of it. Evie sits on one side and Hayley on the other. He tells stories of his week and the two dates it contained.

Just like Wes, always with a story. I'm thankful he kept it PG for this company at least. I'm sure I'll get the unedited version later. "Ready for flight?" he asks after a wink to my Gran.

"Ready as I'm going to be."

Ariana Rose

Chapter Eight

Elijah

It's been a couple seasons since I've been involved in the Hampton club scene. We end up at one of our old favorite stomping grounds. It will be a softer spot to land for me, and Wes seems to rule wherever he's at. We pile in a rideshare from my family's home, and somehow Hayley convinces us to take her as well. She has several friends, along with other NYU students she knows, who are having one last party weekend before class begins next Wednesday.

Upon exiting the car, Wes is immediately shaking hands with security. *What a suck-up*, I laugh. We walk through the door toward the music, and everyone knows his name including the new chef, who is taking a tour through the patrons, and the owner. Hayley gives me a side-glance and rolls her eyes. I chuckle again and pull her close. She knows exactly who he is.

She wraps her arms around me and leans in. "No cockblocking tonight."

"Did you seriously just say that to me? That's an image I didn't need."

"I look hot, and I want to have a good time. Just let me have fun."

"I won't police you as long as you're safe and you go home with us at the end of the night."

"Deal. I'll text my code word in group to you and Wes if I need out of a douchebag scenario." She pushes up to kiss my cheek. "See you at two."

Hayley melts off into the crowd. I follow her white dress and blonde hair to the far bar. She's greeted with what appears to be a couple screams and definitely hugs. She's got her friends. It's time for me to settle into one of my least favorite pastimes of late. Being Wes's wingman.

I tap him on the shoulder and point to the bar farthest away from the direction Hayley went. I won't have to watch the swarm of guys around her, and she won't feel like she can't be herself. It's only eleven thirty, but this place is jam-packed.

Wes leans in. "What do you feel like? Beer? Crown and Coke?"

"Let's go with Crown. Tell them a tall."

A smile plasters over his face. "Eli came to play. Nice." He pats my back and pushes his way to the bar to order. I back out of the way and stand next to the doors leading to the patio. The more things change, the more things stay the same I've found. Being here is no exception.

Everything in the layout is just as I remember. The club is long and narrow. The DJ is strategically placed in the corner. He's doing a great mix so far. It's got that pounding house beat under any song you can think of from Beyoncé to an eighties classic from Madonna, both of which have played since we walked in the door.

There's enough light in the space to make sure you aren't falling over each other, but not too much so it distracts from the beachy nightclub atmosphere. Wes returns and sets my drink in one hand and offers me a shot for the other.

"Fuck. Seriously?"

"Look, man. I know it's a big deal for you to be out tonight. Just loosen up and have fun. A little Fireball never hurt anyone."

"Said no one ever." I look down at my two-fisted scenario, deciding to roll with it. "See you in hell." I clink my shot glass against his.

He smiles and winks. "Talk to me, Goose."

I laugh and we tip the shots back. Holy shit. That burns into my chest. I quickly chase it with my tall cocktail, as if I had any hope of putting out the flames.

Wes tries to shake his off. "Now that you're on your way to Chillville, let's find you a lovely lady to talk to."

"Jesus. You do the talking. I'll do the backup singer routine. I'm good at it."

"Fuck that. Have you looked around? There is so much potential here." A black-haired, petite woman walks by in a dark blue dress that is about as short on top as it is on the backside. She and Wes lock eyes. "Yep, *so* much potential. Last summer, I came here for some business meet and greet thing and had significant one-on-one time with a red-haired, suited executive. No one caught us. There's a private area outside. It's gold, man."

"Public sex at a company function no less. Just when I think I've heard every story."

"I know. I hit the grand slam. She's fabulous. We see each other now and again." Wes takes a long sip from his glass. "Ah, the lovely Hannah."

"Then why are you still looking like a hungry college kid at a buffet?"

"*This* is the skill you have to learn, my friend. Keep your options open."

Keep my options open, he says. Skill I have to learn, he says. "Take me being here as the win for tonight, Mav. Okay?"

"You got it as long as I see you put the ball in play. Sip on that cocktail and get your ass on the floor."

His hang loose personality can be infectious. This is the last weekend of summer, and my new responsibilities start Tuesday. I'm not the president right now. I'm just Eli. I don't have to know who he is to have a good time.

I sip down half my drink while I listen to the full version of Hannah and Wes. His animation makes me laugh. Everything is bigger, brighter, and bolder when he tells it. My mind wanders when a blonde in a white dress catches my eye from the center of the dance floor.

I can only catch glimpses, like images a camera would take. Moments. An arm stretched to the ceiling. An arch of her back as her hair floats to the back of her knees. That's not like Hayley. First of all, she's not that coordinated. Second, this is not the attention she likes. She's a one-on-one type of person not a "Hey world, look at me" person.

I hold up a finger to get Wes to pause in an attempt to get a better look. Pressing my drink closer to my body, I weave into the crowd. My neck bends to the right then the left to see through the sea of raised arms, glasses, and bodies moving every which way.

Right when I think I'm going to break the circle to see the blonde, she moves. The whole circle moves. Finally, a space opens so I can blend into the spectators around her. I can finally say definitively this isn't Hayley. The angel floating across the floor is a head taller than she is.

I take a few moments to appreciate everything about her under the disco lights that offer me better views. Her hair is a wild mess from tossing it side to side. Her arms make the most interesting shapes. They bend and contort in the most free-form ways.

Unlike many of the women here, she is fully covered. Her breasts peek out of her neckline but leave everything to the imagination. Her baby doll dress floats over her middle and the hem settles mid-thigh. Even when she spins, her boy shorts cover every curve beneath. Where I'd expect to find heels on her feet, there are white-on-white sneakers that allow her to move in ways I've never seen.

The club begins to jump again. A familiar tune to me begins to ring through the room. The DJ has put a house beat and mixed it together to a U2 classic, "With Or Without You". The circle around her begins to widen except for me. I want to move closer. The pull of my favorite band and this beautiful woman keeps me planted.

I'm getting looks from people to my right and left. I don't care. I give my nearly empty glass to a server trying to get from one bar to the other. This woman's got me in a trance. Her mix of hip-hop with free-form contemporary is spellbinding, and I want a front row seat. She seems to know the song as well as I do. Her movement follows the lyric.

Bono tells us the thorn twists in our side, and she twists her whole body in my direction. As she does, I boldly step toward her. Her hand rises to my chest but stays a fraction away. She extends the other to meet it, then contracts her body back as her left foot slides in between mine.

Her fingers wrap over my rib cage on both sides, a finger at a time. They ripple up with each beat of the music. I reach for her torso, but she spins twice in my hands then presses tight against my body with her fingers splayed across my shoulder blades.

She's delicate but solid. Her hair whips around and stops across my left shoulder. She rests her cheek over my heart. Her hands guide us both from behind to deeply sway to the music. I'm used to the formal dances my mother taught me. This is *very* different. She's leading. She's pulling me toward her.

The deeper we get into the song, the less I realize there is anyone around us. I hear her slow methodical breathing as the undercurrent to the pulse of the music. We rock forward and back. She's taking me on a ride. The lyric states she's got me with nothing left to win or lose.

I don't know if that's true. I'm not a believer of fate. I don't believe in love at first sight. However, I want to manipulate those lyrics to say I want to win myself back by losing myself in her. Her carefree aura is completely intoxicating, infinitely better than the Fireball still burning in my chest.

She spins again with her back engaging into my chest. This wild spirit pulls my hands around her. She slides her hands down my arms and weaves our fingers together. As she does, she stretches my left arm around to her belly and my right across her upper chest. It's like she's willing me to cage her in.

I feel my hands tremble as my fingers flex over her skin and press in. She gasps. I don't know if that's in response to her dance marathon or to my touch. Her mane is anchored between us, letting the skin of her neck glow in all the colors under the flashing lights. She has a small dark mark on the upper part of her collarbone. It's a beacon calling for me.

I press my lips down on her skin. What feels like an electric shock runs from where we meet and rockets straight to my cock. I can feel it instantly grow between us. This time I know what the gasp is for. She rocks her hips back, grinding a little into me as her hand that was once over mine on her hip grips and tugs at the back of my neck.

As Bono fades into the distance and the EDM comes back in full force, my blonde whirlwind spins inside my arms again. The whirlwind isn't limited to her physicality. Her eyes have a storm I couldn't miss in the darkest of rooms. She cups my cheeks in her hands and pulls my lips down to hers.

I don't even know her name, but I want her. I need her. Her lips are so inviting. I grip over her rib cage so hard, I fear I'm leaving bruises. I reach out for her bare arms. They're a damp oasis. I want to drink off her in every way. I slide my hands up to her face, dragging my fingers in a slow lazy pattern over the apples of her cheeks.

She tastes like tequila and cherry mixed in a potent concoction. This beauty peels her lips away from mine then ghosts them up my cheek to my ear. "Follow me," she whispers. Her hand slides down my arm away from my cheek now possessing my hand, giving it a gentle but firm invitation to do as she asks.

She passes Wes on the way out the door to the back patio. He watches her carefully. As this blonde beauty reaches the exit, she turns for me. Wes leans in but speaks loudly enough for her to hear him. "Get it, Goose. Do *everything* I would do." I give him a subtle head shake as I pass. I don't know what the next few minutes holds, but one thing I know for sure, I feel alive.

Ariana Rose

Chapter Nine

Elijah

The beat of the music can still be felt in the night air. My blonde dancer twirls out onto the patio blocks. There are less than ten people in the wide expanse of the enclosed garden space. In the far corner of the lot is an arrangement of outdoor furniture with large pillars at all four corners. It has two half moons of bench seating surrounding a firepit in the middle.

The heat is too much with the fire. No one is there. She seems to have noticed that before I do. My white vision begins to walk backward to the now fading beat and curls her finger, motioning for me to follow her into what I believe she is claiming as her den.

There are sheer curtains on all sides, blowing slightly in the little breeze we have. I walk inside first at her insistence. Before I can turn back to face her, I can hear the slide of the rings over the wrought iron, enclosing us to the outside world. We begin to circle each other inside the space between the benches and the firepit.

"Goose? *Top Gun*, right?"

"Yeah. It's been a thing between us for years." I can see her breathing catch for the first time. She didn't even do that when she was dancing earlier.

"I like it. It's one of my favorites actually."

"Really?"

"Uh huh." She leans against the white pillar at the back of our hideaway. She glides her hands gracefully up the outside of her thighs and buries them underneath the cotton of her dress. She tugs at the boy shorts I'd admired minutes ago and tosses them to the bench.

It's my turn to have my breath catch in my chest. I stalk toward her. She places her hand out and stops me with her digits over my heart. "Take what's beneath my hand."

From a hidden place, beneath that hand, is a condom. I slowly palm it. With my fingers wrapped around it, I pound the side of my fist on the concrete pillar above her head. I don't want to kill this with a lot of thought or words. I do need one thing. Her name.

"Tell me your name," I breathe in her ear.

She smiles against my cheek as she tugs at my belt. "We'll go with call sign Viper."

I exhale so hard I don't think I have any air left in my lungs. My lips find that dark spot on her collarbone again. Instead of a gentle kiss like before, I give her skin a little nip with my teeth to finish. Viper gives me a soft sexy giggle with all the air in her lungs.

Her hand brushes against my cock as she lowers my zipper. It's been so long since I've felt a woman's touch. Not that I've forgotten, but I'm reminded how fragile the line is between control and desire. The groan I make doesn't even sound like it's coming from me.

I can tell she likes it because she brushes her hand across me again and lingers this time. I pound the side of my hand into the concrete once more. Our eyes connect. She's daring me to hold on and let go at the same time. She's making it a challenge. She wants a reaction.

Her hands ride up underneath my shirt, lying flat against my skin. I palm her breast over her dress with my right hand. She's so soft. My knuckles creak with the tension I'm keeping in them as I knead her over and over. She responds with slow grinds between our hips.

To deepen this seduction, she raises her right leg, digging her heel into my ass, anchoring me to her. I can feel her fingers pulse between us. First, she gives me fractional slides over my cock but then curls her fingers against herself. Oh no. *If you let me, I want that pleasure.*

I slide my hand that was fisted over her head down next to her shoulder. The foil packet corner glimmers between my fingers. She turns her mouth toward my hand and catches the corner with her teeth. With a tense smile, I open my hand and let the condom dangle where I wish my lips were.

In order to give myself the wish, I tear the packet open from its confines. She takes the end I leave her from her mouth then speaks two of the sexiest words I've ever heard. "Let me." *I would let you do anything as long as I can have you.*

I pull her heel free from behind me and bring it to my hip, running my hand from the back of her knee to hook it over my arm. She settles in just like a dancer would. Her body even arches away as her hand works between us. When she finishes, all I want is to devour her.

As she arches back into the pillar, I slide my right hand up her outer thigh then skate across into her inner thigh. She's as smooth between us as the skin on her collarbone. It's unexpected but adds to the growing list of things wholly sexy about her.

My fingers begin to tease her, and she gives me a sweet moan in return. Her arms wrap around my neck as she slowly begins to grind us together like she did on the dance floor. She has ways of manipulating her body so she's a perfect fit to mine.

Viper rises to her toes, reaching her left hand between us to align me to her body. Once she does, her hands force me to lower just enough so she can slide her body onto mine. My eyes roll closed as we connect to my root. In what I can only claim as an involuntary movement, I subtract all the bend from my knees as I straighten up, pulling her body from the ground.

I settle my face in the crook of her neck as she does mine. I can feel the subtle tickle of her hair down my back. Her core flexes and contracts. As we roll together, it transforms into a dance. Not just because it's how we met, it's a dance to hold on. It's a dance to make the moment last. It's a dance to hold on for her. It's a dance to connect. It's a dance to forget. Live in the moment. I've never felt a closer connection to that phrase than I do right now.

I want to memorize the passion between us. I want to memorize her body with my hands. More than that, I want to memorize her face with my eyes. I force open my eyes as we continue to move carefully. She's staring right at me. Her look only spurs me on.

My grip changes on her thigh. It becomes more urgent. I start to massage her skin, sliding my hand deeper up into the small of her back. She arches into me, anchoring her shoulder blades against the pillar. This subtle movement gives me an unbelievable angle inside her.

I plunge so deep I fear I'll hurt her. I don't. With each movement, she relaxes even more. Her jaw goes slack. Her breathing increases. The one thing that's been a constant throughout is the fire in her eyes. As her eyes narrow slightly, she begins rolling against me faster.

Her purrs become more frequent. She's taking her pleasure, and in turn, giving me mine. I know I won't last much longer. I can feel every contraction inside her. I don't know how I've lasted this long. The only reason I have, I think, is because I don't want it to end.

That familiar sensation begins to take over my body. It starts deep in my core then quickly explodes to the surface. With two animalistic groans, I pour myself out into her. I rest my forehead against hers and slap an open palm over the pillar, pulling me deep as I do. My Viper cries out in my ear just before her whole body wraps so close I swear we could be one person.

She doesn't lower her leg right away. We settled like that for I don't know how long. Something happened to me in our time together. I can't put words to it yet. I just know I'm different.

"Are you all right?" I ask her.

"I'm great."

I whisper, "You're stunning is what you are."

After my honest compliment she seems, for the first time, uncomfortable. Viper kisses my left cheek, then my right, before she slides away from me. She kisses the notch at the base of my neck then reaches for her boy shorts on the bench. While she smooths her dress and her hair, I collect myself.

Once the evidence of our liaison is hidden, I turn to find her back on the opposite side of the firepit out of my reach. "I enjoyed our dance," she says.

"I hope we get to dance again," I tell her.

"If you're lucky."

"Where will I find you?"

The fire returns to her eyes as she smiles. "Where you least expect it."

Ariana Rose

Chapter Ten

Elijah

"Wait." I call to her as she walks away. She's so fast, like a mist moving along the breeze. Viper opens the door back into the club. I'm only three paces behind her. I catch the door before it latches back, and Wes stops me with an arm around my shoulder.

"You were gone a long time, although not as long as I would have liked for you."

"Where'd she go?"

"Your dancing queen? She hit the door and poof, man."

"No." I brush past him and begin my search through the crowd. She, by rights, should have only been two yards ahead of me. I should see her. I don't. Finally, the lights help me. I see another group dancing on the other side of the club.

I weave my way through the people. It's not nearly fast enough. When I get close, I know in an instant it's not her. It's Hayley with her friends. She reaches out and grabs my hand. "Hey, everybody. This is my big brother, Eli."

I lean in. "Hayles, did you see a woman walk by you wearing a white dress?"

"Long blonde hair. Pretty?"

"Yes. Where is she?"

"She went by us like thirty seconds ago with her squad and out the front door."

"What? Fuck." I leave Hayley confused in mid-thought. I need to find Viper. By the time I reach the valet stand, there isn't a white dress to be seen. Not even a Goddamn glass slipper.

"May I help you?" the valet asks.

"There was a young woman in a white dress who just left."

"You mean Coop?" he responds.

"Coop?"

"Yeah, Dylan Cooper."

"Dylan. Thanks." When I turn to go back into the club, Wes is standing in the doorway watching. "Get it over with," I sigh.

He smirks. "What do you mean?"

"Your brain is working so hard there's smoke coming from your ears. Don't hurt yourself and just ask."

"You're a pretty grumpy bastard for someone who just danced with one of the hottest women in here."

"I need another shot to put these flames out."

"Mister One Drink and Done wants another shot? Well, fuck yes!" He pulls me to the bar that connects the dining area to the club floor. "This man needs a shot he says. Set him up with whatever he wants."

"Patron with a cherry. Make it a double."

I suck down half the shot before I say another word. Wes is like a dog waiting on a bone. I feed him what he didn't see but keep the most intimate details for myself. First of all, I've never been one to fuck and tell. More than that, I don't want the images of what we shared known to anyone but Viper.

The arch of her back in my hands. The sounds she made in my ear. The fire that burned in her eyes. The fury she created in my body. No. Those details I want for myself.

"I like this chick for so many reasons," Wes exclaims.

"Okay, she's not a chick."

"Listen," he picks up the remainder of my shot, "she popped your post-divorce cherry. She got you outside yourself and inside her. I think that's a total win for both of you. Don't overanalyze it."

"I'm not. I just wish I knew where to find her. I'd like to see her again."

"She twisted you up that quickly. Damn. That's some voodoo she's got."

I don't know about voodoo but there was a definite magic.

Thank God for Uber and Hayley. She was the only one sober enough to get us back home. I know she was completely annoyed with us. Hayles was worried about me cockblocking her when the night started. She ended it by being pissed at Wes.

She'd been talking to a guy all night, and was about to get his number, when Wes started calling her babe and draping all over her. I stood back and just watched. Hayley kept yelling at me to control him. Her potential new beau, after some convincing, did give her his number. Hayley then had a couple of punches for Wes in the back seat.

Hayley and I had Wes dropped off at his parents' place first. Not only did they live closer, but I also know she was ready to be rid of him for the night. After he was gone, she let out a long growl followed by a giggle.

"Sometimes I think he's jealous."

I raise my head from the lean I'd taken to the window. "What?"

"He was acting like a jealous boyfriend."

"That's gross. Don't say that."

"Why? I'm not good enough for him?" she asks.

"Ummm, no. He's not good enough for you."

She laughs. "That was a quick response. Tell me how you really feel."

I toggle from the window to her shoulder. "I had a good time tonight."

"I can tell. I've never heard you slur like this."

"It was that last shot, but it was the best one. It tasted like her."

"Her? The girl you went running after?"

"Yep. That's the one."

"Well, I'd like to thank her for bringing my brother back."

"Me too, Hayles. Me too."

Chapter Eleven

Elijah

The rest of the weekend went well after the hangover wore off Saturday afternoon. My father and grandfather returned from their round of nine about noon. My father tossed me my tennis shoes and tennis racket at about one. He said there was nothing like a good sweat to get the body working again.

I think he just wanted to beat me for once. Even with my head pounding, I got up, tossed a ball cap on, and met him for what I thought was going to be a leisurely game. After a couple of cross-corner shots, I knew he was going to test me. I sucked down two large containers of water in the sixty minutes we played. Dad was right. I did feel better and I let him win.

I drove back to the club alone on Saturday night. I was hoping to run into Viper for another dance. I waited until the witching hour. She didn't materialize. When I got back home, I didn't end up sleeping much. After giving up trying to force it around six thirty, I put on a T-shirt, my glasses, and decided to surprise everyone with a big breakfast.

My family starts filing in one by one by seven. The bacon is the first thing to go. It always is. I could see pride in Gran's eyes when I handed her her special mug filled with her vanilla-flavored coffee. Had I been *that* dead to everyone? I'd always felt like it on the inside, but I thought I'd hid it well. Apparently not.

Hayley and I spend the rest of Sunday by the pool reading, napping, and talking. Even after our end of summer cookout for dinner, we walk the shore, and I make her a makeshift bonfire ring. She brings a bottle of rosé while we listen to the waves roll up and talk more as the stars come out.

She tells me how excited and terrified she is for the coming school year. She wants to be done with it and working already. If I'd asked her a year ago, the answer would have been very different. She didn't want anything to do with the family business. She wanted to venture on her own.

It was always a choice. Mom, Dad, Gran, and Pops would have never forced either of us to follow a specific path. I know the turning point for her. She helped at a fundraising event and saw the impact of what we do in the donation process. Getting the word out is our specialty. Hayley saw the effect something she would create could have.

She also confesses she's really missed me. It's at that point she curls up against me like she used to when I'd read her bedtime stories when she was little. I make her promise she won't allow me to lose myself again. It occurs to me now, I'm sitting out on the beach, the same beach I'd been so afraid to come back to, and I'm fine. I'm more than fine.

It feels odd sometimes to be thanked for simply showing up. It happens to me repeatedly as I am packing to leave. Gran kisses my cheek and pats my chest as she curls under my arm. My parents walk in together. I'm reminded to check my email when I get home by my father. *Ever the leader.* My mother reminds me to text when I get to their house to exchange modes of transport, then again when I get to the apartment, and to send pictures of the renovations. *Ever the mother.*

The last "See you soon" comes from Pops. I lock my small bag in the back of Hayley's car. Turning around, I find he's standing behind me with my helmet in his hand.

"Trying to sneak off?" he says.

"No, sir. I would've found you."

"Tomorrow's the big day."

"For both of us. Are you ready?"

"Yes, Eli. I am ready. I'm excited for you. This is something I've waited years to see come to pass. Do you have any reservations?"

"No, Pops. Just know I won't let you down."

"I never thought for a moment you ever would. If you need me, I'm a phone call away."

I take my helmet from his hand and smile. "You might regret saying that."

"Never, my boy."

I catch him waving to me in my rearview until I can't see him anymore. There's a chill to the air today as I'm driving back. There's that change of season starting. I know it's because of a weather front, but it helps my mindset from the weekend remain the closer I get to the city.

I debated just taking the bike home. After a conversation with the building manager, I'd like to make its new home with me a permanent move. I promised Lauren and Stacey I would let them show me my new digs. I had no say, other than the painting, and I'm fine with that.

I haven't seen them this confident in a design ever. I'm usually the one who sees everything first in all their projects. There's always a lingering piece of doubt. They're artists. It's in their nature. Lauren makes me close my eyes. I roll them hard before doing so. She gives me a good smack for it too.

I can hear the key in the lock, and they each take an arm to guide me in. We round the corner so I'm facing into my living room and dining room space. The smell of fresh paint still lingers slightly in the air. Lauren counts to three then tells me to open my eyes.

The once slightly dated blinds have all been removed and replaced with floor-to-ceiling sheers and blackout shades for the room's length of windows. The palette of stark white and neutral grays has been replaced with a warm oatmeal sofa and three different shades of blue reflected in the pillows and chairs. They've mounted my massive flat screen to the wall over a generous console table, which houses my gaming system, sound system, and newly purchased turntable with all of the best U2 vinyl flanking it to the right.

"Fucking hell, you guys."

Lauren finally asks the question, out of habit, I think. "You really like it?"

"Fuck sake. I'm speechless."

"Write down the date and time. The king of verbose has nothing," Stacey quickly comes back.

I toss one of my new pillows in her direction. "Seriously. Thank you."

The kitchen has become so warm. It was so clinical and modern before. The light pine cabinets are now a rich cherry color. Just like the bottom of a dark glass of ale. The balcony, which was the least used space, has now been transformed to a place where I can have David up for a game of chess or sit and enjoy my music from the inside.

A trail of herbs and plants leads me into my bedroom. For the first time in years, this space doesn't remind me of what was. I thought just changing the bed was enough until I saw the transformation. I realize the entire thing was something that's weighed me down in ways I didn't think it did.

The wood slat framing on the walls right above the bed creates a perfect center for my *Angels and Demons* art piece. It nearly acts like my headboard. "I thought you were going to move the art to the living room."

Lauren takes my hand. "We were, babe. But we thought it was better here. What was and will be again."

They played with the light color of the walls around it with rich gray for my bedding. The girls even tricked out my bathroom with brand-new everything, including a wood bench in the shower.

"I couldn't have imagined this for myself."

"That's kind of the point, Eli. You were stuck. Now you don't have to be."

To say thank you, I cook them dinner for all their hard work. No Italian this time. This calls for a couple of pan-seared steaks with wild rice and a light red. After they leave, I open my balcony door and test out my new favorite sound system with *The Joshua Tree* on vinyl. Out on my new mini couch in the night air, the sounds of the street blend with the music.

It's the perfect way to wind down.

A text from Hayley saying she got to her apartment okay came in. Mom and Dad got home fine. Pops and Gran decided to stay another night. I dive into my email as I promised my father. I need to stay in this habit. I need to make it even more of a religion than I already had.

In my inbox were things I was used to seeing such as meeting requests, seminars for continuing education, weekly reports, revenue projections, to-do lists from my assistant, Anna, and my NYU alumni emails. Mixed in with the NYU emails was a lengthy personal one from Professor Stone.

He has a new request. He needs me to take his class for multiple dates instead of the single lecture I usually do. He's been called to lead a conference in Chicago early in the term. Rather than canceling class, he's asking if I can substitute in his place.

With all he's done for me over the years, I don't think I should say no. I do have to make sure I can coordinate it with my father and with all my new AnSa duties. The timing isn't great, but this opportunity is at the heart of everything I love about my industry. I can also get a jump on vetting the intern candidates.

The familiar downbeat with the haunting vocals spills the softer version of "With Or Without You" across my apartment and out the open door. The lyrics mean something different now. I'll never be able to hear this song again and not think of Viper. She did give herself away to me, but now it's me asking about living with or without her. I do have something to win. I need to find her. I don't know how just yet, but I will.

Chapter Twelve

Elijah

My feet pound the pavement around Central Park. It's the right amount of crisp at five thirty in the morning. The only time I stop on the loop is near the zoo. Even when the gates aren't open, I sometimes stand and imagine I can talk to Bono. He's the only connection to that part of my past I will keep. He's listened to me, theoretically, when no one else could. It's a big day in many ways, and I want him to be a part of it.

Today is a day I look forward to with a great sense of honor, but also a hint of sadness. Pops stepping to consultant is the right thing to do. He wants it. He knows it's time for himself, Gran, but also the company. He's built a foundation that will take us generations into the future. That heavy sense of responsibility is not lost on me.

I stand before the board, with my father sitting proudly to my right, and virtually before all staff, wherever they may be, pledge to be the same person they've come to depend on. While always staying true to the values and interests the company was built on, I make a new commitment to strive for change and growth.

I make sure they understand my desire to expand our presence in not only the clients we represent, but also in our community as a whole. I highlight what we will strive for in this last quarter and what I'm looking at next year to be. In short, I offer a glimpse of what our partnership with my new direction could look like and how we can impact many different sectors.

For a while, I feel like a football coach firing up his or her team. I've done that on a small scale with the interns and my personal staff, but as Peter Parker's uncle once said, "With great power comes great responsibility". Everything falls ultimately at my feet now, good, bad, or indifferent. I need to be mindful of that at all times.

A subtle wink from my father at the end of my address is all I need to let me know he's proud, and I went in the right direction. Next is a meeting with Skye and Anna. I need them to know how much I appreciate them and will continue to rely on their talent. This transition is going to be a steep learning curve for all of us, and I want them to have a free hand on calling me on my shit if I'm not living up to expectations.

First order of business is the reorganization of my schedule. The email request from Will puts a twist in things, but between the three of us and a genuine spark of creativity, we're able to come up with a working solution. Skye will vet all the intern candidates down to about ten so I'm able to find the final four. Anna's moving a few of my meetings to lunches or dinners to maximize each day so I can teach.

Anna also offers to go above and beyond and create the slide presentation for my day one with the students. She's saving me about eight hours of work. By Friday, when I'm scheduled to introduce myself to the class, I feel fully prepared. Will told them his schedule and how I would be involved on the first day.

I feel like I'm the one attending class for the first time by the checklist I go through. Laptop. Check. Presentation. Check. Charcoal suit. Check. Key for Will's office. Check. Anna, just to be a smart-ass, put an apple in my messenger bag with a simple smiley face note.

Will's lecture hall is six rows deep and about fifteen seats across each row in auditorium-style, with running tabletops from left to right. I'm going over my slide notes at the lectern as the students begin filing in. The classroom goes quickly from so silent you could hear a pin drop to a room buzzing with several clusters of chatter. At nine sharp, I begin my address.

"Good morning, everyone. Hope you will trust me as much as Professor Stone seems to, whether that's good or bad, I'll leave up to you. I'm Elijah Sawyer. Will and I have been friends and colleagues in the industry for a number of years. I've also had the privilege of being in your seat with him as my instructor.

"I was told the first month of the term, you would be looking at business models from top ten firms across the nation. Studying how they operate and challenge if their current model could take them into the future. As a president of one of those firms, I can offer our perspective. AnSa International was founded by my grandfather in the late sixties.

"We pride ourselves on making our business about the nonprofit sector and how any voices, no matter how small they may seem, can and will have their causes heard. Most firms generally specialize in, or have, one focus area. We strive for more of a hybrid model. We are able to help facilitate multiple aspects, so continuity of idea and care is maintained."

I finally look up from my notes to quickly scan the crowd. Most are either taking handwritten notes or typing furiously on their laptops. I have a rogue warrior who's lost in his phone, and one in the dead center of the second row back is staring right through me.

I had my glasses off until now to maintain that performance distance for myself. Now that I've gotten my feet wet, I can put them on and continue. As I slide them on my face, the room becomes crystal clear, as well as the one person in the room who is intent on full eye contact.

I don't need to put a glass slipper on her foot to know this is my Cinderella from the other night. Viper has flown back in as promised, when I least, and honestly never, expected it. Her lips curl in the most perfect smile. She is nibbling on the end of her pen. *Oh, that lucky fucking pen.*

Clearing my throat is hard. Moving right now from behind this podium would be even harder and, within a few more seconds, quite embarrassing. "I'm sorry," I apologize. "As I was saying, our company prides itself on being able to consult, take that consult and turn it into developing full-scale communications that will be able to translate in all aspects of the brand, from digital or virtual marketing, public relations, and social media, just to highlight a few."

Viper pulls the pen from the gentle grind between her teeth and raises it in the air. "Excuse me, Mr. Sawyer." I take a deep breath. My name on her lips shouldn't be as exciting as it is, especially not in this setting. "But don't you feel that being the best at one aspect is better than being more than average at all of them? No disrespect intended."

"None taken, Miss..."

"Cooper. Dylan Cooper. Back to my question, doing one thing well has value, doesn't it?" she asks.

"Yes. Of course it does. However, if you really want to get to know someone, you dive in and learn everything. That's the sign of a true partnership. It's more than the surface. It becomes about being inside. If you feel it, your audience will too."

I hear all the words coming out of my mouth, and it's hard to determine now whether I'm talking about business or her. She knows it. She's baiting me the first day, first class to see if I will crack. *I can fly under the radar, Viper. Trust me.*

We entertain this back-and-forth for the entire hour. She listened as others chimed in. She asked layered questions. Her tenacity was inspiring, innovative, and evocative. There were times I gripped the edges of the lectern so hard I heard it crack.

As the students begin to file out at the end of class, my eyes connect with Dylan. She's collecting her things. *It's now or never* I tell myself. "Excuse me, Miss Cooper. Would you have a moment to speak with me?"

"Yes, I would."

She pulls her lip balm from her pocket and swipes it slowly over her beautiful lips. I follow the trail earnestly. "Do you know where Professor Stone's office is?"

"Yes, Mr. Sawyer. I'll be there. Soon."

If Will knew what was about to happen in this room, he'd be so angry with me. Holding the key carefully in my hand, I unlock the door to his campus office. He knew I'd need it in case I'd have to meet with students, do the intern interviews, and weave in AnSa business during the day in order to be able to help him out longer term. I don't think he had in mind a reconnect with one of his students who I danced with and publicly fucked in a club.

I place my bag in the chair as I fumble for the light on his desk. The bag tumbles to the floor at the base of the chair. I crouch down to pick it up and all the contents that have seeped to the floor. "Fuck."

"We've already done that. Shouldn't you at least offer dinner first this time?" My head whips up at her voice, and I take the back of it into the oversized handle on the long drawer. She giggles a bit. "Oh my God. Are you okay?"

I rock back to sit on my heels until the stars in my eyes fade along with the pain. "Shit. This is attractive, right?"

"I think so. I mean. You're on your knees, almost at my feet."

She's so fucking cocky. I'm completely screwed. "Could you close the door so we can talk?"

The lock on the door meets its cradle and the rest of the world is washed away. She bends down beside me. Now I have a closer look in a way the classroom couldn't offer. Her wild mane is tamed today by a dark fabric scrunchie wound all around her curls on the top of her head. The toes of her famous to me white sneakers are peeking out of her sleek side-snap track pants. A soft patch of skin on her shoulder is right next to my lips, as her wide neck sweater sags slightly to the left.

The vanilla scent of her hair mixes with a sweet apple coming from her skin. If this wasn't Will's office, we weren't on campus, and this wasn't technically an interview, she'd be bent over this desk. I've been in her presence less than three hours in total, and she's driven me to the point of madness for her.

"Are you going to talk or just memorize me?"

"Both, if I was allowed."

"We do what we want, right?"

"That's not how my world works."

"Too bad for your world. Want me this close or on the other side of the desk?"

I smirk and play along. "First one, then the other. Let's start on the other side."

"If I don't, you won't make it to the other. I get it."

"Is everything innuendo to you?"

She leans into the desk before she sits slowly. "Is there any other way?"

"Yes. Business first. Do you have a résumé you could send me?"

"Is that your way of asking me for my number?" She pulls her laptop from her bag.

"It isn't, but if it's on there, I may have to use it for more than just business. Have you applied for one of the internships at AnSa International?"

Her face looks up at me in the glow of her computer screen. She has always looked in total control of every emotion, even if it's complete abandon. The moment I mention AnSa, it gives away a chink in her facade. "AnSa? No. I haven't. Why do you ask?"

"I'd like to place you up against... a group of candidates for an interview." She smirks at me again as I put up my hands. "All innuendo aside, I liked how you challenged both the ideas and me during today's lecture. You have a way of looking at things that's quite unique. I'd like to see what you could do in our setting."

Her carefree nature suddenly becomes hidden under a button or two. She slides her finger delicately across the keypad on her laptop. "I didn't know that's who you were that night."

"You sound like you're trying to justify something."

She pulls the sleeves of her sweater down over her hands and balls the weave into her fists, pinning one under her chin. "No. I just want it known I'm not about screwing my way to get ahead. The night at the club was all about fun and living in the moment."

I lean back to rest on the corner of the desk. "I'd like it known I didn't ask you here for that reason either. But, yes, it was." I give those three words their proper pause, as the air between us never loses its charge. "We only give four of these internships out each year. We vet our candidates carefully. The decisions are based on skill, hunger, academics, and drive. Two of those things I can see on a résumé. The other two, I need to hear from you."

"You want to know about my hunger?"

"There are many things I'd like to know about you," I tell her.

"Then ask."

I lean forward. "I'd like to know if you'll have dinner with me tonight."

"Back to hunger. Nice."

"I'll be coming from my office. Is there someplace we could meet?"

She packs away her laptop then stands up from her perch. I've held her body before as it swayed. Now, I'm holding her eyes as a wicked smile dances over her lips. "Of course there is. Your place at seven?"

I cross my arms across my chest as I swallow deep. I thought it would clear the lump in my throat, and if I dug the nails into my side from my hidden hand, it would have the potential to deflate my growing desire for her. "How will I find you?"

"Check your email, Professor," she says after she brushes her hand over my knee before heading to the door.

"Dylan?"

She turns her head back toward me. The left side of her face glows in the amber cast light, while the rest of her remains partially hidden in the shadows. This is a theme and metaphor for us. "Yes?"

"Nothing. I just wanted to see how it felt to say your name."

"How did it feel?"

"Like I want to do it again."

"Trust me, Mr. Sawyer. You will."

Chapter Thirteen

Elijah

Italian is always a relatively safe choice for dinner, and I can't fuck it up. My sauce has been at a low simmer for about thirty minutes. The faint hint of garlic weaves through the air of my apartment. I've opened all of my new curtains to catch the afternoon warmth of the sun and propped open my balcony door to let the still mild air along with the sounds of the city circulate.

Some would say classical music is the way to go for dinner. I'm more of a rat packer myself. Pops taught me about Sinatra, Martin, and Sammy Davis, Jr. very early on in life. Their catalog is massive, and it's always given me a strong sense of confidence and connection to that swagger, even if I feel I've lost my game.

I flip one of my dish towels over my shoulder, resting my arms on the balcony door frame. The sounds of the birds in the trees blend with the horns and sirens below. I rub my hand along the back of my neck. It seems any tension I feel heads straight there.

I haven't cooked for anyone besides Stacey, Lauren, or Wes in a long time. I know that's not my only sense of anxiety. I'm walking dangerously close to a line of landmines. I'm not one to just dive in. I'm not one to act immediately on feelings, but she's got me turned around and inside out. Blue Eyes is giving me a chorus of "Strangers In The Night" when I get what I've been waiting for, a knock at the door.

My heart palpitates as I walk toward it. Once this door is open, there is no turning back. First the click of the dead bolt, then the creak of the door handle, gives me access to her. She dropped her golden hair from the confines of her scrunchie, so it cascades over her shoulders and beyond. It covers portions of the skin that was visible to me earlier as her sweater slides to the left. She's traded her track pants for a simple denim skirt and those sneakers. I never thought I'd love them as much as a pair of heels, but I do. On her I do.

"You're late," I scold her with a small smile.

"Yeah, well I didn't want to seem eager. May I come in?" I open the door wide for her to pass. She opts for walking close, dragging her hand across my chest. "Thank you."

The last time I watched her walk away, I was trying to catch her. This time, it feels like I have. I lock the door, pull the towel off my left shoulder, and whip it across to my right purposefully, letting the corner crack against my skin. "Dinner will be ready in about twenty minutes. Would you like a drink?"

"I can have one glass, yes." I watch her eyes slowly scan my apartment.

"Just one?"

"Yes. One. It's technically a school night. I have a rehearsal tomorrow."

"A rehearsal?"

I twist my corkscrew in the bottle of rosé I have chilling on the counter. She drops her purse in the white, winged, half-moon chair at the head of my dining table before she crosses to check out the view. "It's a senior solo project for the dance students. I'm choreographing a group piece."

"You're a marketing student moonlighting as a dancer?"

Her head whirls back to me as the cork pops. "I'm a dancer moonlighting as a marketing executive."

"You seem to excel at everything." I completely mean that in whatever way she wants to take it.

"Not everything." She walks over to me, taking the half full glass from the tabletop. "Just most things." She licks her lips slowly before letting the perfect pink liquid float over them. I watch her swallow and a little hum of appreciation vibrates from her throat. My cock quivers. It remembers, as well as I do, that sound. It's a sexy tone that's half an octave lower than her speaking voice. "Something wrong?" she asks.

"Wrong?"

"Yes. Wrong. You're staring at me and this glass like you want to crawl inside."

I clear my raw throat. "Well, that's close."

She takes another sip in the silence between us. Dylan backs up about three feet, sliding out of her sneakers. Her bare feet are something to behold. Her toes are painted a pale gray in an attempt to mask a few cuts and bruises atop them. "Mind if I get comfortable?"

"Not at all. I'm going to check the sauce."

"I think I can amuse myself." She smirks, turning toward the music. The breeze from the balcony door catches her hair, blowing it back. As it whirls around her face, she does a double spin in front of the speaker. Fucking hell.

I make it around the corner into the kitchen before I react viscerally. She's like the sun. I just want to get closer and closer to her. I want to feel every bit of warmth she has to offer, literally and figuratively. My dress pants are instantly too tight. Thank fuck I have my dress shirt untucked or the false appearance of control I have would be completely blown to shit.

I call out to her. "I made Italian. I hope that's okay."

"I love Italian." Her voice is husky... and close. Out of the corner of my eye, I catch her shadow. She's standing alongside my tall pantry cupboard. Her sweater has fallen even farther down her shoulder and what has fallen away completely is her skirt. The white tight weave of the sweater hugs her curves and barely covers that heavenly ass of hers.

"Comfortable?" I ask.

"Very," she answers, as she hops up on my counter. The bare skin just below the sweater squeaks lightly as she shifts back, her legs swinging slowly.

"Hungry?" *Answer that. I dare you.*

"Very." She leans in, cupping the back of my neck in her hand, and pulls me to her lips. The spoon clatters to the counter before I slide my hands up her back. Dylan begins to devour me. Her athletic legs squeeze at my sides. My hips pull forward to rest tight against the space between those legs.

She tastes like the sweetest, ripest peach. I sigh her name, "Dylan..."

She nibbles on my ear before she whispers, "See. I told you you'd say my name again."

"It won't be the last time I do either." I reach over with my left hand to turn the burners off. The heat is going off in the kitchen but is about to erupt elsewhere. She brings out thoughts and feelings in me I thought were dead. She leans back and pushes her hips forward. "No. Not here."

"Someday." She smirks.

The devil she carries around speaks to me. "Hold on tight."

She anchors her body to mine. I can feel her ankles lock around my back as I cup the globes of her luscious backside and lift her from the countertop. She arches her back, turning her head just enough so her hair falls away from her neck.

At the base of her hairline she has the tiniest of tattoos. It's the outline of a heart with the pulse of a heartbeat running through it. I run the tip of my tongue across it as we slowly walk across my apartment toward my bedroom. She purrs the whole way. It's the best sounding engine I've ever heard.

I'm not this guy. I've been with three women ever. My prep school girlfriend, the woman I dated before I met Victoria, and then Victoria. All were my girlfriends, one I married. Dylan is driving me to do things I've never done, and I like it. More than that, I'm craving it.

"And there, and there...." Dylan mumbles.

"What?"

"Just making a mental list of all the surfaces we can attempt. In the chair." She kisses the left side of my neck. "On the couch." She kisses the right side of my neck. "Against the glass while the city watches." I gently drop her shoulders to my bed. I expected the rest of her to follow, but her ankles remain hooked at my waist.

She smiles with her eyes, holding me in a trance. She engages her core and rolls her hips perfectly up and down my cock in waves. I flex my hand on the small of her back as my other hand digs into her thigh. Her hair drifts across the once smooth sheets to form a golden cloud across the heather gray.

Dylan folds her hands over the neckline of her sweater and pulls as her eyes close. She's taking in the feeling for herself. Her motion is just as much for me as it is for her. Her sleek up and down motion morphs into slow counterclockwise circles. With each fraction I grow, the room in the confines of my pants gets smaller, but our connection goes deeper.

Even through the fabric, I can feel I've parted her. She gives me another slow purr. My hand slides under the hem of her sweater and grips over her hip. Her skin is warm and even a little damp. I groan my agreement and allow my head to slowly fall back.

Her grip around my back loosens ever so slightly. I lower my chin to catch her sliding her sweater off and over her head. Her breasts are small, round, and exquisite. Her nipples, hard and pebbled, are the perfect pink in the center. I want to taste them.

My keen interest has encouraged her into another gear. She switches directions and rotates clockwise with hard pulses at the top of each circle. I could stare at her forever. My eyes don't leave where our clothed bodies are joined, while I shakily open each button of my shirt before tossing it to the floor.

She's testing me and my resolve as a whole. I can feel every cord in my jaw and neck. The tension in my body is making my teeth grind like she is against me. Her circles become faster and smaller. She begins to pant. Each exchange of air is coming harder. She's pushing herself to the edge.

I place the heel of my palm at her apex to halt her movement. If she's going to come, I want to be fully involved. "Dylan," I whisper. "Not yet."

She opens her eyes, and the corners of her mouth slowly turn up into a wicked smile. "You sure took long enough to stop me," she breathes.

I open my belt, pulling on the buckle. It frees from the loops like a whip to the ground. "*Was* that a test?"

"Mmm hmmm. It was to see how hot I could get you and how close to the edge I could go. It will make falling over it so fucking amazing. It's the best kind of foreplay."

Taking a deep breath in, I let it go in one long exhale. "Fuck."

"Talk to me, Goose. Tell me what and how you feel."

"I don't think you're ready to hear all that. As far as how I feel, I'd like to show you." I reach behind me to gently unhook her heels from my back. Dylan holds the tension in her legs, so they fall slowly bent. I unzip my pants and internally breathe a slight sigh of relief as the added room instantly gives me the space I need. She watches me, holding her legs wide, as she slides her heels up to the edge of the mattress.

Pushing my pants to the floor in pools at my feet, I step out one leg at a time, sliding them to the side with a flick of my toes. Starting with my hands cupped around her ankles, I draw my hands up the outside of her calves. They are toned and rock solid. I let the corner of my nail graze against her skin. I can feel a slight shiver rise and fall through her body.

As I reach her knee, I stop and give it a kiss, just to the inside. Dylan reaches up between her legs and runs her fingers up into the back of my head, twisting my hair around them. "Is this who Goose is or is it the man who pinned me against the pillar?" She gives my hair a gentle pull.

"This is who Elijah is." I kiss the inside of her other thigh. "However, with you at the wheel, I have a feeling I could be steered in any direction."

She smiles again. "Good to know... Elijah." It's the first time she's said my name. Either she's winding so tight or I'm willingly going there, but either way you look at it, I want her.

I slide my knee in between her legs as she lowers her left. She tugs at my hair, coaxing me toward her. I hover over her body. My body instantly recalls certain touches. Her knee at my hip, her hand over my shoulder blade. What's new is how, as my weight presses against her, I feel a transfer of power.

I lower to my elbows. My upper body is planking above her. I reach down and take that perfect pink between my lips. Her hips begin to rotate beneath me. She guides my lips closer and deeper as she curves her arm in to create a new sense of fullness to her breast. It plumps against my cheek and I groan instantly.

Her quiet breaths begin to stutter. Each groan of pleasure I have is mirrored by a sigh from her. Before, she said she wanted to see how hot she could get me and how close to the edge she could go without falling. I'm at that edge. I want her in ways I've never wanted anyone.

I pull up from her body. As I reach my knee again, I loop my index fingers into the sides of her boy shorts and tug them with me. They slide effortlessly down her skin. She points her toes in agreement. The arch of her feet is the same shape of her back.

The strain from me is more than my boxer briefs can even bear. The minute my thumbs flick the elastic, her head angles to the side so she can watch. Her lips don't turn up into a smile this time, but her eyes are doing it for her. I open the drawer on my bedside table and reach inside. Dylan holds out her hand. "Will you let me do it?"

The thought of her hand wrapped around me again turns my hand into a fist so I can release a fraction of the tension. I drop the foil packet into her hand. She takes the corner into her mouth, tearing it with her teeth. For a split second I close my eyes and dream of the next time, so I can have that mouth wrapped around me too.

I crawl onto the bed, straddling at her hips. Dylan pulls up to her elbows. My cock is like an arrow pointing directly at her. She rolls the tip between her fingers, lining it up perfectly, drawing it forward with her right hand. With each fraction of progression, my core tightens.

As her hand reaches the base, she lies back flat with her tongue darting out to coat her lips. That's it. That's my limit. I retreat behind her knees as I lay her legs across my thighs. I rotate my tip at her apex. I want to tease her for a split second like she's done to me from the instant we met.

Her arch toward me tells me she's as hungry as I am. In one smooth motion, I slide inside her. Dylan inhales deeply through her nose as her arm reaches up behind her to grip the blanket folded beneath her body. It wrinkles in the weight of her touch. I loop her right leg over my left arm and rise up. She gasps, pulling me closer. Her fingers dig at my shoulder as I slap my right hand down next to her head. I need the balance. I want the leverage. I crave her release.

I drive carefully into her body. My lips fall to her chest at the swell of her breast. The pattern of noises she's making is like the most erotic song I've ever heard in my ear. I pump harder and faster. Each breath I take becomes deeper and more labored. I can feel this lava-like heat begin to build where we're connected.

We begin to grunt and groan octaves apart in unison. She makes me feel deviant and powerful in the best way. I angle up and her octave drives even higher. *Come on, Dylan.* Each passing second brings us closer.

"Oh fuck... Yes," she cries.

"God... Viper." I use her call sign instead of her name. It just feels right. The same fire and emotion we had at the club is being reclaimed. I rest cradled deep inside her as we race to our climax, first me, then her. Her subtle screams morph into the deepest, longest moan.

She muscles us over, so I'm pinned beneath her. Her golden locks hide both our faces as she strokes my cheek with hers. "Being bad feels good, doesn't it?" she asks. *Yes. It absolutely does.*

Ariana Rose

Chapter Fourteen

Elijah

The sun is finishing its slow descent behind the skyscrapers, casting an orange glow that's fading to the purples of twilight. I turn the stove back on and begin working on dinner again while Dylan showers. While taking slow drags from my wine glass, I stand inside the same doorway she was in a couple hours ago.

The nights are becoming crisper. I don't mind the sweltering heat, but this is my favorite time of year. Football, fall, and family. Now I can add a couple more 'F' words to that trio. Even the street noise and U2 on the wireless speakers can't drown out the pads of her bare feet behind me. I turn my back to the frame, leaning casually against the open door.

She's in white again. Only this time, it's the white of my T-shirt, which nearly comes to her knees on that petite frame. Her hair is about two shades darker when it's wet. It falls in perfect waves against her face and down her back.

"Better?" I ask.

"Mmm hmm. On several fronts."

"I have a fresh glass of wine out here with your name on it, if you'd like."

"I'd love actually. For some reason I could use a glass, along with a big plate of pasta."

"Luckily, I have both." I motion for her to come outside.

She nearly prances toward me like a cat that's gotten a special treat. Instead of weaving through my legs to show her affection, she grazes one hand along my left hip, the other on my chest over my gray T-shirt while reaching up to kiss my cheek.

Dylan crosses out to the balcony for the first time and instantly bends to sniff every flower. "These are gorgeous. Not to be an ass, but this surprises me."

I smile. "You're not an ass. They surprised me too. My friends, Lauren and Stacey, are interior designers. They just remodeled my whole place. The plants were all them. I told Lauren she'd have to teach me how to care for all this shit if she expects it to stay green."

"Pretty nice friends," she responds, as she curls up on the padded bench facing Central Park.

"I've known them for about eight years. They live across the hall. They work and play together."

"Well, the style they gave you suits you." Dylan takes one of her famous slow sips off her glass. I had sex with her a little more than an hour ago, but the sight of that instantly makes me think about going for it again.

"We can eat out here or at the table."

"Here's good. I'm not picky."

She's refilling our glasses as I bring out our bowls of angel hair pasta, covered in my homemade marinara, topped with my grandmother's secret recipe meatballs, and a basket of bread. This is the first time I've even remotely seen her seem surprised.

"Since it seems we have the other kinks worked out," she smirks, "should we try a bit of conversation? Maybe get to know each other while we aren't connected."

I laugh a bit as I pull a chair up, so I can sit across from her and share the café table. "Probably a good idea." I reach over to grab one of the solar lanterns to place at our feet.

"I'm just going to go for it."

"I wouldn't expect anything less," I say, before filling my mouth with wine of my own.

"You help run one of the best marketing firms in the city, if not the nation, you can cook, you live in this beautiful apartment, you're extremely good-looking, and you can have sex like that. I have to wonder when the girlfriend or wife is coming home, because there's literally no way you're single."

She begins winding the pasta on to her fork like nothing just happened. She's expecting me to be with someone, yet she's here anyway. I clear my throat and take a bite of my food before I can even find an answer. "I'm divorced."

"Well, she's an idiot."

I take a deep breath. "You asked me before what I was thinking. There's a lot going on, actually. How much do you want to know? Technically this *is* our first date."

"I don't scare easily, so how about if it gets to be too much, I just tell you to stop and you do the same."

"Fair enough. Well, I was married for about seven years. We were college sweethearts I guess you could say. I came home here one night and found her in our bed with her boss." I mindlessly drag my thumb over where my wedding ring used to be before finding the band of my family ring next to it.

"Shit. Did you kill them? I think I might have."

"It wouldn't have solved anything. I see her now about once a year or so when our paths cross at charity events. Last I saw her, they were still going at it."

"Wow. I'm sorry."

"Nice party killer, isn't it?"

"It's your story. It explains a lot, actually. So that takes care of the wife scenario. What about the girlfriend?"

"You're not only a viper with your sensuality, you're a viper with your questions."

"Elijah, you don't have to answer. Just say too far."

I think for a moment. We've already crossed off the main reason not to. "You're the first woman I've been with since I met her. That was 2006."

"Wow. Okay." I wonder if, in that instant, I've lost her. Reality can be a hard pill to swallow. I know whereof I speak. She takes a beat before she continues with something unexpected. "Come sit next to me?"

I set the bowl down at my feet, padding around the table to sit at her side. "So, you were about my age when you met her?"

I chuckle. "Yeah. I guess so. I hadn't considered it like that."

"So, in a way, this is a do-over. You can go back and do all the things you didn't, or fuck, just have fun again. I mean, I noticed in our meeting in the office you still have a tan line where your ring would be. That means you wore it until pretty recently, right?"

"Studying me that hard?"

"When it's something or someone I want, yes. I didn't fuck you in the club because it's something I've done before. I'm not going to lie and say I'm not sexual, because I am, and I'm proud of it. But there's something about you, Eli.

"You put your hand on my stomach and it was... intense. The way I spun in your hands was fire. I left that night because I thought it was only one night. I was okay with that. Things happen for a reason. I know you don't regret it."

I drag the back of my fingers down her cheek. "The only thing I regret is you leaving."

"My age doesn't bother you?"

Cocking my head to the right, I give her a small smile. "Does my age, divorce, and clear baggage bother you?"

"Everyone has baggage, Eli. It's all about how we deal with it. I've already said you're beautiful, you feed me, and you fuck like a god. I'm good."

I laugh louder than I have in a very long time. "You're so blunt. I love it. Not to mention, you're good for my ego. By the way, my buddy, Wes, already loves you."

"Let me guess. If you're Goose, he's Mav, right?"

"Since day one. I um... there's one more elephant in the room."

She offers me her last meatball. "What's that?"

"Stay with me through breakfast?"

"Only if you let me make it."

Chapter Fifteen

Elijah

It ended up being about one in the morning when we finally went to bed. It was near two before we actually went to sleep. I got my wish about feeling her mouth wrapped around me. I'm amazed my headboard didn't snap under the pressure of my hands. I lay there in a silent haze until I could feel I was near sleep. It was hard to know what to do next. If she were my girlfriend or wife, I'd pull her to my chest and hold on. We're clearly not there yet.

Yet.

Dylan rolls to the right side of the bed. Her hair is all wild and tangled across the pillow. She has the sheet and plush blanket pulled up into her fist next to her cheek. Her left hand extends out into the middle of the bed. I can feel the slight ghost of her fingers at my side. Before I cave to blissful exhaustion, I take her hand in mine, pulling it tight to my chest.

As I let the light in, what I can only assume is hours later, my hand is still in the same place only it's empty. A wave of regret washes over me. She's disappeared again. I sit up and dejectedly pull my legs over the side of the bed. My pants are still balled up where I left them. I slide them on, deciding to make coffee to cure my Dylan hangover, as if that would even remotely do it.

The closer I get to the door, I think I smell coffee already brewing. Is it wishful thinking? I pry the door open and music is what I hear. Did we leave my streaming going? As I listen harder, it's an EDM spa-style set. This isn't anything I have.

"Sleep well?"

Dylan's sexy voice radiates from the floor. She's moved my box-like coffee table over and is stretching out on my rug. My white T-shirt is back covering her body, and she seems to have found a pair of my jogging pants from the chest of drawers. They've been rolled up about three times over her ankles. I can't imagine how they'll even stay on over her hips.

"I thought you'd left."

"And miss the best meal of the day? Not on your life."

"How'd you sleep?" I ask.

"Good. Really good, actually. I was extra tired, I think." I crouch down beside her, tucking a stray hair behind her ear before I kiss her lips gently. "The pancake batter is all set to go."

"Sounds good." I trail my fingers up and down her spine. "What time is your rehearsal?"

"At two. Why?"

"I want to have your special pancakes then drive you home. My turn to sit on the counter."

"Good thing I like to be watched. Help me up and I'll put on a show for you."

"You've already done that more than once." With her hands in mine, she vaults to her feet, gracefully tossing her arms around my neck. I cup her face in my hands and slowly massage the skin just below her ears. "The interviews are on Monday. Are you in?"

"Is that a good idea?"

I reach in with my lips to nibble on her ear. "You tell me. I already know what I think."

"How will this work? That is, if I agree." She wiggles out of my grasp, nearly dancing to the kitchen. I stand in place for a moment regaining my composure and control before I follow her. When I round the cupboard, I find her already concentrating on the stove.

By the looks of my kitchen, she's been up for a while. The juice is in a small pitcher on the counter, with a bowl of fresh cut fruit below it. The place settings are stacked on the counter, and the dishes from last night are already done. I tried so hard to get rid of traces of Tori in this space. In an instant, I won't be able to see anyone but Dylan now.

"Dylan, are you wanting my elevator pitch about why you should intern at AnSa? Because if you are, then it's not the place for you. I told you I think you're a good fit, and I want to see what your ideas would do in the right environment. Most students would take that as a compliment."

"Is that what I am? A student?"

"How do you want to be seen?"

The sizzle from the pan as she flips the half-done pancake over seems to mirror something simmering in her just below the surface. "Interesting question."

I take a step closer to her, leaning against the cabinet. Dylan never looks up at me. When I'm this close to her, she usually stares right into my eyes. It's that sexy version of chicken she likes to play and she wins every time. Right now, she's in her head. It's another first between us. "Does it have an answer?"

The sizzle of a new batch of batter begins. She braces her hands against the stove and rocks back a little. "You know CGI, right?"

"Cooper Group Incorporated. Yes. They specialize in large brand concepts and rebrands from the bottom up."

"Yep. The bigger the dollar signs, the more my father is interested."

"Paul is your father." Instead of towering next to her, I cross behind her, hopping up on the counter where she sat last night. "I should have put two and two together."

"Eli, you asked me how I want to be seen. I want to be seen as me. I have my own thoughts and ideas. My father likes notoriety and dollars. He's not a bad person for wanting that. I get it. It's the nature of it for him. He wants to be able to say he made them soar. Cool. If I have to end up in this industry, I want it to mean more than that."

"End up? This choice to come to AnSa is about much more than the decision of here or there, clearly. Okay, perfect world. Where would you want to be next year?"

The shock on her face that I would even ask is evident. The answer flows out of her like water over a dam. "I want to be a principal in a contemporary dance company until I can't dance anymore. Then, I want to get the word out about the companies after, so I can still be near it. I want to contribute by making the arts and causes known so they can help more people. What does changing the outside of a soda can do to make that happen? Nothing. If one charity, one program, one dance company can change one life, that's everything right there."

The rubber spatula scrapes against the bottom of the pan, giving a little chill, creating sound that echoes off the walls. I rest my comforting hand around hers. "Have you ever said that out loud before?"

"No. Never."

"How did it feel?" With that same hand, I reach my fingers up to tilt her chin to look at me.

"Honestly? Pretty fucking great."

"Why aren't you a dance major then? Selfishly, I'm glad you're not or AnSa would lose a great candidate, but if that's your passion, you should give it your all."

"Going all wise professor on me?" she teases.

"Take it however you want but answer the question. It matters."

Dylan plates the last pancake before switching off the stove. She gently forces my knees apart so she can walk in between them. I smooth the hair back from her face, massaging her blushed cheeks with my thumbs. Her fingers walk up my thighs to my rib cage, subtly tracing them over and over. "It's not that I don't want to be part of the industry my father's in, but we have very different philosophies and timelines, as I've said. Dance is a hobby for them. It's breathing to me.

"He's very *my way or the highway*. That doesn't work for me in business or in my life. If I do well on this senior project, I'll get an audition for one or more companies, depending on the interest in me. My parents don't know about it. If I do decide to interview with AnSa, I don't want them to know that either."

"I wouldn't tell them. It's not my place. I don't run into Paul unless it's at a conference. Look, you need an internship to graduate. I'm offering you a shot at a place where you can carve your own path and have a voice. If that appeals to you, I'll set the interview up."

"*You* appeal to me." She pushes up on her toes to ghost her lips across mine. This trust and vulnerability she's placing at my feet right now is hotter than her body in my hands. "Yes."

"Yes, you'll interview?" She nods her head slowly before resting it against my chest. I wrap my arms tight around her. In such a short amount of time, I feel so protective of her. Not that she needs it. She's fiercer than I've even given her credit for. "Dylan, one more thing. I would like to continue this, whatever it is, we have going on between us. The only thing I would ask is that we keep our relationship out of the office. I owe that to my grandfather, my father, my staff, and most importantly, you."

"So, quickies while the blinds are pulled or tossing me down on a conference table are out of the question?"

I smile. "I'll make up for it in other ways."

After we finish eating, we linger, woven together for about an hour on the couch as the sun ducks in and out of the clouds washing light over us. Our conversation is surprisingly easy. I don't toss up any walls and neither does she.

I want to know everything about her dancing since it's what drew me in to begin with. The longer she talks about it, her demeanor changes. She's still this innately sexual woman I'm completely attracted to, but she also has this childlike excitement when she's talking about movement or the emotion behind it.

Dylan talks about how she feels about being an artist and how she uses her body instead of words or paintbrushes to create a story. I'd never thought about it like that. However, I know Aristotle did. He said, *"Dance is rhythmic movement whose purpose is to represent man's characters as well as what they do and or suffer."* Without knowing it, she's created another kinship for us.

Instead of taking her home, she had only enough time for me to drop her at the rehearsal space. I let her keep the joggers. Not only did she look adorable in them, she could go straight to work on her piece in them, and in my mind, I would be with her. I don't want to think too far ahead. That wouldn't be good for either of us.

We sit together in my car until the last possible second before I lean over the console and give my Viper a long, slow, deep kiss that I wish could have lasted for days. I took *her* breath away for once. She exits and runs up the sidewalk. Dylan offers me another double spin and a smile before she disappears behind the side entrance door.

My head falls back over the headrest with a low groan. I said I was fucked before. Now, I know I am for sure. She's headstrong, smart, sensuous, and sexy. I push the search button on my steering wheel, waiting on the next choice in my music shuffle. I'm greeted by the ferocious strum of a guitar and one word, yeah. I'm taken on a ride with Bono singing about desire. I just watched mine dance away. For now.

Being alone so long is truly leaving me mindfucked at the moment. After Tori, I wasn't good company for anyone. I had too many things to work through. I was content enough going to work and coming home. I had what I felt was enough contact from being at the office, running in the park, and spending time with Wes and my family.

What the last couple of weeks have shown me is, I couldn't have been more wrong. Now that I've had a taste of the flip side, I don't want it any other way. I would be happy if Dylan would come back and simply stay. I didn't notice the quiet before. It's now the loudest thing.

I spend the majority of Saturday in my office. I have my speakers on low with Sinatra and Nat King Cole as my music of choice. I fade in and out of work to flashes of her. Her hand. Her hip. Her cheek. Her lips. I find myself twisting my pen over and over between my fingers then my teeth.

"Your mother would be furious to know we're both here on a weekend like this, and you're attempting to ruin the dental work we paid for."

My father's voice pulls me back from the sexiest daydream on record. "Dad. She doesn't know about me but you, yes, she'd be pissed. Why are you here?"

"I got an email from Natura. They had questions. My notes contained the answers and I hadn't scanned them to the file yet, so I had to get a visual to respond. Why are you here?"

"Getting ready for the intern interviews on Monday and meeting with reps from a new potential initiative on Tuesday. A friend turned me on to the idea. You know me..."

"When a friend calls, you run." He smiles. "Is that all? You seemed in a non-workspace when I walked in. It was very similar to how you were in the Hamptons."

I tug on the back of my neck, rubbing back and forth before I lower the volume on my music. "Am I still that transparent?"

My father tucks his hands in his pockets as he strolls to the open seating on the other side of my desk. "Well, it's the same distracted look, and pair that with Sinatra."

Tapping my pen on the open palm of my hand, I open my confessional. "I met someone. It's very new, obviously. I've forgotten how to do this." I chuckle.

"Where did you meet, that is if you wish to talk about it?"

"I think I need to. Wes has already given me the green light. He is very singularly focused, shall we say, in his assessments. I'm not going to sit here and tell you he's wrong, but I also know I'm looking for more.

I didn't realize I missed being part of a whole instead of the whole on my own. Dammit, I'm not making even a little sense."

"You find yourself thinking about her more than you feel you should. You would want her beside you right now, if you could. Am I right?"

"Jesus, Dad. I feel like this is the adult version of me coming to talk to you about Lisa in prep school. But yes, you're right, I absolutely would."

"That's not necessarily a bad thing."

"Isn't that too fast? How could I feel this way already?"

"I went on one date with your mother and always knew I'd marry her. Love works in mysterious ways."

"I didn't say I loved her."

"Eli, you never said you didn't either. It's none of my business either way. I understand your apprehension. I also feel like you're going to do something you're not known for. Why you're built for this industry is you have some of the best instincts I've ever seen.

"You trust your gut and go for it and rarely miss the mark. Because of what you endured with Victoria, you will, maybe rightfully so, second, third, and fourth guess yourself in matters of the heart. Maybe just this once, trust the heart we both know you have that's bigger than your fear."

My father's words ring in my head for a long time. I'm the luckiest son in the world to have Jackson Sawyer for a father. Even in my darkest, he is right beside me helping and holding me up by doing the hardest things. He forces you to think for yourself. He will offer his opinion but always in a way where you don't feel less than, even if you're as wrong as you could possibly be.

His encouragement is on rewind, even as I'm calling Dylan's number. In the first ring, I think about hanging up. In the second ring, I decide I'm in this for the long haul. She answers in the middle of the third ring.

I can picture her smile as she speaks. "I thought of about five different movie quotes I could have answered with, but I'll go with a simple hi."

"Hey, Dylan. I took a lady's advice and called the number on the résumé."

"You're assuming I'm a lady."

"If memory serves me, you absolutely are. How were the rehearsals?"

"Long. I staged the whole thing then decided I didn't like it, so I'll pick it apart on Tuesday. Miss me?"

To tell the truth or not tell the truth; that is the question. I ended with Tori on a lie. Remember, be bigger than the fear. "Actually, yes. I can't stop thinking about you." There's a long pause. I can hear a bit of faint music in the background, but I can't make out what it is. "Viper?"

"I'm here."

"Have I freaked you out?"

"No. Honestly, I hoped you'd call." The husk is back in her voice.

"Where are you right now?"

"My apartment."

"Are you alone?" I ask.

"I will be, until you get here."

I'm already searching for my keys somewhere between the words until and you. My messenger bag is over my shoulder, and I'm switching the lights off. "Text me the address. Barring traffic, I'll be there in twenty minutes."

The elevator takes me to ground level and out toward my parking structure. GPS says four minutes. Even better. I pull out of the garage and take a left. I make it out and over the bridge toward the campus without hitting one light. The traffic gods are ever in my favor. Dylan gives me the code to her parking garage, as well as the code for her elevator.

I feel an unfamiliar tingle in my chest. I can't wait to see her. The elevator slows to the eleventh floor. The bay seems central to the building. As I exit, there are four doors: two to my right and two to my left. 11D is hers. D for Dylan and D for desire.

Casually propping myself against the doorframe, I give two quick knocks before crossing my arms over my chest. I wait and hear nothing until the slow rotation of the dead bolt and the creak of the door give way to my blonde beauty. Her bright orange sports bra makes an excellent pairing to my oversized joggers on her frame.

"I know I said twenty. I hope I didn't catch you off guard."

"Not at all. Come in." She reaches for my messenger bag, lifting it from my shoulder, then backs up for me to pass by. I inhale deeply as I do. Fucking hell. She saunters behind me step for step into her kitchen. I don't know what I expected her apartment to look like, but this surprises me.

Every wall is exposed brick with some knocks to random ones all over. This place has seen some history. The entire space is dotted with large pipes and valves, in and along the walls. Most of the lighting is from backlights attached to the brick. It shines straight up giving sundog effects in every corner of the room. Her furniture is sparse but colorful.

Her small sofa is a bright blue with seafoam and black floor pillows stacked on either side of the round white coffee table. Her television is on a corner console, opposite the kitchen island that separates the two spaces. She has three barstools at the counter, one orange, one yellow, and one lime green.

Her kitchen is complemented in all stainless steel with hints of seafoam and black. Behind the sofa is a large, nearly thirty-by-twenty, hardwood space. Ballet bars run the length of both walls with eight-foot-high mirrors that reflect every bit of light and movement in the entire room.

"Where do you sleep?"

She sets my bag down carefully on the kitchen counter before extending her hand to me. Dylan walks backward down a short hallway through a frame with no door. Her bedroom is massive. It's the full length of the loft. It's divided into four distinct areas. The upper left corner is the bathroom. The old two-person clawfoot tub is the centerpiece with a rigged rain shower attachment and a full wraparound shower curtain.

"That looks like fun." I smirk.

"We'll try it later." She holds my palm up and kisses the center, while staring with her blue gray eyes right back at me.

The upper right-hand corner is her queen-size bed. The mattress and box spring are angled into the corner, with flowing curtains that part to the sides over the top third of the bed. The flowing canopy reminds me of something straight from a Persian fairy tale. I'd like to be part of that world.

The lower right corner is two giant bean bags with a large audio system. The speakers are nearly two and a half feet tall each with a woofer besides. She has everything she'd need to mix her own music. Then just inside the door to the left are two ten-foot racks with a large chest of drawers between them. On the floor are two racks of shoes. There are sneakers of every shape and color on one and most of the other, but oh that other half rack. Seven pairs of fuck-me heels: one for every damn day of the week.

"This is home," she says, breaking me out of my erotic fantasy.

"It's great. I've learned so much about you by just being here."

She slides up, pressing her body against me. At first, her cheek does a dance against my chest. Then her hands join in at my waist, followed by her hips gently swaying in my hands. It's only then her eyes look up for me. That's when I smirk and repeat her words to her. "And there… and there…"

"See. It's easy to do, isn't it?"

"And oh so hard," I growl in her ear. Everything inside me is twitching. I can hardly be near her and not touch her. "I want you so much."

"I know." She smirks.

So. Damn. Cocky.

She kisses the side of my neck and does what Viper does best and slithers away. Dylan then calls from the kitchen. "Need a drink? I don't have wine but how about whiskey?"

"I'll take one. Make it a double."

She giggles. "Coming right up."

I take about three deep breaths before I can safely move toward her voice and body again. She's kicked out the barstool for me on the corner. I sit down as she slides the glass across the counter to me. "There you are, Goose. Tame those flames."

"Wes is going to love you."

"Meeting the friends already?"

"Only if you want to."

"What do you want?"

My mouth is full of amber as that question rolls from her tongue. One hard swallow later and I'm no closer to a definite answer, at least one I'm ready to share. "Besides you naked next to me? I want you in my life however that looks. Look, Dylan, I've been broken as fuck. Outside of the office, the time I've spent with you has been the most alive I've felt in longer than I care to admit."

"That's pretty clear, Elijah."

"What do you want?" I ask.

"You like to ask me that question, don't you?" she responds.

"It's what you should be asked. If it's not right for you, it's not right for me, as well as the reverse. I had to learn that lesson the hard way."

"You blame yourself for her cheating, don't you?" I suck the rest of the whiskey back, letting it burn back down what was bubbling up. "You don't have to answer that. I have my answer by the look on your face. I'm here to tell you, and show you, that's not true. I said she's an idiot and I meant it.

"There is such a thing as fucking communication. She could have told you she wanted out. She decided to be the worst kind of woman and be all, 'I'm going to fuck someone else in our bed and get caught instead of talking it out.' Fuck that. You deserve better. I think you're realizing that the more time you spend with me."

She's right. I am.

Dylan is, without a doubt, the strongest woman I've ever known outside of my family. She's fearless when it comes to speaking her mind and making sure she's heard. I fold up a bit after she told me I deserve better. She is right. I'm slowly realizing it, but I need more time.

Everything in me wants to stay with her in her apartment. She digs in the back of her freezer for her hidden pint of mint double chocolate chip ice cream and with two spoons we finish it. We talk for a long time about everything.

I tell her about my family and how much they mean to me. She hasn't had that same experience. All her grandparents have passed, and she isn't close with her remaining family. She's also an only child. This leads to a conversation about Hayley.

The longer we talk about her, Dylan realizes she knows her. They've had certain classes together the past two years. It is by pure fate they don't share a seminar this semester. Will was ready to take Hayley, but in true Hayley fashion, she decided that she knew him too well and wanted the separation. She's so independent and I'm so proud.

"It's interesting how you talk about family."

"Why do you say that?" I ask.

"It's just so different from what I'm used to. Is that what you want someday?"

"For myself?" I look down into the empty pint and give a sad little smile. "Funny you ask. That was the beginning of the end of my marriage."

"She wanted kids, and you don't?"

I tilt my head away from her, resting my head on my fingers, as I twist the empty spoon in the cardboard cup. "Actually, the opposite. We were on the same page, at least I thought so, until I found the pill packets in the bedside table when we were supposedly trying."

Dylan's hand comes into view, softly stopping the nervous movement of my spoon. "Do you dance?"

"I think you know the answer to that already."

"Not club dancing. I mean real dancing like USO, nineteen forties big band, slow dance style. Ballroom and shit."

"I'll do anything that involves you."

"That's not what I asked, but I like the answer. Sometimes when there aren't words, movement helps."

I've studied words forever. Motivation helps me understand how to do my job better and help my clients achieve their goals. I want to try it this way through her eyes. "What do you have in mind?"

She tugs on my arm and drags me for the first time onto her dance floor. Dylan pulls me in close and calls out to the air around us, "Play mood."

"Play mood?" I ask.

Her electronic assistant begins to pipe out a subtle vibe starting with Norah Jones. She also just so happens to be one of my mother's favorites. I lean into Dylan as she leans into me. As I slide my hand into the small space just under her shoulder blade, she runs her hand the length of my arm, resting her hand at the top.

She looks as though she's going to say something, but I catch her off guard by pushing forward with my left foot, taking her backward. I pivot her slowly across the hardwood in time to the music. Once in a while, my shoes squeal like I'm on a basketball court, but she doesn't seem to mind.

With every turn, she leans farther back into my hand and her body softens. She looks different. She's so elegant and regal, even in my joggers and an oversized top. Dylan stays on her toes even in those sneakers she wore the night we met. She lets me think I'm leading. I know I am for the most part.

The song gives us the last few notes. I know they're coming. I slowly turn her under my arm twice then pull her in tight. We stand there just barely breathing hard, unmoving. She pulls the fabric of my sweatshirt into her hand and finally looks into my eyes.

"You played me, Goose. Where did you learn to dance like that?"

"Mom and Gran. Not that anyone outside my house knows, but I could waltz before I went to prep school. I know just enough about every ballroom dance to be dangerous."

"It's extremely sexy. I like a man who knows how to move."

"You knew I could already." I rest my forehead against hers. "I should go."

"You want to leave?"

"No. I don't. If I don't though, I might never. I'm scared of how intense this feels between us."

"I can think of a thousand other ways to be scared. We'll get to those in time."

I take a long, cold shower before I go to bed alone. I can still smell her on my pillow after two days. Rolling to my stomach, pulling her scent into my arms, I go over my game plan for the interviews. I have five in total for three spots, four really. Dylan will get one of them, no matter what.

She's perfect for the slot; no one could argue her grades, obvious passion, and talent. The bonus of her working at AnSa is twofold. She'll be close to me most of the week and we won't lose her to a rival. I know where her heart is. She is like me in many ways. A difference in one person's life is all that we need to be happy. That will make her successful in this industry when, and if, she chooses it. I want to see to it that when the stage lights fall, she will rise on the other side just as bright.

Yet another Sunday night without much sleep. I'm awake before my five thirty alarm, with my arms still wrapped around the pillow. My brain is already on overload. How will today go? Will Skye have the same opinions I do about the hires? Will Dylan agree to work with us? Will she be attracted to the work version of me, which is very different from what she's seen? I guess there's only one way to know the answers to all these questions.

My run is longer today than I intended. David was in the park for an early morning game with his partner in crime. It had been a few weeks since we'd crossed paths. It was nice to take twenty minutes to catch up with him. He keeps sipping on his coffee but peering over the top of the cup. I'd ask him what he's staring at, but I already know.

The steam from my morning shower helps soothe the ongoing dull ache I have. My tie is still woefully crooked as I lock up and run for the subway. I am not the look of a corporate executive today, that's for damn sure. Anna takes one look at me as I breeze past her desk at quarter past eight and laughs.

"If I didn't know what day of the week it was, all I'd have to do is look at you."

"Very funny, Anna. I know it's not in your job description, but can you help fix this thing around my neck, so I don't look like an idiot for these interviews?"

"Okay, Eli, you need to calm down. I've padded your calendar this morning because I know you. The Monroe meeting is pushed until eleven. You have the first intern at nine thirty, the second at ten fifteen. I've ordered lunch in so you can breathe, then you have the last three back-to-back from one to three thirty, with our meeting at four to go over the final details for the quarterly tomorrow morning, and your call agenda for your new client tomorrow afternoon. I've got the outlines done to get your new hires up to speed, so all you have to do is relax and pick them." While this pep talk is going on, she's managed to make my tie perfect.

"What would I do without you?"

"I hope you never have to find out. The files for tomorrow are loaded on your desktop for anything you need. I swapped your normal espresso for tea today, so drink it. You have thirty minutes until your meeting with Jack. So, settle in, it's Monday."

"Thank you, Anna."

As she leaves, I do just that. I take a deep breath and go to my Zen place, as Hayley would put it. I dock my cell on my wireless charger and put my headset on. Here goes Monday.

The day goes by in a whirl. My father came in first thing and took copies of the intern résumés out of pure interest. I'm anxious to hear what his thoughts are, purely from the papers. He also had an update for the Monroe meeting, which was critical.

The intern candidates were a kaleidoscope of personalities. Everyone on paper should have been a fit. Some, as always happens, were not. My first one was bright, chipper, and eager. She's definitely in the running. The second and third were fine but tentative. They were not advocating enough for themselves. If you can't sell yourself, how can you market a brand?

That left me with Levi, who in all honesty, reminds me of me about ten years ago and finally, Dylan, who was on her way back. The chill that had been around all day quickly vanishes with a knock at my door. I quickly clear my throat and rise from my desk. "Come in."

I expect Anna to come in, but Dylan is there and she's alone. "Hello, Mr. Sawyer. Your assistant said I could come back."

"Yes. Yes, please, Miss Cooper. Come in and close the door."

The door latches and the temperature rises nearly ten degrees in an instant. I was so in my head about what differences she'd see in me, it didn't dawn on me what she would come in like.

I want it on record that, while I would cross the desert to remove her from a dance bra and leggings, what I see before me is infinitely better than that. Dylan appears in a form fitting navy suit, with the skirt long and lean hitting just at her knee. The single-breasted jacket hugs every curve she has and sits right at her waist. The pop of color across her breasts is the same seafoam color as the pillows in her apartment.

Her normally wild blonde hair is tamed into a sleek ballerina bun at the base of her neck, with a few stray hairs wisping around the subtle bronze glow of her cheeks. My eyes can't turn away from the glossy pink fullness that is her lips. *Dear God, don't look at her feet. Stay away from the feet until this interview is over.*

"Did you close the blinds on purpose?" she asks.

"They've been closed all day. Less distractions."

"Until me, right?"

"Yes. Forgive me, but you're stunning."

"Is that Eli or Mr. Sawyer talking?"

"Both. They're both giving you compliments to be sure, but one of them is definitely thinking much dirtier thoughts."

"I like whomever that is. How do you want this to work today? Will you be asking me anything or just staring?"

"I have one question, then yes, thirty minutes of staring."

"What's the question?"

"What time can you be here in the morning?"

Chapter Sixteen

Elijah

Her navy blue jacket is carefully folded over the white chair in the corner of the room, on top of mine. That long, lean skirt is lying across the arm of the same chair. My suit pants are a rumpled mess beneath it. Her seafoam top is in its own pool on the floor, with my tie woven through it. Those heels were ignored as promised until they came to my front door at about six.

I asked her to leave them on, to which she responded yes. They now reside one at each corner of the bed. My hand lazily strokes up and down her spine, as the weight of her body pins my torso to my mattress. Her bun was pulled away pin by pin in a slow seduction, before her suit ended up where it is now.

As my fingertips cross her right hip, she sighs. "That sounded like it came from your toes."

"That's what happens when your fantasy comes true."

I smirk against the top of her head. "Which is?"

"You in that suit was the climax of my professor fantasy."

"Interesting choice of words."

"Here's another one for you then." Dylan gives the air between us a dramatic pause before she rests her chin on my chest. "How long do we have before the pizza gets here?"

As I answered the door for the pizza delivery, Dylan raided my closet again finding my old lacrosse jersey. It sure as hell looks better on her than it ever did on me. She greets me in the hallway snatching the pizza box from my hands. "I'll take that."

"Hey!"

"Oh, calm down, grumpy. Go in the kitchen and get us some water. I'm going to set up an indoor picnic."

She pushes the living room furniture into a configuration of her liking, then plops down cross-legged on the floor. She winds her wild mane around her hand, laying it down her back. I stare at her from feet away and I know, for my sake and hers, I have to find a way to be near her and not want to be near her.

I settle in beside her with my legs fully stretched out and my toes weaving into the rug. My bare feet on the carpet is one of those self-soothing things I've done since I was a child. "Since we didn't get to talk much this afternoon due to my clear distraction, may we do that now?"

"I figured we would. I didn't know how you'd respond to me today. Once I saw your obvious reaction, I kind of played it up. Watching you sweat is becoming one of my favorite things."

"You're the only one who gets that response from me. Feel honored."

"I absolutely do." She takes a glorious bite out of her pizza with a groan of approval I've grown to love. "So, what should I expect tomorrow? We'll be in a group setting, right? I imagine I won't see you much."

"Actually, I supervise all the interns. That's why this will be delicate. As it turns out, you and your teammates come at a good time. AnSa is taking on a more personal project of sorts. It's for a friend of the family."

"Who is it?"

"Have you heard of Sam Roark?"

"Hockey player right? From what I've read, he's said this is his last season. Is it for him?"

"He and his fiancée actually. She, and his family are heavily involved with the foundation he started a couple of years ago."

"A class Hayley and I were in together last year used them as a model for a project we did. We were supposed to look at athletes and their causes. I liked how open he seemed to be about his past and how he wanted to work hard in his hometown giving the kids a place to go instead of possibly getting into things they shouldn't, but then also introducing them to experiences they might not normally be able to due to their circumstances, no matter what they are. I feel like they do most things really well, but I think there's an opportunity here."

"Like what?" Dylan licks a bit of sauce off her bottom lip and pulls it in. "Go ahead. Say it."

"You really want to know what I think?"

"Of course I do."

She licks the bit of grease off her fingers while she cocks her head just a bit to the right. Dylan usually has the words ready. Sometimes the words are ready before she is. "Having all the visibility they have in the NHL is great. That hits a huge market, especially in the area where he's playing, and it's different from the NFL. But I worry some demographics are being untouched. I'd like to see some cross promo to reach them.

"I know the kids Sam's foundation can help come from tough places. Some need extra help and care, so do some of their parents. But if some of them had arts outlets, or allowed the arts to bridge a gap between the kids and parents if needed, what might that help? There are so many studies showing the positive correlation between music, art, and dance therapies and mental healing along with education. We need to reach those people and get their time, money, and interest involved. These can be bonds they take with them, no matter where or how old. They can even repair families."

"Why do you dance, Dylan?"

"I dance because I don't know how not to. I dance because it's a part of me. There are two ways I can get every bit of my emotion out, and that's the one that's acceptable in public. Well, unless you're us that is."

"I want to see how you, Levi, and Candice work together. If it goes how I think it's going to, I want you to pitch what you just said to Sam and his family. Don't change a word of it." I suddenly feel this burst of energy. My finger waves in the air as I get up and start pacing. "What is the New York community known for? Broadway and the arts, right? So, we build our connections by going into those plays, musicals, dance companies, and we draw the artists out. It can be an auction for time with the artists, tickets to see them. Paintings to purchase. The list is endless. We start here, where we know, then expand to his city. The more people we have on board, the easier it will be for others to say yes.

"Then we have performances along with the auction to showcase the talent they could, or would, get. We have some of these kids locally come and watch. It could be the beginning of sparks or mentor/mentee relationships. I think we start with a huge fundraiser though. Really kick it off."

"You got all that from what I said?"

"Not only could we raise awareness but also bring in a shit ton of money. I don't know if you're aware but his family comes with a built in network. Sam's father works for a company with several connections of his own. AnSa could be the East Coast coordinator and secondary sponsor. If they go for it, you will have to perform."

"Me? You're crazy."

"Why? It's no crazier than not doing it. No crazier than us."

"Us? We're an us? Less than a month and you're already there?" she asks.

"Generally speaking, my dear Viper, when there's a you and a me there tends to be an us."

"You want to pitch this as a side hustle to the general marketing package."

"*We* will be pitching this, but if you care about me at all, you'll do me a favor."

"What's that?"

"Don't pull your hair all the way back like that, and wear pants instead of a skirt. Then I'll only think of your ass and not the easy access I can take to toss you on my desk."

"You're all talk! We have to keep things professional, he says. We need to hide things at the office, he says. Then you say things like that."

"It's going to be so hard. You're like... gravity."

Ariana Rose

Chapter Seventeen

Elijah

Sam, Lucy, Sam's parents, and everyone who joined the call from the Roark Foundation were as wowed by Dylan's lead on our presentation as I was. She was poised, polished, eloquent, and equally passionate. I feel so many different things right now. Behind the wheel of my car as I sit in traffic, it plays back like a movie in my head.

Dylan centered herself in a way I've never seen from her before. The placement of her hands. The depth of her breath. Her eyes morphing from closed to open. Her calm demeanor washed over the boardroom. I had an agenda prepared. It was given to everyone in the room locally and where our participants were. I made the introductions and she soared.

I wanted the interns to begin to get comfortable in pitches. It's the heart of what we do. It's about listening and observing. Coming in with a plan but being able to change that plan based on your gut. This whole idea came from Dylan. It was based inside her. It was only right she gave them the same words she gave me.

I could see people I've known for years flash their eyes over to me in a look of wondering how I could simply sit back. I kept my usual stone face as I watched Dylan go through our presentation slide by slide. I could feel a smile slip every so often. I watched as one by one, the room here and virtually, leaned in completely captivated by her.

I know the feeling.

Even after the meeting adjourned, even after the cameras were off, there was nothing more I wanted to do than throw my arms around her and pull her close to me. Her black wide-leg trousers would have brushed against my herringbone. Her red heels would have dangled millimeters from the floor across my shoe tops. The deep floral pattern of her blouse would have partially disappeared inside the edges of my jacket, as my nose would have disappeared near the high-collared bow around her neck as I'd drink in from her obvious deep well of power.

The thought of it made things inside of me shiver and twitch. I was glad I was in the car alone. I could shift and adjust as necessary in a vain countdown until she could meet me at my door. The elevator from the parking structure couldn't move fast enough. I fidgeted with my keys the entire ride up.

As the doors open, Dylan's figure arches along the wall at the end of the hall. Her bag dangles at her side. Her shoulder blades touch the wall as her hair cascades long and straight over her left side. Her hips are thrust out as she seemingly poses for me outside my door.

I'm tugging on my tie from the minute we lock eyes, as she drops the handle of her bag, pulling on the bow around her neck. The keys to my apartment dangle next to her ear as my hands capture her flushed cheeks in my hands.

Her hands slide under my jacket, gripping over my rib cage. I fumble with the lock, as all I want to do is devour her. Her soft giggle against my lips is one of the sexiest sounds she makes. We fall in the door and I kick her bag as the lead. Dylan slams the door behind us; we're finally enclosed alone.

The frenzy begins to allow our skin to meet. Her hands that were once on my back are now sliding up to push my jacket to the floor and complete the removal of my tie. Her top is like a maze I have to solve. She's begun the work by allowing the bow to fall, however, the twists and turns around her neck make it difficult for me to achieve my goal.

By the time my fingers finally find her neck, every button on my shirt is open, leaving my chest bare for her lips. As she allows me to enjoy the sweet taste of her skin, she lowers the side zipper of her top in one slow motion. With one step back, she raises her arms sexily above her head, letting me know it's my turn to free her.

The silken fabric pulls away from her skin easily and is next in a trail from the front door. The ivory lace that blends with her skin is delicate in contrast to the strength she radiates. My hands slide down over the fabric, taking it with me. I have myself the pleasure once again of committing to memory everything that she is. Strong yet soft, petite yet powerful, and in this moment, one-hundred-percent mine.

We back up slowly into the living room, tasting each other while she works my belt buckle. Her teeth tug at my bottom lip. "Fuck. Today was such a rush."

I groan. "I could have taken you on that boardroom table."

Dylan maneuvers us with the infinite grace she possesses around the coffee table and pulls us to fall onto the sofa. "I thought you said work only at work."

"I'm already breaking several rules with you. So since I'm going to hell anyway, I might as well go out with a bang."

Her deep laugh is just as hot as her girl-like giggle. "I love your choice of words." She arches backward underneath me as we both fight with our zippers in the rush we're in. "Look under the books on the table."

I knock them back to find a short string of help for when we're not near my bedside table. "Now I know what you were doing the other day when I took a bit longer in the shower."

Her hands slide into my waistband, gripping me tight as the fabric of my pants slips lower on my legs. "I told you I had plans."

As I rise up to my knees, Dylan arches back to slide her pants off, tossing them with ease behind the couch along with her shoes. They hit the hardwood with a thump, followed by a second. She lifts her arms over her head, and they playfully disappear over the arm of the sofa as her breasts push toward me and the sky.

I rip into the foil with the same growl I have just at the sight of her. If only I had three or four hands right now. I could finish protecting both of us while getting to touch her body. I'm jealous of her hands as they play with her breasts. Her legs slide back and forth slowly between mine. "I could watch you all day."

"I hope that's not all you do."

"Oh hell no," I assure her.

With my hands finally free, I let one disappear between us as I lean forward and plank over her. Dylan reaches up and pulls me to her lips, as my hand travels a frantic path to give her a taste of what my body feels. Her beautiful body rolls into the vibration of my fingers.

She responds nearly instantly. I can already feel from her what I feel inside. I can't wait any longer. She pants as her eyes lower to watch as I align us. Every time with her is like the first time. That same anticipation and deep-seated desire always burns right below the surface. As I sink inside her in one slow, full motion, we both exhale. It's a sigh of relief.

I lower closer to her; my knees bear the weight. My arms wrap around her heated body to anchor her to me. I'm tethered between wanting to race to the finish because my entire being is telling me to and yet I want to make this last as long as I can. I've never wanted a woman so much. I've never been this driven to be connected in this way.

My hips thrust forward and back in time with the beat of my heart. No amount of breathing is going to slow the rate. Her nails claw up the fabric of the couch before she wraps her arms around my back. I pin her frame to the pillows. Each pulse of my body brings a noise from her.

What begins with a slow breath becomes a gentle moan in my ear and is climbing to a constant string of pants, some of which contain my name, which is only making me drive harder to the finish line.

"Ohhhhhhh fuck…" she groans in a high pitch. "Eli, I'm…"

"Viper. Wait. For. Me," I growl. I can feel the battle. There's no loser. I make it last, we win. I give in, we win.

We stop communicating in words. She knows my body now nearly as well as her own. She can feel the shake in my shoulders, the tightness of my abs, my harsh breath on her neck. Dylan and I release our fiery passion for each other and this day in a way that makes me grateful for the noise of the city.

"Did you want me to order in, instead? I think you might be too tired to cook." Wes's voice echoes in the hallway as he crunches on an apple.

"What the fuck, man. Don't you knock?" I ask, as I try in vain to free the blanket from the back of the couch to cover Dylan and me.

"Do you think you would have heard me? Yeah, right."

Dylan starts laughing beneath the protection of my body. "Maverick, right?"

"In the flesh." Wes winks as he makes himself at home in the chair on the other side of the coffee table.

Dylan slides up as I try to cover us, but she wraps the blanket around my lower half and not her. "Well, Mav, since you're too late to join in, I'll go toss on a T-shirt and cook for you both. I'm suddenly very hungry."

With a kiss on my cheek, she wriggles out from under me walking slowly to my bedroom with the same sway I got the first night we met. Being caught didn't faze her. Being naked in front of Wes didn't faze her. I'm equal parts stunned, and not, by her reaction.

As we hear the bathroom door close, Wes leans in with his mouth hanging open. "Dude, she's phenomenal."

"Don't talk about her like that. Ever," I warn him.

"Jesus, fuck off. I meant she's amazing. Most would have been eeek and run away. She was all take a picture it'll last longer. Fucking phenomenal. Oh, and a favor please, can you put it away?" I look down at the blanket edges hanging open and quickly stand up to wrap it like a towel at my waist. "Blonde. Wild hair don't care. Is that Viper?"

"Her name is Dylan Cooper but yes, that's her."

"You've been holding out on me, you asshole. This wasn't a booty call. Give me the short version quick before she comes back."

I sigh as I rub the back of my neck, which I'm sure is either red with embarrassment or with marks from Dylan's nails. "She turned up in Will Stone's seminar I do every year. There she was second row center. I called her to his office after to talk."

"You're knocking all the fantasies off with one woman. First it was fuck in public, now the teacher/student vibe. Who are you and bravo."

"Jesus Christ. Locker room later, which by the way you're not getting any play-by-play. After the seminar, I invited her to dinner here. Dinner turned into dessert, which turned into breakfast, which...." I pause.

"Which what? Don't leave me hanging," he begs.

"Made her a part of this year's AnSa intern class." Before Wes can say a word that matches his I fucking knew it smile, I continue, "Don't even say it. I can see it in your fucking grin. She's brilliant, passionate, and amazingly intelligent. She's already going to head the revamp project for Sam's foundation."

"Damn. She's wound up in you. I mean awesome, but..."

"But what?"

"I don't need to say it. You already know."

"Maybe he does, but I don't know if I do. Tell me what you're thinking, Mav, that's if you have the balls to say it to my face," Dylan challenges Wes.

He quickly puts his hands up. "Look I don't want to start shit. I just don't want to see Eli hurt."

I take a step forward when Dylan shoots me a look. It's funny how, with some people, it takes years, and sometimes never, to understand thoughts without words from someone you care about. Dylan is so open and honest. I've never seen her hide. She feels what she feels and says what she says with sass blended with kindness. She's completely unapologetic and it's one of the sexiest things about her.

Dylan steps in between Wes and me. With a fierceness, she crosses her arms and looks him in the eye. "If you don't want to start shit, don't. I don't need to fuck to get things. Eli and I are having fun. I know what he's been through. We've talked about pretty much everything. He can be who he wants to be with me. I think he's even figuring out that there are things he wants he didn't know he did. So, if you want to get to know me, and how we revolve together, stick around. If not, you know the way out."

Instead of waiting for his response, Dylan turns with a kiss for me on the cheek. "I left the joggers for you this time." As she walks toward the kitchen, she hollers back at us, "I hope chicken and veggies are okay."

Wes stands stunned for a split second before a wicked smile and silent chuckle wash over him. "Like I said, fucking phenomenal."

Ariana Rose

Chapter Eighteen

Elijah

Wes and Victoria knew each other from day one. They were always friendly to each other. They cared about one another. The one thing that was always missing between them however was respect.

Tori didn't always respect my need for time with him. He's like a brother to me. We've been through more things than I care to think about on his side and mine. When I spend time with him, it's family time to me. She saw him as a rival in many ways.

Wes didn't respect her, because I think over time, he watched my flame go out. I felt it. I didn't want to acknowledge it. My marriage model was about compromise and making it work. Clearly, in the end, Tori was not of that same opinion.

Watching Dylan and Wes is a different experience. His respect for her was instant. I could tell she held back at first. That's her defense mechanism, but by the end of dinner, she let him in as well. There was a playfulness and synergy between them I was so grateful for.

Dylan's voice cuts through the stillness I feel before sleep. "You haven't stopped smiling."

"I'm just happy."

"Can you tell me why?"

"I've never seen someone handle Wes the way you did. He loved the hell out of it and so did I."

"I don't like the feeling of having to prove myself, so if I end up in that place, I make it go away fast. I wanted him to know where he stood with me and how you and I are together."

"You did that and more, Viper." I stroke her hair back from her cheek with my fingers in tiny feather light pulls. "When are your rehearsals this weekend?"

"I'm going over costume design at lunch tomorrow after class and before I finish the afternoon at work. I decided to give them Saturday off, but we have a late three-hour marathon Sunday night. That's the only time I could book the space. Why?"

"Can you fit some overnight things into a backpack?"

"Yeah. Where are we going?"

"Back to the start. I want to go to the Hamptons overnight. The drive should be stellar with the leaves changing. One last ride for the season."

"Ride? Like on a motorcycle maybe?" I can feel the pleased curl of her lips against my skin.

"Does that surprise you?"

"More like excite me."

"I like when you get excited." I slide her body on top of mine.

"Oh, I know." She smiles.

We leave the city in our rearview at about five on Friday. Unfortunately, or fortunately, depending on how you look at it, Dylan didn't get a chance to change before we took off. Just outside of the prying eyes of the city limits, she unbuckles and dives into the back seat of my car.

With the skill of someone who might have done this before, she goes from my project manager to my Viper in five minutes flat. Flat was the key word. She'd smile then disappear from view for a second. Her heels were a tease as they flew over the seat at me.

I heard the zipper on her backpack about the same time as I saw her flip her hair in my rearview mirror. The hair tie was gone; her wild waves were back. I reach up to tilt the mirror so I can take in more of the show. First her skirt disappears, and her jeans rise. Then as she catches me watching her, Dylan smiles at me with her eyes before opening her blouse one button at a time.

I'm blessed with red silk today. Her tank top slides on so easily, just before my favorite white sneakers come barreling over to land beside her heels. She nibbles on my ear as she climbs by and puts her seat belt back on. "You're bad," I tell her.

"You like it," she responds, as she pulls her toes up to the edge of her seat. "So, are Jack and your mom going to be there?"

"They have dinner with friends tonight at six. My mom is not fond of being late so they should be gone."

"Do I get a tour of your parents' house, specifically your old room?"

I laugh. "Maybe next time. I'm a little nervous. It's a big deal we're taking this small risk."

"I get it, Goose, but think of it as foreplay."

"Everything you do is."

I park in my spot in the driveway, leaving the keys in the lockbox where the key to my bike is. "I'll give you Hayley's riding jacket and helmet to wear. I think you're about the same size." I hold the helmet while she slides into the leather. There's only one word that comes to mind once she's set.

Fuck.

I've never been so hard on a ride before. The events are on loop. She flips her hair and tightens the strap under her chin. She straddles that bike like it was made for her. Her arms wrap around me and each time she changes her grip on a turn, it sends rapid fire straight to my cock. Every once in a while I'd hear her laugh in the wind. I love the pure joy she has of being in each and every moment. God this was a good idea.

I let Dylan off the bike with our packs before I back it into the garage once we reach the Hamptons. She pulls off her helmet and begins to check everything out. "Welcome to the family home," I tell her.

"Damn. It's beautiful and huge."

"My gran and pops wanted it big enough for four or five generations to stay here at one time. It's kind of a dream for them."

"Nice dream. Show me inside?" She extends her hand and we walk up the path as though we've done it a thousand times before. Dylan leans against the paned side window, while I do the keyless entry and security system.

"It's all high-tech. Set to seventy inside. Pool set to eighty-eight. We'll have to roll back the cover, but go for a swim after dinner?"

"I didn't bring a suit."

"Somehow Viper, I don't think that's a problem."

"You're right. It's not." She smiles.

"Let's get takeout from Sam's. We can eat deckside until the air cools and then get warm in the pool."

"You have the best ideas."

"All my best lately revolve around you."

I didn't know what it would feel like to have her here. She never seems bothered by the inevitable ghosts. I'm so glad I got rid of most of them at the end of summer. I do the quick order from Sam's then take her on a full tour of the house.

She spins and twirls on all levels of the house where there's an open space. I sorted in my head, on the way out here; I don't want us to stay in my usual room. That wouldn't be fair to her or me. My parents' room has a beautiful big balcony so we could sit under the stars if we choose.

Sam's brings us the best thin crust garbage pizza on the planet, along with a six-pack of end of summer ale. We each sit cross-legged on the edge of chaises facing each other, with the pizza box in the middle and the beer on the ground.

Her body isn't the only thing I would cross a desert for. Her laugh, her smile, the way she listens and thinks. We've known each other for about six weeks, but in that time, we've built something I don't think I've had before. She's made me question everything, and for someone who already questions everything, that says something.

In the dark, we bob up and down in the pool for about an hour. Dylan's tank top is like a second skin. It moves over her every curve. The cool night air makes things stand at attention, including me. I climb out first, holding out a thick oversized towel for her to blanket in. She quickly hops out and runs into my arms.

"Your lips are blue," I laugh. "Why didn't you tell me how cold you were?"

"I was having too much fun."

"Let's get you inside and warm you up."

I run a hot bath in the oversized Jacuzzi tub in the en suite. I leave the canned lights barely up so we can watch the stars through the skylight. I thought about putting music on, but in a rare change for me, I decided to leave it quiet. However, I like the sounds I do hear. Her body separates the water and the stillness as she settles. A few random birds in the nearby trees. The wind rustling its way through the leaves.

As I settle in behind her, I catch her watching me. "What is it?"

"It's not sexy but it's a conversation I feel like we need to have."

"Okay. I'm listening."

"My costumes have been finished for weeks. I lied. I went to my doctor and had an IUD put in and got tested for us. If you're okay with it and healthy, I don't want to use condoms anymore. Part of being as sexual as I am is knowing what I want. I only want to be with you. If that were to ever change, I'd tell you. I know I just dumped a lot on you, but what do you think?" I sit with her in between my legs, holding on. I'm speechless. "Eli?"

"Yeah. I heard you."

"I'm not asking for a title or a commitment, other than we're monogamous. I'm still me. We're still this, just without the hood, but only if you're comfortable." She spins around, straddling my lap. Her arms pull up lazily around my neck. "Do you trust me?"

"I do. I have to." I sigh. "This is a hot-button issue for me. I was tested every six months for two years because of Tori. That's not an issue. You're the only woman I've been with since her. You know that."

"I won't hurt you Eli."

She could, but I want to tango on.

I take a while getting ready for bed. I don't know why, but this triggered me in a way I didn't expect. It shouldn't. I know better. Dylan is the opposite of everything I'm used to. She's honest. She's brave. She took charge of herself. It's amazing and sexy. In that same breath, it touches a point of anxiety I've not yet been forced to look at.

I massage underneath my eyes and around my temples before I put my glasses on. When I open the door from the bathroom, she's there, patiently waiting. She's got a pair of red flannel pants with hearts on them hanging just at her hips with my U2 T-shirt. The door to the balcony is open, and she's taken an extra duvet from one of the other bedrooms and put it on top of the one we already have.

"Elijah, I know I just tossed a lot at you. I can tell you're working something out in your head. You don't have to work it out tonight. In fact, I don't want you to. I've made the bed for us. I've made a little nest. I want you to lie on my chest and let me hold you for once. I've opened the door hoping during the night, any doubts you still have will escape and you'll get clear."

I bring her hand to my lips, kissing the back. She leads me over to the bed, pulls back all the blankets and climbs in. She settles herself in the middle leaving her arms for me. Without hesitation, I climb in to rest my head on her chest. My hand rides the outside of her thigh and crosses to her belly.

I can feel my heart rate slow as Dylan pulls the blankets back around us. My legs slowly vine with hers. She carefully reaches in and removes my glasses. Even with my eyes now closed, I can feel her watching me.

Her finger slowly traces down the side of my face, around my chin, and back up again. It's one long leisurely pattern. Her body tension releases into the pillows as her hand rests over mine. The last thing I remember is her fingers in my hair along with the rise and fall of her chest. She's given me the one thing I needed more than anything. Peace.

We both wake in the morning still in the same position we fell asleep in last night. If she wanted to move, she didn't. Her hand is still on mine and my ear is still resting near her heart. Dylan offers to make breakfast but that's not what I want. I have this strong sense of needing to do everything together today.

It starts with breakfast. We keep it simple. The food is simple. The conversation is simple. One of the best things about us is not having to read between the lines. I haven't yet figured out whose doing that is, but I'm sure as hell not questioning it.

Instead of taking the bike for another spin, I grab the keys for Pops's classic sixty-four and a half Mustang. It's a fucking work of art in all its powder blue glory. With the windows down along the water, it's a bit chilly but the sun makes it a perfect drive.

We find some juicy burgers for lunch and take one last walk through the LongHouse Reserve for the year. Somewhere in the middle of all this, it occurs to me I feel like we're on a real date. Something other than dinner hidden in my home or hers. Something other than our work in and out of the office. Something other than the chemistry we clearly share.

It feels good.

"I have an idea," I tell her, as we wander through the gardens.

"Uh oh," she giggles.

"Stop!" I laugh. "This feels like a vacation today. I'd like to roll with that."

"Okay. Sounds easy enough."

"Except for what I want to do, we'd need to go shopping."

"The problem with that is what exactly?" She twirls under my arm.

"I was hoping you'd say that. So you'll let me spoil you?"

"You don't have to do that, Goose. I can handle myself."

"Never argue with your wingman. Let me. What do you say?"

"I say poor credit card," she giggles before running away to get me to chase her.

Dylan could look good, and does, in anything. From her dance gear to jeans to a casual dress and sneakers to a suit, which is my favorite, to my clothes to nothing at all, she is unbelievably beautiful. However, the sight of her walking down the stairs to me tonight would stop any Formula One race in its tracks.

Each step coming toward me gives me the opportunity to see something new. First are the flesh-colored pumps she chose. Good God. I want to see those up close later. The white background of the dress sets off the bit of bronze her skin still has from summer. The indigo pulls out the rich color of her eyes. The powder blue is an exact match to the car and the pink pulls me to her lips, which glisten over her smile.

Her hair is perfectly cascading around her shoulders. The hem lies just long enough for the imagination to work overtime, but short enough to see her legs in all their athletic glory. As she reaches the bottom next to me, she extends her hand out and lays it on my chest. "I like this sweater on you."

"Thanks for picking it out. I have an extra for you. The owner said they would look perfect on your ears. I'd say I tend to agree." The dangling opalescent teardrop earrings will accent her ears, which I love to taste, but point me to her neck, which I love even more.

"I always wanted to be Cinderella. Thanks for making it happen."

"You're better than any princess I can think of." I offer her my arm. "Shall we go to dinner?"

"Yes, Prince Goose." She leans into my ear. "Do yourself a favor and walk behind me on the way into the restaurant. You won't be sorry."

Fuck.

The leather jacket she borrowed from Hayley is the perfect opposite yet perfect complement to the dress she has on. It's also her clear way to tease me. I can't look at her until we are in public. The heightened anticipation is setting me on fire.

As we pull into the valet station, her door is quickly opened. I hand off the keys and grab my ticket. By the time I reach her side, she's removing her jacket in the sixty-degree weather, just to give me the show I was promised. The jacket hits me in the chest as she walks as if she's on a red-carpet runway.

She sweeps her hair over her shoulder to give me the full effect. The neckline has two capped buttons, which give way to two thin straps that fall effortlessly over her shoulder blades. The back of the dress is completely open.

She has one small mole on her back. I've seen it. I could find it in the dark. It's barely still on her back. That mole is staring me in the face just to the left of the top of the zipper. Watching her like this, I feel exactly like I did the first moment I saw her. I have to touch her, and I have to touch her now.

As I give my name to the host, I slide my hand into the small of her back. "Just wait until we get home," I whisper in her ear.

She looks straight ahead with a taunting smile. "With our new rules, you might not have to."

Jesus.

I know what I'm going to need to put out the flames. It's time to let her taste the drink I've named after her. I hold her chair out, as a proper gentleman would, for her to sit. My thoughts are anything but proper. I choose to sit at her right against the window. The tables in the corner are a bit farther apart and my cover, so to speak, won't be blown.

"Let me order for you on the first round."

"All right. This should be interesting." Within a couple of intense silent minutes spent staring at each other, mentally going over my options for later, our drinks arrive. "Okay, Patrón and two cherries?" She laughs. "Clue me in."

I slide one two-shot tumbler her way. "It was a whim. I'd just gone to find you after you ran away into the night, and Wes wanted to buy me a victory cocktail."

"First, I didn't run, I walked. Second, it wasn't running away, I was going home. And third, I should have known it had to do with him."

"The Patrón may be him, but the cherries were all you. I could still taste your lips. After I found out your name, the only way I could keep that for myself is to add two cherries. I'll never eat a cherry again without it reminding me of you." For the first time ever between us, she blushes. "That was beautiful."

"What was?" she asks.

"Never mind. I'll keep it to myself."

The restaurant is less than half full. I'm not used to being up here this late in the season, so it is nice to have something a little more intimate. We inhale every course straight through to dessert. The conversation never slows. We talk about everything from school, music, dance, work, art, and more about our philosophies on life.

As the check comes, Dylan is doing a little stretch of her neck. Her eyes are lowered, and her long lashes greet me in a wave. The power she has over me is back. I don't care where we are or who may see us. I reach for the delicate curve of her chin, tilting it to look at me. "I..." I pause.

"You're perfect." I rise a little from my seat to taste the same cherry, but now mixed with chocolate and all things inherently Dylan.

"Let's get out of here. I'm feeling things I won't be able to stop and don't want to. Thank you for dinner... and that kiss. I won't need the jacket for the ride home."

My hand explores every curve of her leg beneath the hem of her dress on the short distance home. The less than five miles, in time, however, seems like an eternity. Dylan stands between the keypad and me at the front door. She kisses my neck with her hands at my waist, as I try in vain to enter the six damn numbers.

We stumble in the door laughing. Once the outside world is closed out, our laughter fades and I can finally react. I weave our hands together, tucking her right arm behind her back as I rest her against the door. My right hand cups gently over her throat as I press against her before tasting her lips once more. Usually, she tries to weave away. This time she leans into it, giving in to my lead. Our bodies gently grind together against the paneled door. Each soft moan from her or groan from me bounces from floor to ceiling in the foyer.

"Hey, Eli! I saw the bike in the garage and saw the 'Stang was gone. I wondered when you'd be back. How was the ride?" A female voice begins softly in the kitchen but soon mixes with the music we're making in what we thought was an empty house. "Um, hi" are the last two words I hear before I feel Dylan freeze inside my touch. To my left, out of the shadow of the kitchen, stands Hayley.

"Shit, Hayles. What are you doing here?"

"I needed a quiet night to work with the monitors in Dad's office. Um, clearly I'm interrupting."

"Eli? Do you want me to go or...?" Dylan asks.

"No! No. Stay." I take a breath before I address my sister. "You are and aren't interrupting. Hayley, I think you two know each other. This is Dylan Cooper. Call sign Viper."

"Hey, Hayley."

"Viper? Like *the* Viper?"

"Yes, Hayley. Now that this cat is out of the bag, it has to go back in the bag and stay with you. We don't want this public knowledge," I tell her.

"Jesus, why not! Oh my God, Dylan. I wanted to thank you weeks ago. Now I can for real. I can't tell you how happy you make him. He's not so fucking sad and down on himself. You gave me my brother back. You guys do you in whatever way you want. I'm cool with everything as long as my Eli stays. If he gets hurt again though, it will be a whole different story."

"Whoa, Tiger, back down!" I grumble. "This one doesn't scare easy, but damn." Dylan slowly goes from not knowing quite what to say to a giggle fit. I kiss the back of her hand to break her laughter. "What's so funny?"

She responds. "I didn't believe you when you said how you two were together. It's fabulous. If I had a brother and I walked in on him like that, I don't think I'd be as cool about it."

"I'll pay him back for it one day," Hayley says.

"Um shit, no! Just no." I walk away into the great room.

"Look, Eli. I'm in the other wing. Just pretend I'm not here. I'm a big girl. I get it. I'll just catch you at breakfast. Mom sent a quiche and pastries. There's enough for all of us." Hayley asks Dylan, "May I give you a hug? Seriously."

"Sure." Dylan nods.

I only saw Hayley and Tori hug once. It was on our wedding day. It should have been a sign. I know Hayley was young, but she is beyond important to me. Bond with her. I think the older Hayley got and the more she was out in the world, she came to understand what was coming for me before I did. Wes being in our corner was one thing. Hayley knowing and approving sets a whole different tone. Dylan and I just hit another level.

Dylan offers to go upstairs to give Hayley and me a second alone. I watch her back until I can't see her milky skin any longer. "You absolutely never looked at Tori like that. Not like *ever*. Holy shit, Eli."

"Please don't make more of this than it is right now."

"And what's that, Brother? Tell me? You like her. You're clearly having lots of sex with her. She makes you smile. What more is there?"

"Look, I just want to keep things light and fun. So does she. There is another piece to this that you're missing. She's one of my interns. Dad would flip out and Pops would be pissed. Please just keep this to yourself. If you need to dish, call Wes."

"You're worried about me and *he* knows?" Hayley laughs. "You're joking, right? His mouth is almost as big as his ego."

"I hadn't intended on anyone knowing nor did she. It was something we decided together. She's got amazing ideas. She's in the top of her class. She's got passion for days."

"And you *like* her. Don't freak. Your secret is safe with me. Do you need me to make a pinky promise like I did when I was a kid?"

"No, Kiddo." I press my lips to her forehead. "I don't."

"Go be with her, Eli. I promise I'll keep my earbuds in." She smiles.

I point toward her room. "Shut it. Go."

I climb the steps slowly until I hear Hayley's giggles fade and her door close. My focus then switches from my sister to what is on the other side of my bedroom door. The solid French doors are open just a crack. As I push them wider, I see Dylan standing on the balcony in the moonlight. She's swaying a little forward and back, as if she was standing on the bow of a ship. She's my Rose.

As I shut us in and lock the door, the sound of the click carries into the night and her. She turns her head over her right shoulder a bit. "So... you like me?"

I take a couple steps forward before answering her, "Yes. I believe I do."

"That's good to know." She steps out of her heels, leaving one on the balcony and one in the doorway. She literally walks right out of them. Her steps become more catlike as she pulls her hair back over her right shoulder again. Dylan eases the loops over her covered buttons, letting her neckline dangle loose.

We meet barely an inch apart in the center of the room. She reaches out and tugs underneath my sweater to free my T-shirt, giving access to her skin on mine. A chill shoots through my entire body. She begins to slide both pieces up as I grab hold of them from the back. As a team, we pull them off and to the floor.

Dylan artfully takes her thumb and traces a line inside my belt buckle before loosening it and letting it hang against me. The tiny straps from the back of her dress are calling for me to move them. I pull them back like strings on a bow to lower them past her elbows. They only fall so far without an assist from the barely-there zipper.

That's not the only thing that's bare. Her chest is bare beneath the confines of the dress, as well as what's beneath the two ruffles of the short skirt. I exhale in a rush at the sight of her as the fabric floats down her body to the floor.

"Jesus Christ. You were like that the whole time?"

"I decided if we were going to start a new eight count, I wanted you to remember the first beat."

"Viper, I never forget a good lyric."

I physically can't stand being separated from her anymore. My arms wrap her up at her waist and just under her arm, pulling her off the ground to press her into me. She's slightly chilled to the steam I nearly feel radiating all around. I walk with her in my arms, setting her gently on the edge of the bed.

Dylan slowly lies back, allowing her arms to splay over her head. As I simply stare in awe at her perfect body, with a smirk she rotates in the center of the bed. Her hands reach behind her and she slowly winds her fingers around the slats of the footboard. Her toes tug at the fabric of the duvet while her knees bend slightly and move like palms in a slow breeze. I know her body. This means she's ready. She's been ready.

My shoes find a new home deep under the bed, as I free myself from the confines of my clothes. I climb up and over her body. My knees part hers as I settle back on my heels. I can feel my chest heaving as I look down the bed at her body open and waiting for me.

"Do you know how powerful you look, Eli? How beautiful?"

"You do this, Dylan."

She looks like an angel lying on a cloud. Her hands are stretched through the wood rails holding on. The tension in her body calls to me. "Let me watch you just for a minute," she requests.

I'm already nearly painfully hard from the stunning sight laid out before me. I don't think I'd ever deny her a thing. I rock back to my heels and allow her eyes to laser focus on me. I need to palm myself and give in to the tensity.

The full, long strokes of my hand build another peak I want to climb before I reach the summit that is her. I slowly twist left. Over and over.

My hips begin rolling in slow clockwise circles. There are only two things that would be better right now, her fingers in place of mine, or finally fully feeling her for the first time.

The second option is what I crave. I obsess over it as my mind goes to another place. My breathing goes from deep full breaths to slow steady pants. "Eli…" Her voice washes over me in the dark. "Come. Here."

The moonlight from outside beams across her eyes. They're dancing in anticipation. I gently let go of myself. The edge was close. Too close. We both knew it. I take a deep breath as I walk my hands down the bed by her sides. As I lower toward her, our bodies align without us having to do a thing.

I can feel my tip ride along the line of my personal utopia. She feels it too. The slats creak under the grip of her hands as she arches her back. As she does, I slip a fraction inside. She's so inviting; I could easily drown inside her.

I rest my head on her chest as the room spins for a fraction of a second. "Don't fight it, Eli. Just don't. I know you know how to be nice and slow. Show me your other side."

Dylan's eyes narrow in a challenge. It's one I will accept on behalf of the part of me who is starving to taste her. I clamp my hand around hers and thrust inside. The room fills with our own music. She's this side of a scream every time I plunge deep. I'm this side of a roar each time I claim her completely.

We ride this wave over and over. My free hand plays down her chest with each roll and arch of her body. I'm still fighting. Even with this power, I don't want to go too hard or too fast. I want to reach the finish line, but I'm not in any hurry. The thrill of drinking her in like this, the way she's stroking my every need, is the ultimate desire.

She tenses her thighs, and it sends us to another level. My hand that was once free has now joined my other over the top of the footboard. Even in her relentless pants, she marries it with a wicked smile. She knows what she's doing, always.

My new restrictions inside her are my fingertips on the edge of a cliff. The harder I try to hang on, the more futile I know it is. I use my fingertips to leverage my last bit of power and push as deep as I've ever been. Her cries are the sweetest music I've ever heard.

"Oh. God. Dylan." Each crack of the wood, and loss inside her, brings a different word. I'm on a train that won't stop. Her climax rushes in before mine. Her whole being cries out as her nails dig into my skin. Our combined pleasure consumes the air around us.

I'm completely frozen as the pulses move up and down my spine. With each shake, shiver, and sigh from her lips, I slowly lower my body down to hers. My hands are unwavering on the bed frame, even as my arms resemble Jell-O.

Dylan reaches over to my shoulder with her lips. "You can let go now."

"I don't know if I can."

She smiles. "Let me."

I do. I am. I will.

Chapter Nineteen

Elijah

I'm in the mood for steak is our new code when we're around other people. She's even dared to use it at the end of a meeting when we're all filing out of the conference room. The first time she did it, I choked. I think Anna picked up on it. It's becoming apparent we're not as skilled at hiding our connection as we once were.

Dylan's always been able to read me. I'm still not certain if I'm that transparent, she's that intuitive, or both. I do notice everything about her. What I'm noticing lately is her spark is just a shade dull. As we wrap our final meeting for the Roark Foundation brand relaunch in a few weeks, I ask Dylan to stay behind.

She stands back toward the top of the room while I close the door. "Will you sit with me?" I ask.

"Sure. Is something wrong?"

"I'm not sure. That's what I'd like to talk about. As your boss, you're forgetting details I'm not used to seeing you forget. You're about a half step behind where you usually are. As someone who cares about you, you're not smiling as much. On the Dylan scale of one to ten, you're at an eight when you're usually consistently an eleven. Talk to me please."

She sits down while wrapping her hands around her neck in a vain attempt to rid a bit of her evident anxiety. "Right after the Hamptons, the day after my marathon rehearsal, I found out my unicorn dance company's director is going to attend the showcase at the end of the month."

"Holy shit. That's great, right?" Dylan doesn't respond instantly, so I prompt her again. "Right?"

"No. I mean yes, it is. Except yesterday I had to let one of my best male dancers go because the school found a banned substance in his things. He's on probation. I can't have that near me, and neither can the school. His understudy has like a week to get up to speed and my alternate has to take his place.

"I've been doing so many extra practices before class, during my lunch breaks, and some nights after I leave you, instead of going home. My piece could fall apart, and I could lose a real shot at an audition. This is everything, Eli, everything."

"Hey. Hey. Don't panic."

"I don't panic. I just marginally lose my shit." I don't mean to, but I burst out laughing. "I'm glad you're finding humor in this, Eli."

"I'm sorry. Truly. First of all, you should have said something before. Second, let me help you."

"What are you going to do? Put on some tights and learn the choreography?"

"As much as I know you'd secretly love it, no. As your boss, I can alter your schedule so you can dedicate more time to your preparation and sleep. As someone who cares for you, I'll make sure you have the space to care for yourself and be there for whatever support you need. I want this for you too, you know."

Dylan finally releases her neck, reaching for my hands. Her fingers trace the back of mine, playing with my ring. "Do you know how long I've waited for someone to tell me that?"

"Longer than you should have, Viper. As much as I would like to spend tonight with you, I want you to leave and head home. Do what you need to do. If that's sleep for twelve hours, do it. If that's have an extra rehearsal or two, do it. If you don't want to sleep alone, call me, I'll come to you."

"She really was an idiot," Dylan whispers.

"What did you say?"

"Nothing. Plan on that sleepover."

I'd heard what she said. I asked her to repeat it to see if she would. The fact she didn't tells me something. She's making decisions about us like I am. We aren't sharing them yet because of our own fears to be sure, but I know it's happening.

I run into my father while packing up for the day, and he invites me to the house for dinner. I haven't been going as much since the end of summer, for obvious reasons, so tonight is the perfect night to correct that. I convince him not to tell my mother so I can surprise her.

My parking spot is hidden from her view in the kitchen. Dad and I arrive at the same time, so she thinks it's just him coming in the door. I quietly set my messenger bag down on the bar in the front room and watch Mom from the doorway.

Sometimes I think she's happier in the kitchen than anywhere else. Classical music fills the spaces left between sizzles on the stove. I walk up behind her, kissing her cheek while I steal one of the cherry tomatoes she's slicing. "What's for dinner?"

"Eli!" she screams, as she swats me with a towel. "Shame on you for startling me, but I'm so happy you're here."

I wrap my arms around her, apron and all. "I'm sorry it's been a while. Things have been busy."

"So I hear. Your father tells me this gala event you're working on is going to be wonderful. Would you like something to drink, sweetheart?"

"You don't have to wait on me, Mom. I'm good until dinner."

"That's in five minutes. I've been reading the materials your father brought home. I think the whole thing sounds amazing. My son is a superhero."

"I'm not Superman, but we're sure going to try," I tell her.

"It sounds like you have an exceptional intern class this year. Also, will you please set this bowl on the table and call your sister? She's upstairs."

"Sure, Mom." I walk into the formal dining room, setting the bowl down before I do something I know will wind Hayley up, and most likely get me in trouble. I yell up the stairs, "Hey, Princess Hayley Jo! Get your tiara down here! The peasants would like to eat."

"Elijah Jackson!" I'm scolded from behind me. "If I wanted to yell, I could have done that myself."

"Come on, Mom, have a heart. I like to pick at her once in a while."

"She told me you did that recently. It's not like you to go to the Hamptons lately at all, let alone in the off-season."

I'm a bit stunned. I wonder what else dear sister said. "Jesus, Eli. Dramatic much?"

"So you mentioned I was in the Hamptons?" I can feel the color in my face change the minute Hayley walks in the room.

"Yeah. I didn't think it was some big secret."

My mother reaches in from behind me and settles the basket of bread on the table to my right. "You might have mentioned to your mother that you were seeing someone. Why was I the last to know?"

"I... What?"

My father comes strolling in, clapping his hands. "Smells delicious. What's for dinner?"

"Looks like a huge slice of crow for my sister to feed that big mouth of hers."

"Elijah. What a nasty thing to say." I'm scolded again.

"I asked her to keep one secret. One and she couldn't do it."

Hayley blasts me. "If you'd shut up and listen for just one second before you get your panties in a bunch, I can explain. So grab some wine or beer or whatever will chill you out, and I'll tell you what we've been saying."

"We? Shit. This should be good."

"Eli. Enough," my father chimes in. "You're both acting like school children. Sit."

As dinner begins, we're all silent. I'm sitting directly across from Hayley like we're in some super cage match main event. We eat slowly, savoring the time the food occupies our mouths so we can't talk.

My father breaks the silence first. "Can we have a conversation about this? I know it's not the way you assume it to be, Elijah."

I end up picking at the last remnants on my plate while I speak. "How is it then?"

"Your sister returned from her study overnight and told us she'd seen you with a date up there. Hayley said she met her and liked her. She also said you looked happier than she's seen you in a long time. To which I added you'd mentioned a young lady to me. Is it the same woman?"

"Yes, Dad. It's the same one."

My mother reaches for my hand. "I just want to know if what your father and sister say is true. Are you happy? I don't need to know any other details than that if that's what you want."

Her petite fingers fold inside my much larger hand. To comfort her, I give them a gentle squeeze. "We met that last holiday weekend in the Hamptons. She splits her time, much like we do. She's beautiful, intelligent, and yes, she does make me happy. We're keeping it light and fun. This is how I need it to be for now. I hope you understand."

"You're a grown man, Elijah. Just don't feel like you have to hide."

"See, Eli. I'm not such a jerk, am I?" Hayley sneers.

"When I'm wrong I say I'm wrong. I'm sorry, Hayley, truly. And just so you have a name because you don't have a face. Viper. I call her Viper."

I got the phone call from Dylan as I was driving home from my parents' confirming I should come sleep with her. She reiterated just sleeping several times. There's that eight again shining bright. I'm glad she feels comfortable enough to show me when she's off. Her eight, however, is better than my eight any day of the week and twice on Sunday.

She's fresh from the shower when she answers the door in an oversized sweatshirt and not much else. Her hair is still damp and very wild as she folds into my arms. Dylan barely moves once I have hold of her. I work to get the door closed and locked behind us.

"Was it that bad or that good?"

Her voice mumbles against my chest, "Both."

"All right. Bed for you."

She nods and doesn't fight. On the Dylan scale, her eight is sinking fast to a six. I need to hold her until she feels right again. Dylan wanders through her seating area and kitchen to shut off the few lights, and I notice she's limping a bit. "Jesus, are you hurt?"

"I always hurt, Eli. That's the name of the game."

"You're limping though."

"My left calf is strained, and my toenail ripped badly on that same foot. I'll live."

"Not acceptable." I run my hand down her back, scooping her up to cradle in my arms. "Ice pack. Where is it?"

"The freezer compartment in the mini fridge next to my bed. You don't have to baby me."

"There's a difference between what you call babying and what I call caring for a downed wingman. Remember, Viper, I said don't fight me."

She slides inside my jacket for warmth as we walk into her darkened bedroom. The only glow we have is from rows of soft white twinkle lights that wind above her bed. The path trails down through sheers and near her mattress.

I tuck her down beneath the comforter and elevate her injured leg. After wrapping the ice pack in a light towel, I place it on the pillow under her. She hisses at the cold at first, but when the pain relief begins to set in, Dylan slowly relaxes. "Your joggers are hanging on the back of my bathroom door if you want to wear them to bed."

"I know control is your thing, Viper. I'm fine with it except when I'm not. This would be one of those times. Rest. Heal. Sleep. You've taken care of yourself for so long, you don't seem to trust anyone else to do it."

She pulls the comforter up to her chin and turns slightly away; her hair falls to hide her eyes. She hides her physical pain. She hides her fear, which I understand. What is she hiding now?

I sit down beside her on the mattress and pull her hair gently back. That's when I see the tears trickling down her face. I've never seen her anything but happy. Her strength is cracking. I know this face. It's one of: I've been strong for so long I need to not be for a while. "What's this all about?"

"I'm. Just. Tired. I'm tired of my body hurting. I'm tired of fighting people, who are supposed to love me, for a piece of my soul. I'm tired of doing this alone. I'm tired of being tired."

Dylan being so vulnerable breaks me and energizes me in the same breath. She's showing true faith by telling me she's afraid without having to say it. I quickly peel out of my jacket and dress shirt, my shoes make a quick exit, and I toss my pants over her chair. I want her to let me take the weight until she can carry it again.

I climb over her and slide into bed. Without moving her leg, she curls tight against my side. I brush her hair in long strokes with my fingers. As I tuck a few strays behind her ear, I offer her a soft place to land.

"Your body will heal, Dylan. It will. You know this. You're not going to class in the morning. You'll sleep until you wake. You're not tired of fighting. You're tired of fighting alone. You aren't alone. I'm here. I can't dance for you, but I'll do everything in my power to make it easier for you to try. You're not alone."

Chapter Twenty

Elijah

The past week has been hell. Her lowest point was the twelve hours she slept in my arms. From nine to nine, the only movement she made was her chest rising and falling in her breath. She woke to eat and soak in her tub. I sat at her breakfast bar on my laptop for my meetings. I told her she wasn't alone, and I meant it.

I ordered a late lunch for us, and she slowly began to practice on her own stage. Her new lead dancer video called her, and they were able to work on his part remotely. Her spirits were higher, and a bit of her spark was back by the time I went home that night. I gave her the two days at the end of the week off, the day before and the day of her performance.

That Friday, I sent her a care package to arrive first thing in the morning. Enclosed with my note was a travel size bottle of our tequila, a jar of cherries, and a model fighter jet. The note read *"To add to your bravery, Viper. Break a leg."*

I wanted to wish her good luck at the venue, but she told me not to. It's too much for her. I get it. Selfishly, I want to be the last person she sees and the first one after she performs. This isn't about me. It's about her. I am the only one she knows in the audience. No friends, no family, just me.

This is her moment. This is what she's worked her life for. This is the shot she wants to take. On the flip side, I've been in this position before. I gave every ounce of support I had to Victoria and then it ended. My own fear is becoming powerful again.

I find a seat on the center aisle, way in the back, for a myriad of reasons. One, I don't want her to see me while she's performing and get distracted. I know the pressure she's under for perfection. Two, *I'm* too nervous. I don't want that kind of energy for her. Three, I want to be able to take in the performance as a whole. I can't do that if I'm front and center. Last and certainly not least, I have certain acquaintances in the building. They think I'm watching as an alum, which I am, but I'm also the doting partner of the most beautiful and gifted dancer in the building.

There aren't many seats left in the auditorium with just five minutes to curtain. The two next to me are open. I hope they stay that way. I don't want anyone to overhear me in case I make an ass out of myself. My luck runs out as a pair of spectators breeze in just before the lights fade. I stand up, stepping into the aisle so they can file past me.

I don't pay attention to if they're man, woman, child, or animal. My focus is that black velvet curtain and when it will part. I lean forward with my elbows on my knees, twisting my hands over and over again. An arm reaches over and a gentle hand with long fingers covers mine. "You'd think you were asked to dance. Chill out. She'll be amazing."

I glance up the arm to find it belongs to my sister. I whisper, "Hayles, what are you doing here?"

"I picked up a stray, and we decided to come cheer on your girlfriend."

"A stray?" I ask as I lean in.

I see a wicked smirk pull forward from next to her. "Picked up a stray? I'm the best date you've had in your life," Wes corrects.

"Jesus Christ. I will kill both of you."

Hayley smacks my arm with the back of her hand. "Get a grip. She deserves to have a crowd. You deserve to have support."

"Me?"

"Don't bother calling him on it, Hayley. He'll just deny it."

"Call me on what?"

Before I can get an answer, the lights dim, and the music rises. There are four performances before hers. I want to enjoy them. I try to enjoy them. There's so much talent in this department. I didn't realize. Then my thoughts drift to her parents. This is a huge deal and they don't know. I can't imagine having something like this without my parents by my side.

The fourth soloist completes their piece. The applause dies and the lights raise enough to alter the set slightly. Dylan wanted a couple of light props for the staging. Her whole piece is about the evolution of light to dark then the fight to choose a side. It's pretty powerful, heady, and fucking poetic.

She wouldn't let me see the finished product before today. I've had these images of what it would look like in my head from the ways I've felt her move dancing with me, in and out of bed. I don't know if it's true, but I think I want this for her nearly as badly as she does.

Hayley reaches over and threads her fingers with mine. As much as I was determined to sit here alone, I'm glad I can share it with her and Wes. The music starts soft and low. There are twelve dancers on stage. Six male and six female dancers are all staged in pairs, wearing costumes that fade from white at the top to full black around the ankles.

The women move first. Their costumes flow away from their bodies like mist over the mountaintops. The men wrap their hands at their waists, raising them effortlessly into the sky and carrying them like clouds shielding the light. The spots come up like rays of light and shine through the pairs casting shadows across the stage.

I'm struck by equal parts beauty and sadness as I watch. I think anyone who's in the audience can look at what the theme embodies and find something they relate to in it. I know I certainly can. I'm lost for a moment focusing on one couple then the next.

Where's Dylan? At first, I think I see her then a movement or gesture tells me otherwise. About a third of the way in, the music builds like a giant rain cloud as she bursts through the center in a pale blue flowing dress. She floats across the stage so effortlessly.

Her toe simply points, and she's vaulted into the air. Her touch can be so poignant when she wants it to be. She gently gathers the players together with her movement. It's almost like she's hypnotizing them to drive the darkness into the floor, casting it away.

The cast isn't listening. That is the point of the piece. She is the heart and they aren't listening. It dawns on me in that moment the true meaning of the piece for her. It's a commentary on her relationship with her parents, the struggle she feels between the two worlds in her heart.

I feel this pull to *her*. I can see her face in the light. It's covered in pain. It's not the pain of acting to convey a message. She's leaving her heart on the floor, and this time, not in a good way. My right hand balls into a fist, and I settle it just in front of my lips at my chin.

Hayley's grip on my hand changes. I can feel a quiver to it. I'd look but I can't take my eyes off the stage. Dylan's movements become heavier and more direct, for lack of a better word. The ethereal quality is leaving, and the strength is in the force. She's fighting.

Fighting herself.

Fighting for what she believes in.

Fighting for what she feels in her heart.

Her group of dancers spreads out and copies her movement exactly. They've seen the light and are fighting alongside her. In the end, they hold her up in the silence. There's a fraction of a second before applause begins where everyone sits stunned. This wasn't a simple performance. This was a soul put on display and that moment of silence was the respect for it.

I watch the crowd stand one by one in an ovation for the cast and all their hard work. The minute Dylan is brought to the front, the roar in the room goes to the next level. Wes breaks out his patented whistle. Hayley is wiping tears away from her cheeks. I feel this warmth in my chest. I'm beyond proud. I can't wait to put my arms around her in private and tell her everything I'm feeling.

After the showcase, Wes, Hayley, and I wait in a corner of the auditorium. It's the best place for me to go unnoticed. Everyone will be filing out. I crack my knuckles over and over again as I pace slowly in a tiny circle.

"Would you stop?" Hayley scolds.

I lean back against the wall doing the only thing I can continue to do, which is be patient. Dylan gave me an idea of what might be going on after the performances. The audience at these events are packed with the scouts, for the lack of a better term, she talked about from dance companies all over the United States and some globally.

If they're interested in a particular dancer, they notify the director and he'll make the introductions. This is how the students get their shot at jobs after graduation. Her unicorn is here. They'd be lucky to have her and stupid not to take her. She has an amazing gift. As much as we would like to keep her at AnSa, I would like to keep her, this is where she should be.

There's one other cluster of patrons still left besides the three of us. Time is ticking by so slowly. That's when I see her. She's standing at the top of the stairs, stage left. Dylan's still in costume. I can tell it's caught her off guard that I'm not alone. I hold up my hands in a silent gesture of 'well?' Her hand, from softly at her side, holds up the number two.

I wink and motion for her to come to me. She pads quickly off stage charging in my direction. Dylan leaps from a yard away and I catch her. My arm at her back cements her to my body. My hand cradling her head anchors her to my heart. She nests in closer with the tip of her toes brushing across the tops of my shoes.

I whisper in her ear, "I'm so proud of you."

Wes drapes his arm around Hayley's shoulder and whispers something in her ear. "What was that?" I ask him.

"Just a running commentary, friend. It's nice seeing you like this."

"Like what exactly?" I ask, as I set Dylan back on her feet. There's a piece of hair floating across her forehead. I gently push it back into place.

"Fucking happy."

Something happens I've rarely seen before from Dylan. The mention by another person suggesting that she makes me happy makes her blush. She can dance hard for hours and be dripping with sweat; she can make the innuendo gods smile with the dirtiest of suggestions, but she's never blushed over either one.

She does make me *very* happy.

Hayley reaches up and takes Wes's hand while rocking forward and back on her feet. "When are you going to tell her your surprise, Eli?"

"Come on, Hayles."

Dylan looks between us. "What surprise?"

I sigh defeated. "Thank you for letting the air out of the balloon, Hayley. Your timing is impeccable."

"I just wanted to see you tell her."

Dylan begins tugging at the cuff of my sleeve. "Tell me what?"

"I've been a witness to how exhausted you've been. We've been working hellish hours to get things ironed out for the gala. When you weren't at the office, you were in the studio. With a long holiday weekend upon us, I thought we could take a run up to Vermont before the craziness begins."

Wes chimes in like a chorus, "My family has a place on the slopes. There's skiing, a hot tub, pool, sauna, numerous surfaces to do whatever it is y'all do." He dangles the keys in front of her. "Unman him with my blessing, Viper."

"Seriously? Wow." Another first. She's lost for words. "My instincts are screaming at me to pop off with my usual snarky personality. I... um... it doesn't fit right now. Look, I've felt unsupported in dance and what makes me happy for a long time. I've danced for strangers since I was about sixteen.

"Knowing Eli was out here was awesome. But then finding you both," she pauses then smiles, looking down at the keys she's palming in her hand, "it means a lot to me that you cared enough to come support me, not to mention help with this. Thank you."

Then she smiles with a look that's as wicked as it gets. "I won't unman him because, well, that's no fun for me. But we will take these keys and your permission. When do we leave?"

Ariana Rose

Chapter Twenty-One

Elijah

I've done this drive so many times I could do it with my eyes closed. Wes's family has owned this home in Vermont since we were sixteen. I remember the first weekend my parents let me go with his family. He and I stayed in the room that had the bunk beds. Wes's mother was not sure she ought to let us be on one side of the house alone, but she did it anyway.

They went to bed early, so we snuck into the beer refrigerator in the wet bar off the kitchen. We learned quickly they would only glance on the inside and never count, so we became experts at facing out the cooler. We'd sit sideways on the bunks, his over mine, and we'd talk about what it would be like to have girls up here.

We tested that theory after graduation. They let us come alone. The girls snuck up later in their car. Wes took one side of the house and I took the other. It was three days of "Don't ask and don't tell until you get home". It's been about five years since the last time I was there. It'll be nice to be back.

Dylan yawned her way through about ninety minutes of playing DJ until I told her to give in and go to sleep. She was up so early; she'd danced to perfection. She can relax now until after break. About an hour ago, I reached into the back seat and pulled my ski jacket out to cover her up.

She'd pulled her knees up, curling into the perfect ball in her seat. Dylan's head rests on the padded console. Every so often, I reach over and stroke the apple of her cheek. Either she curls up tighter with a little noise or she doesn't move at all.

We pull into the driveway about two in the morning. The housekeeping staff had been here and left a couple of lights on for us. I can't wait for her to see our surroundings in daylight. We went from skyscrapers and slush to fresh powder nesting into a mountainside. God, I love the East Coast.

"Dylan," I whisper. "Hey, beautiful, wake up. We're here."

She groans. "Just five more minutes, Mom."

"You can have as many minutes as you want once we're inside."

She stretches like a cat after a long nap from her fingernails down to her toes. "I'm sorry I didn't stay awake."

"I'm not. Now you don't have any excuses not to get into the hot tub with me."

"Damn. That was my line."

"I know." I kiss her nose. "I'll get the bags. Put that coat on. It's cold outside."

"The boss is here too? Nice. I've taught you well."

She's right. She has. I spent a number of years with Tori, and since Tori, thinking I could only be confident in one place. Dylan taught me I can be as strong as I am in business when I'm at play. Merging the two is not a bad thing. For us, it's only been good.

"This place is amazing. They renovated it about seven years ago. I can't wait to try the sauna and heated rain shower."

"My knees could use both."

"Are you still sore?"

"I can't name a dancer who doesn't have something."

"Well then, let's see if I can fix that again."

We open the front door, and I turn off the security system. There's a glow coming in from the back of the house. The chill of the late-night air is quickly dimmed by the warmth of this house. I reach for her hand, leading her to the back. "There are so many cool things to see. You'll notice in the morning, as the light comes in, you're surrounded by mountains on all sides. We're kind of in a little valley. We have a private entrance to the downhill runs on the other ridge, and if you look out this window down past the deck, there's our first stop, the hot tub."

She rests her head back on my chest. "Do we have to worry about neighbors?"

"None to speak of for a half mile."

"Naked and loud. I like this idea."

Dylan follows me slowly down the hallway to the master suite at the back of this wing. She stops about every three feet to look at another picture on the wall. There are a lot of small giggles with one-liners about Little Mav and Little Goose. She seems to especially like the one of Wes and me at our prep school graduation. Maybe I look more familiar to her.

"You were eighteen."

"Yeah only," I reply. "God, we were young. Sometimes that feels like another lifetime."

I set our bags on the long white bench at the foot of the bed and turn on my bedside lamp. Dylan has yet to come into the room. She lingers just outside. "What is it?" I ask.

"Do you really feel that way? Like it was another lifetime?"

"Some days I do. So many things have changed. So many things have come and gone."

"Our age difference never hits me that often. When you said that, it was like a hard punch. I've only seen you as you. It's easy to deny it. When I see you like you are in that picture, it's real that you've lived a whole other life."

"That's really intense for this late at night. Would you like wine? Water? Beer?"

"White wine would be nice, Eli. Thanks. I'll be down in a few minutes."

The downturn in her mood is screaming like neon. I didn't mean to be dismissive of her revelation, but it's never far from my consciousness. It's something I carry around with me. I don't want her to dwell on it. I don't.

I found an excellent bottle of dessert wine nested in the middle of the wine cooler. While it's breathing on the bar, I activate the heat lamps along the path leading to the hot tub. The shovel is where it always rests, on the hook outside the door. The motion lights pick up the sliding door as I step out and feel a gentle crunch under my feet.

The shovel feels good in my hands. I don't get the opportunity to push snow around very much. I don't count the gentle brushing away that my balcony gets once in a while as real shoveling. We need a dry path to the tub. I clear that with about four passes, and what I didn't get, the heated tiles absolutely will. Per Wes's instructions, I should only have to remove the tub cover and power it up.

Quickly the jets begin to circulate and the steam rises, blowing back across the newly fallen snow. Oversized thick robes hang from the back of the bathroom door just inside the sliding glass. This bathroom is new since I was here last. It has a heated rain shower in it with a wide bench and sauna.

As I'm admiring the tile work and hidden features, the sound of bare feet behind me alerts me to her presence. I tug down on my outstretched arms over the glass, giving a much-needed pull to my tight muscles. The cotton of her robe brushes against the skin on my back before her lips meet my shoulder blade.

"I see you're ready," I tell her.

"I'm sorry I got all moody."

"You're allowed."

"Today was a lot, you know?"

"Trust me, I do." I turn around, allowing my arms to fall around her. "Let's unwind a little bit then go to sleep until we feel like getting up. If we don't get up, that's okay too."

"Sleep all day, food that's bad for us, all the alcohol and sex all night. That sounds like the perfect getaway to me."

"There's my girl."

My girl.

Those words fall out of my mouth without thinking. I haven't asked her if that's what she wants to be. We've certainly never said the 'L' word. We have all these unsaid agreements between us, all these unspoken truths. What happens if words are put to them? I know I can take that next step. Can she?

The chill hits her body under the robe on the walk to the hot tub. I purposely walk behind her so I can see everything that happens. She points off in the distance at a pair of deer just on the tree line. I set the wine glasses down on the deck, resting my hands on her shoulders. She watches in wonder until they disappear into the night.

I tug on the ties of her robe. "Need help?"

"I won't say no."

Chill bumps rise from the base of her neck down to her navel as the thickness of the fabric begins to fall away. I can tell she feels the tingle elsewhere too. Dylan slides her hands inside the robe over mine, which have begun to explore her skin. With my cheek moving slowly against her temple, I draw a line from her hip, down the crease of her leg, into the top of her barely-there hairline.

"Are we staying out?" he breathes. "Or are you getting in?"

I laugh a little. "Both. Equally. Test the water. Let me watch you."

"I know it's your favorite thing."

"One of them anyway."

She shrugs out of the robe and lets the cold air blanket her. Instead of shrinking up, as most would, she extends her arms and goes with it. Her abandon is back. I can get drunk so easily from it. With a smile over her shoulder, she climbs the three stairs, steps out of her slides, and disappears into the steam.

Dylan sinks her whole body down until her eyes, nose, and top of her head is all I see. She trolls around the top of the water like a shark waiting for her unsuspecting prey. I'm not naïve to her existence. I'll willfully play her bait. My Viper pushes herself to the far side when I start my ascent. I set my robe over the corner. I can't see her mouth, but her eyes give away her smile at seeing my pale skin against the snow.

The heat takes a minute to get used to. Sensitive areas need to be met with extreme caution. However, once the shock wears off, my body begins to relax in ways I'd forgotten how. I reach back for my wine, all the while keeping Dylan in my sight. She moves a little to the left then a little to the right. It's the dance she prefers.

"That nap did you wonders."

She swims over to me as if she was in a full-size pool and treads water, just out of my reach. I sip my wine in gulps and rub the back of my neck with my hand. I can feel the beads of sweat begin to collect at my temples and trickle from my hair down my back.

I thread my fingers through the damp strands, slicking it back the longer the steam plays at it. With the last sip of my glass, Dylan smiles with her eyes again and disappears below the surface. I soon feel her hands on the outside of my ankles, and they rise at the same pace her body does between my spread knees.

She floats her body forward into my waiting fingers. Her legs slide along mine until she's straddling my lap. Her mouth parts slightly as she sucks her bottom lip in between her teeth, for in her mission to be in my lap, she's discovered her success.

I flex my fingers over her back, leaning in to kiss the swell of her breast. With my lips ghosting her skin, I offer her a confession. "Dylan, you were inspiring and breathtaking today. I was in awe of you. I thought you deserved to know that."

Her movements cease. I can see I've caught her off guard. She's fighting saying anything. Her breath tells me so. The pound of her heart confirms it. Looking into my eyes is too much for her. Dylan turns over in my arms, resting her back against my chest.

Her sleek hair trails down my arms as she pulls them tight around her torso. My fingers dig at her skin. The bubbles from the jets tease in every direction. They ping-pong between us as we simply touch each other. Dylan's hands become mine and mine become hers.

She guides us up the center of her chest, letting us drift both right and left. Our fingers weave together over her breasts. Her body arches back, forcing them even deeper into my hands. I push from underneath. They crest as Dylan rolls her hips back. My cock is straining beneath her. She rides the bubbles over me, giving it extra sensation.

I run my hand back down her, letting it disappear under the water. I want us to be so desperate when we leave this water that we'd consider laying in the snow to make the ache stop. Her thighs respond to my deep tissue touch. I knead into them, pushing in slow circles, higher and higher toward her apex.

I strum my fingers over her. I tap each one over her delicate skin for her to push against. Every time I let her grind down for just a second, she exhales. Her grip over my hand at her breast begins to grow stronger and more frantic with each passing second. She has this one spot, halfway down her shoulder, where if I kiss it or give it a little nibble, she nearly loses it. As much as she wants me to stay away from it, I know she loves it.

With the second slight suckle over her skin, she starts pulsing like the driving drumbeat in the sexiest song you've ever experienced. Each downward drive builds a tension in me I'm not sure I can control. Who will break first? I know who I want it to be.

Everything is burning. The fire between us, our skin tender by the water, and I burn. I'm willing to be burned by her. I press the heels of my hand tight against her core and begin to rock. The heat is dizzying. Her body weight is so easily stroking me.

"God, Eli..." she cries out. My name echoes off the trees into the cold, dark night.

"I know. Ride it out." She pushes my hand so tight it suctions to her. I can feel every individual pulse from inside her. She's hungry and I'm starving, starving to be inside her. It's selfish. I want to feel that. "If it wasn't dangerous, I'd take you right here." My brain and body are on overload. I won't let passion win out here. "Fuck it. Fuck. It. Shower. Now. We'll come back."

We rise from the water in a cascading tidal wave. The ripples wash over the side, and heat sizzles against the frozen ground. We put our slides on but nothing else. The twenty-foot sprint is not enough to bother with the robes. Once we hit the doorway, our foot coverings fly to the four corners.

We tumble back to front and front to back along the wall. My hands dive up into the base of her hair, pulling and tugging on it. She reaches down and over the globes of my ass, pulling me as tight as our bodies will allow. Each thud of someone's back pulls the air right out of us.

The bathroom lights are on over the mirror. The backlit shadows trail to the floor. I pull the shower door open, programming the water from the electronic pad. Time, pulse of the water, temperature. Now all it needs is us.

"Climb up on the counter," I tell her. She turns and places her foot flat against the cabinet and pushes her body up. As she does, she begins to caress her skin. Dylan rides the swell of her breast with her fingers, tracing down in between them. Her hips pulse forward and back.

I knew we would end up this way. She's the sexiest vision I've ever seen. The water from the overhead nozzles creates the sound of a storm. It's the way the rain would hit the asphalt or concrete. The steam is pouring out of the open door like an arrow pointing the way.

"Keep moving just like that. Watching you on the edge is almost as beautiful as you are."

She offers me a gentle whimper as her teasing travels south. Dylan rocks back and lets her fingers walk down, parting herself. I watch as she hooks her fingers in, and through her skin, with a deep roll to the right.

She keeps slow at first. Her eyes watch me give myself a couple good pumps as an appetizer.

I take a step closer to her. "Faster," I whisper.

She groans as I can start to see the vibrations in other parts of her body. Her left hand grips over the top of the sink next to her. She raises her right leg up, resting it on the drawer handle. I know her signs. I know her. She won't stop if I don't stop her.

Dylan starts to pant. Her toes curl over the brushed nickel. That's my cue. I step between her shivering legs and grab her wrist. She opens her eyes with a stunned whimper. I don't offer her time to be disappointed. I align my body with hers and ease my way in.

My right hand folds over her hip, pulling her close and allowing myself deep inside. My ring clicks against the mirror behind us as I hold her wrist to it. I pull forward and back in a passionate rhythm, the timing driven by the beat of my heart.

Her noises morph into fractions of words. The echoes give me long oh's and the accent of the end of my name. Just when I can hear her at the edge again, I stop and rest my head against her chest. I've never been her edging tool.

The first time she showed it to me, I was so turned on I could hardly breathe. She called it the best kind of foreplay. I wholeheartedly agree. She pants with her lips capping my shoulder. The only word I understand this time is, "More." I must hold myself back. I have a fantasy in mind.

"I won't stop this time, Viper. I won't. Dive over that cliff hard."

We push back into overdrive. She hardly has time to register what is happening. We drive as one, together, into each other. The doors and drawers of the vanity beneath her are rattling with our desire. The sound of our skin dances in the sound of the falling water behind us.

Dylan's groans become longer and deeper. "I'm going to…." are her last words before I feel the pads of her fingers dive deep into my right shoulder. I stop moving immediately. A fraction of movement from me would send me over the edge, and that's not where I want to be yet.

My eyes are focused on her, everything about her. The back of her right hand flexed against the mirror, her damp hair creating art in the fogged mirror her head rests against, the driving beat of her heart I can see in the pulse of her neck.

The flush of her skin. It's morphed from an inviting ivory to a vibrant pink. I can feel her body grip me from the inside. She doesn't want to let go, which is a good thing. I'm not finished yet.

I release her wrist as she begins to relax and wrap her body around mine. "Hold on tight. I'm not letting you go."

Her sweet little giggle signals she's more than okay with that. Lifting her from the counter, we turn and slowly walk through that shower door into a wall of steam. I lower her to the floor under the falling rain. Spinning her slowly away, I draw her back to my chest. The wet strands of her hair lay across us like a connecting tattoo.

My hands trace over her from the top of her head, down her shoulders, ending with my hands pulling back across her chest. I caress over her breasts, allowing my thumbs to tease her. She shows her appreciation in a gorgeous sigh and the shifting of her weight beneath her. Dylan desires the friction again.

She slides her hand across her torso and over her belly button in a direct line to relief. "No," I tell her. "I want that." Leaning in, the water rushes down my back, the heat charges me. I whisper in her ear, "Bend forward. Brace yourself on the wall."

Her back arches gloriously forward. As my fingers slide down her spine, she turns her head back over her shoulder to watch me. I don't make eye contact. That's not where I'm focused at the moment. I want to watch myself enter her this way. I want to see the twitches in her body as I reach around to invite my fingers to feast.

Dylan's anticipation amplifies as I caress down her hair then anchor my hand around it. As I give my bouquet of locks a tug, I push back inside her. The path is easy and wholly erotic. How I am with her is not how I've been with anyone before. I have this amazing feeling of power. When we met, she had all the control and I was more than content.

She's changed me. A woman can trust you to be a husband, boyfriend, or partner. A woman can trust you to be a father and caregiver. Dylan has given me one of the ultimate shows of trust. She's trusted me to have a bit of power over her body, which in turn, makes me feel more connected to her than I have to any other woman ever.

I push into her over and over again. The gentle, and sometimes not so gentle, sound of our skin melts with the murmur of the water raining over us. I can feel her abs tighten as my hand falls over them on my way to her sweet spot. Her knees buckle slightly as I vibrate back and forth. She's sinking into every feeling. Her raw emotions are one of the most seductive things about her.

"Shit. Eli... Eli..."

I know. I know. My teeth grind and my own pants give way. "Yes. God. Yes."

My release plunges into her, spurring another wave of her own. My arm quickly wraps at her waist as her body gives in. She's given me every ounce of her. That was the fantasy I wanted. Dylan let go in much the same way she's gotten me to do. *Desire* has become *All I Want Is You.*

Chapter Twenty-Two

Elijah

My body is beyond fully relaxed, but my mind is spinning like a top. But like with her spins, they always come back to center. My center is over one question. I asked it of Tori and got a lie in return. I need to ask it again but this time from Dylan. I need to for myself and to have the knowledge to move forward.

"Hey, beautiful," I whisper. "Are you still awake?"

The soft apple of her cheek nuzzles against my chest. "Just barely," she mumbles.

"Awake enough to talk?"

My heart is pounding softly. I know she can feel it. To her credit, she says nothing. "I can be." Her hand trails from its position under her cheek to stroke down the side of my rib cage. She permits her fingers to move slowly up, down, and over the ridges.

"Where do you see yourself in five years?"

Her fingers stop moving as her head pops up. "That's a deep question for this time of night, or should I say morning."

"I mean it. I have a lot of things churning around in my brain. I know you want a career in dance, but what about the rest?"

"The rest? Ask me a better question, Sawyer. You know damn well that's not the one."

We've lived in the land of don't ask, don't tell for months. We've stayed at the carnival, ridden the rides, played the games, and excelled in the fun house. She scolded Tori for being a coward and not having the conversation because it was too hard. I need to know if she can practice what she preaches.

I wrap my arms around her tight and anchor her to my chest once more. My courage, or sheer idiocy, breaks the silence. "Do you want to be married? Have kids?"

I can feel her breathing stop just for a second before she speaks. "Those aren't simple questions, Eli. They're just not."

"I never asked for something simple in return. It can be hard, complicated, or even I don't know if that's the truth. Just tell me your answers, whatever they are."

"Marriage can change people. I've seen it. You can be a couple and have fun, travel, experience life, and all the things, but then once that piece of paper happens, it changes everything."

"So, your short answer is no."

"I didn't say no. There would have to be, I don't know, rules, I guess. Like, I don't want to go to bed pissed off unless I'm guaranteed make-up sex. I would want to know my dreams won't be sacrificed or theirs either, for that matter. We'd promise to try and grow together and be understanding of change."

"Those are some pretty tall orders."

"You asked me. You're the only one who ever has. I have a question for you though. Aren't you scared to get married again?"

"I know how good marriage can be, but I also know how quickly it can turn to shit. That doesn't mean that, for the right person, I wouldn't be willing to try again."

"I know you want kids."

"I wanted two by now. That hasn't changed. I've always known I wanted to be a father. I want to pass down all the traditions to my own kids that Pops and my dad gave me. I want to be able to sit at my desk and hand the crest ring over to my son or daughter. I want to play bad tennis and hack a round of golf. I want to teach the waltz and wear a tiara, if I'm asked, for a tea party. I want a child to take over for me as I am for my father, should they choose."

"When you have good models for it, that comes naturally. I'm on the other side of it. When you don't get the support you need, or feel like you can count them, you doubt your own ability and desires to pass that along." She finally pulls her head up, resting her chin on my chest. I can't see her eyes fully in the darkness, but every once in a while, I can catch their shimmer. "Where is this coming from, Eli?"

"Nowhere in particular. I just wanted to ask."

"To answer your question, someday I would like kids, when I'm done dancing that is. I don't want to ask what might have been. That's not fair to me or the kid."

I start stroking her back again. "You're right. It's not."

Dylan

My eyes start to hover in that amazing place between sleep and awake. I can sense it's still dark in the bedroom. I'm so warm beneath the down comforter; I don't want to move. My short conversation with Eli faded into silence, then I fell asleep to the rhythm of his fingers. If I think about it hard enough, I can still feel them moving.

It's so quiet here. I have zero concept of time, which is fine by me. I've worked so long and hard all semester to keep up with my classwork, AnSa, and the showcase, I'd almost forgotten what sleep is beyond the one day Eli forced me into it. I can feel the blankets riding across my cheek nearly hiding my eyes.

I turn my head under the duvet so the first thing I do see when I open my eyes is Eli. My hand reaches out to touch him. The bed is cold and empty. "Eli?" I pull the blankets down just enough. He's gone. His pillows are in his typical V shape, one on each side of where his head would be, but he's missing. "Eli?" I call his name again with no answer.

After rolling to my back and flipping the blankets off, I'm immediately freezing. I don't remember where the lights are, so I grab my phone, finding the flashlight. The time on the clock also catches my eye. It's one thirty-seven. It's afternoon. Shit.

The robe from last night's hot tub adventure is at the foot of the bed. I wrap tight inside and dig inside my bag for anything to cover my feet. Instantly life is better. My phone guides me to the door. The natural light from the outside floods the hallway. I follow it back to the family room and the kitchen.

Eli is curled up with the television on low. Hockey is on the screen. He's in his gray sweats with a vintage Minnesota Twins sweatshirt, no doubt gifted to him by his grandfather. His hair is a beautiful mess with a one-day, unshaven face. He's toying with the bow of his glasses between his teeth as he watches the puck travel up and down the ice. "Hey," I say quietly.

His warm smile greets my voice. "Hey there, beautiful. I was beginning to wonder if you were going to wake up at all today. Feel okay?"

I slowly shuffle, bundled with my arms around me, to his side. He moves his feet so I can tuck in close to his body under his waiting arm. "I think it all hit me at once. Sometimes after big shows, I end up sick because I've been running on coffee and chocolate."

"Do you feel sick now?" he asks.

"No. I'm okay. Just groggy."

"I won't let you run on just those things so the spoiling starts right now."

"Starts? What was last night then?"

With a look of satisfaction, he states, "Purely selfish, I assure you. But this is *your* vacation. I have a few things planned. We'll start with being lazy all day. We can stay just like this, and I'll feed you."

"Okay, again you hit the two best things. You told me I'm beautiful, and you're going to feed me."

He settles his glasses back on his face before he kisses my forehead. "You're more than beautiful. I'm going to get you a glass of orange juice. Would you like breakfast or lunch? I have options for both. I'm a whiz with online grocery shopping."

"Unless you have plans already, I'll take an actual lunch, and we can have breakfast for breakfast tomorrow, if it's my choice that is."

"You always have choices. I love many of your choices, actually. Don't move."

Eli leaves me on the sectional covered with a large fleece throw. I can hear the refrigerator door opening and closing along with the rattle of dishes. "Elijah? I'm sorry about last night."

There's nothing for a minute or so. I just assume he can't hear me. I rest my head on the back of the sofa to stare at the game. His gentle tone then rolls in from behind me. "Why would you say you're sorry?"

My bed of spinach appears with sweet and spicy tuna and a bowl of sliced apples. "Well, I fell asleep before we finished and... I know it's not what you were hoping to hear."

"All I wanted was the truth, Dylan." Eli slides back into his spot including tucking me under his arm.

"So that's it? You're satisfied?"

"We've only known each other for a few months. We're still getting to know things and what the future might hold. I remember you saying that not having the conversation is worse than anything that could be said. I agree. You were honest with me. Nothing bad can come from that.

"More than anything, I choose you. I'm the best version of me when I'm near you. That's in every way. We don't have to have all the answers right now. I just need you to hear I choose you."

I choose you.

It's fucking incredible, the feeling you get when you hear those words. You get chosen for schools, programs, jobs, and auditions. You can be chosen to be a friend or a person to confide in. But when you have a person you have feelings for and have given yourself to in many ways say I choose you, it tells you you're good enough as you are.

You don't have to change. You don't have to wear some mask or be someone else. I'd rather hear I choose you than I love you. Love can have conditions. You can love someone and not choose them. Choosing is investing. I'm his choice and he's mine.

Wow. He's *my* choice. I hope he can't feel how scared I am. For all the jokes I make, the clear innuendo I sling at him at every moment possible, the vibrato I've taken great pride in creating, I'm a girl at heart.

I reach forward, setting my plate on the coffee table, then swing my legs over his lap. My toes dig into a little slot between the cushion and his hip. His hands slowly slide over and adjust the fabric of my robe. His sleepy eyes meet mine from behind the dark brown frames of his glasses. My fingers trace through the stubble on his jawline as I give him a gentle pull toward my face. His hand slowly draws up my body to rest just below my ear.

Our lips do a delicate dance together. "Eli, I choose you too."

We sit quietly against each other watching the rest of the second period of the game. About midway through, after I'd finished my lunch, we lay down together on the couch. I curl up on his chest and pull my hands under my chin. He fans the plush blanket out, cocooning us.

"I do have one other confession. It's not a big deal but I should tell you, tomorrow is my birthday. I didn't want to say anything, so you'd feel like you were supposed to fuss or something."

"Or something. I like the vagueness of that. Your birthday. So many possibilities. You let me worry about the or something. You simply breathe."

With my ear against his chest, I can hear his heart beating. It's slow and steady. It's the best downbeat for a slow waltz. I let my eyes close and listen. It reminds me of us dancing in my apartment. The rise and fall of the dance are now the rise and fall of *his* chest in breath. It's so soothing, the light dims, my breathing slows, and the horn signaling a goal fades into the background.

Chapter Twenty-Three

Elijah

Those who suggest a weighted blanket calms your body have obviously never slept with Dylan as a blanket. I was wide-awake, watching my favorite teams battle, then the next thing I knew, it was two hours later and another game had begun.

Dylan had gotten up at some point, gone to shower, and returned. I catch her covering me with an actual blanket before I pull her down back to where she should be. She smells so good. It should be criminal actually.

I ask her if she knows how to man a gas grill. I have a menu for tonight that will require a bit of assistance. I woke up with several other ideas for tonight and tomorrow. I get the sense she doesn't really care for her birthday. My mission is to spend the next twenty-four plus hours changing that.

She wants to get a light workout in today to help warm her injuries. After I'm sure she's set up on the lower level, it's shower and go time. I call in a favor to the nearby ski resort for a couple of surprises I hope will mean a lot. I didn't have time to prepare. I only know her. My instincts will have to do.

The doorbell is ringing within five minutes of my shower. Gabe came through in the clutch. I got two of the largest boneless pork chops they had with their secret sauce for plating. They sent a dozen bacon wrapped asparagus, and all of what I'd need for wild rice pilaf along with a white baguette. My secret requests have been granted, those as well will be unwrapped with time.

"Did I hear the doorbell? Who knows we're here?" Dylan shuffles past me to snoop in the bags on the counter.

"Back away from the counter, Viper. That's an order."

"Whoa. That was also hot." She winks as she slinks away to a stool on the other side of the island. "Thanks for the few minutes of alone time."

"You never have to ask for that. I hope you're hungry. I have a late dinner and a few surprises on tap. Are you comfortable in what you're wearing? I need you to be absolutely comfortable. Just call it a rule."

"Well," she grins, "I'm most comfortable when I'm naked, however, that's not good for cooking. I think I'll torture you with being naked under my robe. Sounds like a good plan to me."

I growl, "Me too. Pile your hair up as well. That will be a big help later."

"Ooh. Promises, promises, Goose."

She nearly skips away like a school age girl. She thinks she knows what she's getting into. She has no idea.

Up until now we've been playing a pretty great game. It's been tit for tat. Even thinking that in my head right now I laugh, but it's true. I've made her dinner; she's done the same for me. We've made love more times than I can count. She supports me and I support her. I want tonight to be about more than that. I told her I choose her. Instead of telling her I choose her, I want to show her.

Dylan descends the stairs about ten minutes later and I've transformed the kitchen. A fire is roaring low in the fireplace. I've found a Michael Bublé station on music streaming, which is the perfect playlist for the light snowfall that's begun outside. I've set up a string of candles just under the overhead lights, which I've turned down only leaving it light enough to cook.

I've set careful places at the short end of the counter lined with linen napkins and a glass of wine ready and waiting for her lips. Her gentle gait reaches the landing and slows. She's taking everything in behind me. I close the oven door and lay down the mitt, pretending I don't know she's there. "What did you do?" she asks.

"Created a special meal for a special woman. Park it on the right. The pork has about another seven minutes, as does the asparagus. Enjoy your wine. If it's too sweet, we can get a different one."

"This is too much, Eli. I said no fuss."

"Hush. Sit. Drink. Let's talk, if you're okay with that."

"Okay... Is there a topic list?" she asks.

"Tell me about your favorite birthday. When was it?"

"Tomorrow." She grins. "Aside from that I think it was my eleventh birthday. I got my first pair of pointe shoes that year and a couple of private lessons to go with it. She was the prettiest dancer I'd ever seen. She was a prima ballerina in the company where I wanted to work, until I discovered the dancing I do now. I think that's where I find my parents' decline."

"They wanted you to stick with ballet and you wanted contemporary. Is that what this is all about or something else?"

"See, to them, I'm not going to make a company so why bother trying. They don't understand that dancing is who I am, not what I do. Jesus, I must sound like a broken record."

"No. Sometimes you need to say a thing multiple times before the other person will buy it. You don't have to sell me on it. I've seen you in action. I've seen your heart. When was the last time they came to a performance?" Dylan settles back in her chair. If she has to think about it, it's been a long damn time. "How do you feel about asking them again?"

"How did you learn to do that?" she asks.

"Do what?"

"Not tell people what to do. You realize it's a useful skill, right?"

"Dylan, I spend all day, every day, telling people what I need done or think they should do."

"That's not what I mean. Ever since we met, you've given me choices. I feel like even if I chose to walk away from all this, you'd let me."

This conversation took a different turn than I expected, but it feels like a sidetrack that needed to happen. I know her biggest touchpoint, not that I didn't before. She knows my biggest fear without me saying it. "If I couldn't make you happy, I'd want you to go. The only thing I'd ask is that you'd tell me first, instead of disappearing." Just then the timer goes off on my phone. "Time to check the meat. I'll be right back."

The bite the air is giving me is what I need. Where I was out here in a jacket before, I don't want one now. I want to feel the cold. I've only ever wanted honesty from her. We've never lied. We've never called something more than it was. It wasn't so much about how she said what she said. It was *what* she said. I wasn't expecting that.

I would walk away without a fight. I would. I don't want her to feel trapped. That would kill her spirit, which would hurt me more than being without her. As I close the grill and collect myself before finding the door, she's there in the window watching. When I approach, she doesn't move except to open the door.

The gentle touch of her hand slides the door and a bit of snow blows in around her face. My hand lays over hers and closes it behind us. I'm pinned between her stare and the cold at my back. "You do, you know," she whispers.

"What?"

"Make me happy. I've never done things the way we're doing them, Eli. Sometimes I handle it better than others. I wasn't trying to tell you something or ruin the dinner. I was only making an observation. That's it. I like that I can be who I am with you and have it be okay. What I was more trying to say is that's not just a me thing. That's an everyone thing and I think it's awesome. No wonder people are drawn to you."

"It's definitely a you thing. You make me happy. I choose you, remember?"

Dylan nods slowly. "Yes, I remember."

"I'm starving. Let's eat. You're not running on coffee and chocolate while I'm around."

The rest of the dinner is much lighter. She asks me about some of my more memorable birthdays, which means we talk about when my birthday actually is. It was the week before we met. She is quick to make the joke about how she blew out my candle instead, which gets a huge laugh and an even bigger kiss.

We each turn in our stools until we're facing each other. The tie on her robe begins to loosen and the sides fall open. She inches toward me until my only option is to pull her onto my lap. Her feet dangle on either side of me as my hands explore over her heated skin. She's right. Knowing she was naked under the robe was torture.

Back on course, Goose. You have another maneuver to make.

I try to hold Dylan at arm's length while she's relentlessly rolling her hips in a slow figure eight against me. "Viper. I want this. Oh, how I want this, but I have a plan. You'll want the plan. Trust me."

With a little groan and a bit more coaxing, she stops her pursuit. When I'm able to fully move without difficulty, we walk hand in hand up to our bedroom. I switch off all the lights and direct her to sit in one of the low wingback chairs along the window.

I disappear into the bathroom and return with a bottle of lavender lotion, a tiny pale pink bottle, and a vanilla patchouli mixed candle for light and scent. "What is all this?" she asks.

"For your pleasure. Just sit back and enjoy."

Dylan perches herself back in the chair and just before she curls on top of her legs, my fingers restrain her and pull her ankles toward me one at a time. The Cheshire grin she now possesses lets me know the light bulb has gone on and she knows what's coming.

I settle on the footstool and lightly press into her right arch. Her arms slide the length of each side of the wingback chair, until her hands grip over the ends. Her toes point and her eyes close. The purr from the depths of her soul could shake the fresh snow loose from the trees outside the window. This is going to be better than I could've imagined.

I angle my other thumb into her left foot, so it doesn't feel ignored. As I pull both of my hands back, her eyes open to small slits. "I hope you like pink. I know I do. All shades of it. The pink that covers the tops of your cheeks right now, for instance. Or the deep pink your nipples are, teasing me at the moment. Or better yet, the pink I know that waits for me later."

She takes a deep breath as she pulls the top of her robe open even wider. "Were you always this dirty in your poetry?"

"It's a new trait I've acquired. I wonder how that was inspired? Now, lay a foot in my palm. I'm going to try another new thing. Painting on a very small canvas."

"Remember when I said how sexy I thought you were in the Hamptons? How powerful?"

"I do. Vividly."

"This is up there."

"See if you still feel like that in thirty minutes."

"You think it will take you that long to paint ten toes?"

"Seven for the toes. Seven for the massage."

"That leaves sixteen minutes."

I grin. "It does, doesn't it?"

I meticulously paint each and every toe. I don't miss a stroke or paint outside the lines, even while she squirms a bit. My hand folds beneath the back of her knee and softly glides over her skin. Her heel cradles down into my palm and I go to work. Beginning softly, I blow on her toes under the veil of drying them. I know better.

Her thighs press tight and slide fractionally back and forth with every puff from my cheeks. I further her torture with a rounded slide of my thumb over her arch again, this time pressing deeper. Dylan's toes curl over my hand and hold on. Her breaths begin to have the pulse of a heartbeat. I'm giving her pleasure I thought I only could give another way.

That realization only possesses me to keep going. As I abandon her right foot for her left, that fraction in between tells me quite a few things. She likes her present. This simple act of care is pushing her to a sexual edge. It also tells me, when I get to those last sixteen minutes, I need to pace myself. Not only for her, but also for me.

I repeat the process on her left. I watch as she anticipates every move as if it was a movie she's seen before. She knows what I'll do and when. I try to change it, but her smile guides me back in the same direction. We've hit our mark.

With one last puff over her perfectly pink beauties, I gently tug behind her knees. As I do, the fabric of her robe catches on the fabric of the chair and it slides open. The entirety of her body is exposed to me. It only takes a moment to marvel at her before I need more. "Don't move," I order.

Gravity calls me to my knees in front of her. Her right leg drapes over my shoulder like it was born to be there. My index finger, like the rest of me, wants to play. I start a line from the top of her big toe, running slowly down and over the arch of her foot. She wiggles and twitches. I'm not willing to analyze right now if that is because she's ticklish or firmly something else.

Over her slightly bruised ankle, up her calf, and to the back of her knee, I pause for a second to let my lips taste her. I can feel the chill bumps rise beneath them, even with her skin so warm. Each imprint I leave is deeper than the last. The next step is her apex. I can audibly hear her inhale and hold the breath. She's waiting. I am too. I have been.

Dylan

The time between the last kiss on my thigh and the next time I feel his lips touch my body feels like forever. My eyes are wide on him. I want to see the moment he touches me there. His confidence is erotic. Everything he's done tonight has led to this. He wants to set me on fire. He's absolutely succeeding.

A hint of his stubble grazes against the tender skin just beneath my own. It burns in the sweetest way. I don't focus on it too long. I want to feel everything he wants to offer. His lips kiss up and down my line. The tip of his tongue parts me and my back instantly arches.

His hand holds firm over my belly. I roll my hips up into his touch and allow his tongue to plunge inside. He flicks and rolls in tight little circles with a gentle suckle at the end. There isn't anything I don't enjoy about being with a man. Foreplay is my absolute favorite. The buildup of tension is sexy as fuck.

This, what he's doing right now, is different. He's on his knees. This man, who doesn't realize his own strength and power, is on his knees at my feet. He's willing to submit in a way to give me a gift. I've dreamed of him inside me like this.

Sometimes it would wake me up when I wasn't with him and even sometimes when I was. I could feel this relentless pulse between my thighs. It would be so strong I'd have to get rid of it or it wouldn't go away. If I were with Eli, I'd have to have him. I would wake him or wait until morning when I was even more amped and then pounce.

When I was alone, I'd imagine him there with me. My fingers were his. My vibrator was held by him. I'm the queen of wanting to edge it out. On those mornings, however, I would wake in such a sexual rage that I couldn't get off fast enough. That's what I feel right now. One lap from his beautiful tongue and I want to come.

I deserve more than that. He deserves more than that. The nails on my left hand drag over the chair covering with the sound of a rip as my moan mingles with it. I clamp my other hand down over his on my belly. I need to feel his skin but also add weight to try and squash my urge to explode.

He doesn't restrict me. He never has. He doesn't ask me to hold still. He's always cared about my freedom and my needs from the first moment. He slides his tongue forward and back slowly. The ridges it creates catches inside me. The shocks are powerful. My hips slide up. I can't help it.

His patterns are slow at first. When he feels me start to contract from the inside out is when his passion bursts. I can feel him smile as he moves faster. Every time I moan, he does, which in turn makes me moan even harder. The low guttural growl from his throat is a sound I will never tire of. It's another thing I crave.

I can feel my clit pulse with every pass over it. My head hits the back of the chair so hard I see stars. If I'm honest, I was seeing them before that. The skill at which he's baiting me right now is like nothing I've ever felt. Every ounce of my body is tingling.

I reach in and grab the back of Eli's head, tugging not so gently on his hair. His growl and accelerated mission tell me he wants me to give in. I'd love to play the game and hold out. I would. But there's no way. I love to have control in everything sexual. I'm learning with Eli that he has a hold on me like no one ever before.

His short flicks send me into overdrive. The wave begins in two places: the tips of my toes and the roots of my hair. They roll up together, greeting me where Eli is coaxing them. I'm moving so much he wraps his hand from underneath over my thigh, so he can keep going.

The harmony from our vocals mixes and fills the space. "Oh. Fuck. Oh. Fuck. Oh. Fuck." He moans in the spaces between my words. As I come, I arch up as he suckles me deep. He's drawing me out. The sounds he's making are nearly the ones I hear when he comes. Eli is getting as much pleasure as I am.

I feel like I'm floating over the both of us, in what I can only imagine is what people think of when they talk about out-of-body experiences. I know in my heart and soul this is the most intense orgasm I've ever felt, hands down. I don't remember the next few seconds.

When I'm able to realize my surroundings again, he's kissing up past my belly button, then between my breasts, and finally my lips. I can taste myself on him. When my lips have had enough for the moment, I pull him away just enough so I can whisper one thing, "My turn."

Ariana Rose

Chapter Twenty-Four

Elijah

I'm not sure how her birthday turned into a gift for me, but it did. We didn't watch the sunrise but came damn close. I should have been exhausted, but instead, I felt energized. After a few hours of sleep, we made that breakfast she wanted and hit the slopes for a couple hours. She'd never been skiing before.

It was fascinating to see how she learns. It's the same way she seems to dance. She watches, observes, asks a million questions, processes, and moves. It's amazing. We were able to slowly slalom a couple of the steeper hills. I could hear her laugh the whole way down. It's a beautiful thing to know you can bring joy to someone. If I can make her smile like this forever, I've got a life.

Whoa.

Forever.

We pack up and leave mid-afternoon. The whole way down the drive I catch her looking back. I can't place the emotions I read with her. When she's ready, I hope she tells me. Dylan follows the same pattern she did on the way up. She's able to play DJ for the first ninety minutes or so then slowly falls asleep against my shoulder.

Once she's out cold, I turn the music off. The only things I want to hear are the road beneath the tires and the gentle sound of my beautiful girl sleeping. As we reach the city limits, Dylan begins to stir. "Where are we?" she asks.

"About thirty from your place."

"Since it's still my birthday, I still get to choose, right?"

"Yep. You do. What is thy bidding?"

"Take me home to your place. I want to stay with you. Practically, we have a shit ton of loose ends to work on for the kickoff gala in two weeks. Selfishly, I want more of last night every night for the foreseeable future."

I smirk. "Have I created a monster?"

"I always was one disguised as an angel."

"Viper, you can stay with me as much as you want."

She wraps her arms around mine and exhales so deep. "Good."

Her body immediately relaxes again. I almost wonder if the conversation we just had was in her sleep. My lips are drawn to the top of her head. With my imprint still fresh on her hair, I whisper three words. Three words I thought were only in my head. Three words I wasn't sure I'd ever say again. Three words I'm not ready for her to hear while she's awake.

Having Dylan with me nearly all the time is easy. We don't feel the need to have conversations constantly. She's turned my entryway and part of the living room into her alternate studio, which creates the sexiest shadows as the sun sets. We move and dance around each other like we've done it for years, not months.

I'd thought a lot about how we'd mark our first holidays together. This used to be my season with Tori. I'd been going along with whatever my family wanted with just a little less heart. I haven't decorated my home since she left. I know the holidays aren't especially fun for Dylan either.

Her parents prefer to travel instead of staying home. They were flying out on Christmas Day this year, so it worked out that we spent Christmas Eve with our families. After Dylan dropped her parents at the airport, she came back to my place and waited for me after brunch with Wes and his family.

I walk in the door to a chill. As I round the corner, I see the balcony door open and Dylan bundled up on the floor just inside. Outside in the lightly falling snow is the smallest tree I've ever seen, with one string of lights from her loft wound in and through the branches.

Crouching down at her side, my lips find their way to her temple. "I thought you didn't like the holidays," I tease.

"I don't, but I wanted to try it your way. Do you like it?"

I climb inside the blanket with her. "It's very Charlie Brown. I love it." We sit in as much silence as the city offers us until I work up a bit of courage. "I know we promised no gifts, but I was shopping for my mother and saw something that reminded me of you. I couldn't resist."

Leaving her for the briefest of moments, I dig behind my vinyl collection for the rectangular box with the pale blue bow. Dylan turns toward me with the tree glowing behind her. I've seen her look beautiful every day we've known each other. This moment stops my heart.

Her childlike smile is the only gift I need as she pulls on one end of the ribbon until it all falls away. The crinkle of the tissue pulling back reveals an eight by ten antique plaque depicting Degas' *Ballet Rehearsal*. Dylan audibly gasps as her fingers run across the front. "You remembered."

"I remember everything you tell me, Viper."

We make love nearly from Christmas through New Year's Day. The office is closed. We're able to be as close as we want and give each other space to simply be as well. It was exactly what she needed to finish her recharge.

The new year brings Dylan back to her exceptional performance level at the office. Sam, Lucy, and everyone helping with Roark are so taken with her, they want to help gain additional funding for a dance school she talked about in addition to the other arts programs linked to the Foundation. A portion of the proceeds from our gala kickoff will help fund it long term.

When we're not at the office proper, she's in school or the studio or eating and sleeping, we're breathing this project. We've had massive differences of opinion, pillow fights, dinners that turned into nearly breakfast meetings. There was even one night where I woke us from a dead sleep with an idea. I'm glad she's not a violent person, because I deserved a throat punch for the way I sprang up in the middle of the night. I think I got the best of that deal afterward.

A week before the event, I surprise Dylan with what she's told is a final errand for the décor. It is a personal shopping experience to find a dress for her to wear. She's going to be my date for the night in the eyes of the company. She's going to be my angel in my eyes. I want her to look exactly how she wants to look.

I stand for a long time staring at her in the mirror as I attempt to zip her dress up. That's not the way I want this zipper to go. Her black and rhinestone strappy heels look like those pointe shoes she told me about.

The hem of her dress is multilayered and short in the front and trails to the floor in the back. The gown folds over and over with all layers meeting at her petite waist, with a rhinestone belt to match her shoes.

Her beautiful shoulders angle perfectly out of the sleeveless top. I'm surprised at the simple elegance of this dress. Again, I'm having trouble with the zipper. I stop midway up her back. "Is something wrong?" she asks.

"Not wrong. I want you out of this dress before you're even in it. We're going to get found out for sure tonight. I won't be able to hide it."

"Zip it up, Sawyer. I need to finish you off."

"That sounds like heaven."

She spins around in my arms like she did that first night, only her hair is in a sleek braid down her back. "You look like we just finished a quickie in the coat check," she giggles.

"That's a fucking great idea. I want to make that happen. After they announce our funds raised and the band is back playing, we're so doing that."

She fixes the last button on my vest and straightens out my tie to perfection before she buttons the top two on my jacket. "You want to risk getting caught?"

"For you, yes."

"Tell you what. Since we made this a black-and-white ball tonight, I got a little something for you." She pulls a white pocket square from the pocket of her dress. "When you want to request that flyby, you tug on this and you'll have Viper's undivided attention," she whispers in my ear. "I will be the one bare and waiting for you."

I don't think I stopped twitching, even after we got to the venue. I'm constantly distracted by the thought of what isn't under her dress. She works the room with such ease from the moment we step on-site. She has her mental checklist and is running through it step-by-step.

We have our breakdowns of what each of us are responsible for. It's divide and conquer on the vendors and back together to greet all our VIPs. When my family arrived, it added a layer. I could see a bit of tension for the first time in Dylan. Her shoulders were up, and her breathing was a beat faster. No one would notice but me, or maybe Hayley.

My father leans in as we watch Dylan work the room. "She's quite impressive, Son. I've gotten rave reviews from every person she's come in contact with. This idea of hers is quite amazing."

"She's a natural. We're lucky to have her."

"One thing I need to ask. Did you invite Victoria?"

"Tori? No, why?"

"She's here. She's with him." My father motions over my shoulder to the entryway. There she is in glittering silver, which I'm assuming is her version of white. I'm certain it's a new design of hers, or his, for that matter. She's got a large glass of wine in her hand, and I can tell it's not her first.

"Fuck," I mutter under my breath. "Dad, this is a disaster for a number of reasons. Many of which I can't get into. She needs to stay away from me and the staff."

"Your mother and I will run interference the best we can."

"Thanks, Dad. I need to find Dylan."

"You won't have to look far. She's right behind Victoria."

My radar zooms in and he's right. They're nearly back-to-back. My guts twist inside. I'm not prepared to have my past, present, and hopeful future collide. There's too much at stake. "I'm going on stage to kick off the donations early. I'm going to call Dylan up. Please intercept Victoria."

I rush to the stage. Hanging on to what little bit of composure I'm still maintaining, I grab the microphone. "Good evening, ladies and gentlemen. Before we continue the evening, I'd like to call my partner and co-chair to the stage, Miss Dylan Cooper." Applause fills the room as she takes careful steps forward toward me and away from Victoria.

She glides toward me with purpose, distancing from the minefield that lies just behind her, none the wiser. I lay my open palm out for her. With the grace of a dancer, she offers me her hand as she climbs the stairs. When she's safe at my side, I continue with her hand in mine, "Just one quick announcement. AnSa International will be matching all donations collected tonight.

"We're all here for one reason, the children. The children can thank the woman standing next to me. This idea was born and bred by Dylan's passion for dance and the arts. With your donations this evening and corporate sponsorships, we can make true differences in many lives. Here's to a fun and fruitful evening filled with conversation and giving. Dylan and I will be available for any questions about our partnership with the Roark Foundation and its mission. Thank you all for coming and please enjoy."

I lean down and whisper to Dylan, "I need to talk to you. Alone."

"That time already?" She smirks.

"No." My one word erases any trace of playful attitude she had before she follows me to the balcony, just beyond the west end of the stage.

I thrust the door open into the cool air. "Jesus," she cries. "What's eating you?"

"I need to tell you something. Tori is here. She's here with the man who... she's here with her boyfriend. I didn't invite her. He might be representing his fashion house and brought her. That's neither here nor there. She's here, and she's got a mouth when she's had too much to drink. I fear that's the case."

"Say it plain, Sawyer. What's the deal?"

"I don't want you two to meet, interact, or have her know you exist."

"Fuck. Calm down. I can handle her, Eli. I'm not afraid."

"I am." Those words fly out before I can even dial them back.

She takes a step back from me. "Wow. Did you just really say that?"

"I thought I was in a better place with it, but I have this weird level of panic. It's triggered by him and by my need to protect you and us."

"Who are you right now, Eli? I don't know this person. I don't care what she thinks. I don't care what she knows. This isn't about that. You've never once made me feel you were ashamed of me or being with me."

She turns to walk away, but I grab her wrist and tug. She spins back easily into my chest. "Viper, I'm not ashamed. Ever." With a quick glance to make sure we're alone, I tilt her chin up between my thumb and my index finger. My thumb begins a slow circle, massaging into her skin. "Ever. I'll always put you first."

Dylan slides her hand into mine and draws it down out of sight. She rests us together on the inside of her thigh before leaving me to explore on my own. There is a warmth, a heat under the confines of her dress. "I want you to remember this. Remember the last place this hand is until our flyby. Our dance is coming."

I grip her thigh and higher between us. Her sigh breathes in a rush before I take her lips with mine. Our tongues and mingled moans stretch on and on. I start to feel that familiar shift in her weight and mine too. I want that flyby now. We would have had it too, if I hadn't felt the vibration of my phone in my jacket pocket.

Dylan and I separate breathless. Her lipstick is smeared beautifully and while I'm proud of its placement, it's a dead giveaway to anyone around us. "I've messed up your perfect lips. I'm sorry."

She traces her finger lightly over them. "I'm not. At all." She wipes away any evidence from my face then sucks on the pad of her thumb with one last bit of temptation for me. "I'm going to sneak down the back hallway to the ladies' room and reapply. Next time, I'm using your pocket square to clean up, so you have a souvenir. Be glad your jacket is long. I'll find you inside."

I growl a bit as my hand separates from her skin but smile as she walks away. I turn my attention to my phone as it vibrates again. *Fuck.* The incoming texts break the walk in the clouds I was in. It's from Wes inside. The message is clear.

Tori 911.

Instant reality mixed with anxiety kicks in. I reposition my jacket as I weave my way back into the main room. Wes and Tori are easy to spot. She's hanging all over him at a secluded table, along the bank of windows near the stage. He's trying to keep her calm and seated, which isn't working. Her boy toy is nowhere in sight.

When Tori stresses, she tries to chill with a glass of wine. One glass would do that. She's on I'm guessing glass three. Glass three Victoria isn't easy to reason with. Glass three Victoria is dangerous. "Jesus, Eli." Wes leans in. "She's... in a way."

Her makeup is a little streaked on her cheek. Her wine glass in front of her is nearly empty. "Thanks for keeping her company. Victoria?" I can see she's winding up. Her eyes narrow in my direction. I lean back into Wes. "Get me a cloth napkin, two glasses of water, and a strong cup of coffee, black. Do not stop for anyone."

He nods and quickly leaves. I sit down beside her, trying to assess the situation further. "Tori. Are you alright?"

"Do I remotely look alright? Jesus. He left me here." She slams her handbag on the table. "Can you believe that? His whore calls and he's off after writing a big check. He told me I'm a big enough girl to get myself home and he'll meet me there later, if I'm good."

"I'm sorry about that. It's not kind, what he did."

"And then, there's you." She tries to smooth the hair away from her face.

"Me? What about me?"

"I saw your speech. You always could take charge of a room. Your co-chair, as you called her, she's pretty."

"Yes. She is. What are you getting at?"

"I saw you. I. Saw. You."

It all starts to click. The texts came in the middle of my kiss with Dylan. There were no physical witnesses, but I never considered behind the darkened glass. "What did you see?"

"Not the Eli I know. Hidden hands and tongues. She's a little young for you, isn't she?"

"Leave it be, Victoria," I growl.

"There. See. I knew it. Your eyes don't lie. Does the rest of you?"

"Dylan has nothing to do with this. You've had too much to drink. Wes is going to bring you some water and a coffee to sip on. Once you're sober enough, I'm going to put you in a cab and send you home."

"Home? Alone? Not a chance in hell. I'm going to stay."

"No. You're not. Not like this."

"Make me a better offer. I would go home with you though."

"You can't come home with me. No. That's not how this is going to work."

"I know how much you hate scenes and confrontations. Please don't force us into one. Dance with me." I've been so busy playing damage control I didn't notice the music had gone from dinner appropriate to after party. "Things haven't changed that much, have they? You can do one dance. I know they're still your favorite. If you do one dance with me, I'll go quietly. I promise."

Ironically, U2's "One" is playing in the background. I don't want her to ruin Dylan's night. I don't want her to cause a scene that inevitably I'll have to explain. I'm hoping Tori will keep her promise and one dance will guarantee she'll leave quietly.

Dylan

I love the small battle scar of lipstick across my face at Eli's doing, but he's right. It won't do for tonight. Later however, I just might have to put it on so he can smear it off anywhere he wants. I can still feel the pulse of his fingers on my thigh under my dress. His sign for a flyby isn't too far behind. After what he just gave me, it can't be. I'd say we have a window of about thirty minutes very soon.

The thought of that excites me to no end. I hope for Eli it will take away some of the anxiety he's feeling. I wish I understood why he cares so much if she's here. I guess the point is that he does and it's not for me to understand why. As I'm about to pull the door open, I hear U2 faint in the background. It's perfect. We can get a dance in, then with a whisper from whomever cracks first, we can sneak off quickly to have a small secret to carry the rest of the night.

I walk back in the ballroom down the short staircase. By the second stair I see it. In the center of the room, silver sways in my line of vision. Everything comes to a halt in that one second when I realize another woman's hand is in the hand that just touched nearly inside me. Her head is resting on the shoulder that belongs to me. Eli's other hand is in the small of her back. Dancing. *They're* dancing.

I can clearly see a familiarity with them. He knows how to hold her. They move like one. People don't stop and stare when they're near each other. Tori. It has to be Tori. His wife. They fit. They *still* fit. Every insecurity I've had is playing like a movie right before my eyes. I stumble down one more stair before running literally into Wes.

He's at the bar. He looks at me then follows my line of sight. His eyes scrunch up tight, muttering one word, "Fuck."

"Yeah. Perfect word."

"Viper. It's not what you think."

"Or it's *exactly* what I think. Dicks before chicks, right?"

I can feel Wes quickly behind me, as I want to get closer so Eli can see I'm watching him. The closer I get, the sicker I feel. I've never seen him intimate with anyone before. I've thought about it, but seeing it is way different. Standing there, looking at her in his arms, is worse than if I would have caught them in bed. I wonder if he understands that?

We lock eyes and a chill washes over me. I don't think there are any words that can fix this. I turn away from him, him holding her. I vow to make sure I finish the business at hand for the foundation and tonight's event. That's bigger than me. But that's it. That's all I'll be able to stomach.

Wes cuts into their dance. I get a long, well-placed smirk from the silver wrecking ball. He's trying to keep Tori occupied long enough so Eli can try to talk to me alone. "Please listen to me."

"I can't listen. I don't want to listen. Do what you're going to do with her. *Maybe* I'll be ready another time. But not today. I'm going to stay to see the evening through for Sam and his event, then I will say my polite goodbyes. I'll be the only one not making a scene tonight."

"Viper..."

"No." I hold up my hand. "Just no. You, of all people, should understand what I just saw and how it feels." I have to walk away with some dignity before I cry, before I scream, and before he truly sees how much he just hurt me. Although with what I just said, there should be no mistaking it.

Ariana Rose

Chapter Twenty-Five

Dylan

I stayed up all night doing the only thing I thought would calm me down. I rehearsed. Ballet. Contemporary. Lyrical. Crump. Hip-hop. I even made a fusion of the five. It all sucked because nothing can take back what I saw, how I walked away, how I hurt him, and how he didn't come after me. Simply, I hate how Elijah and I left things yesterday.

I've only had one love in my life. Dance. That's the only thing I have to judge love by. It's the only love I trust completely. It never lies to you. It makes you free. You're never confined to one being. You're allowed to take on whatever spirit moves you from the music.

That's what I should have told him. It's not about her. I'm more confident than that. It's about the dance and what seeing them together represents to me. Elijah has never lied to me about anything. I should've listened.

I look around inside my studio apartment and he's everywhere. I didn't realize how much. His tie is hanging over my ballet bar. His slides are next to mine by the door. The scent of the candle he bought me because I said it smelled like him, still lingers in the air.

We're twisted together.

I'm in love with him. It's not just about the dance. I love him.

I need to see him. I need to apologize for getting so angry and tell him why. He didn't try to hurt me. I just didn't want to listen. I was angry at myself and not him, because I was actually insecure about her, when all I had to do was trust in what he's always said. I need to tell him I believe him. I need to tell him I've chosen. I need to say I love you before I lose my nerve. I start digging in my duffel bag for my car keys. I should take the subway, but when you suddenly realize how you want your life to be, you want it to start as soon as possible.

The entire drive over to his apartment I'm talking to myself. I'm deciding what I'm going to say and how I'm going to say it. I swear to God I hit every light between my place and his. With each stop, I'm rescripting what I want to say. I think the poor guy, who was next to me at every light, thought I was fucking crazy by the time I got to Elijah's.

The morning doorman is there to greet me with a wide smile. The ride in the elevator is the last few seconds I have to practice the final version. What it boils down to is: I love him. That's it. Simple. Straightforward. *God, I hope he says it back.*

I walk, and partially run, down the hall to his door. It's early, like 8:00 am, early for a Sunday. I hope he's not on a run. Maybe he's cooking his special breakfast. *Jesus. Breathe.* I take a deep breath while I pull my hair down from the bun on my head. I'm sure I look like a wild mess. Then I think for a moment. It will be how I looked the first night we met.

Reaching up, I knock on the door, softly at first. The longer it takes, the more my heart sinks. I come to say I love you and he's not even home. This is my luck. Just when I decide to leave, I hear footsteps inside. He is home. *Oh my God. Oh my God.*

I hear the chain falling away from the door and the dead bolt turning. As the door cracks open, his vintage *Joshua Tree* T-shirt hits my line of sight. Only, he's not the one wearing it. It's the shirt I was wearing just the night before last. She's got flawless olive skin, dark eyes, and wild dark hair. She looks different than she did last night. She used to have his last name. Tori.

"Hi. May I help you?" she says.

I'm surprised I'm able to form a full sentence. "I'm looking for Elijah. Why are you here?"

"The question is, why are you? You left last night quickly, from what I recall, leaving Eli to finish the night on his own. I stepped in."

"That's what I need to discuss with him. Where is he?"

"My *husband* went for a run. He should be back soon. Is there a message I can leave or would you like to wait with me?" She opens the door wider. I can see a trail of her coat, handbag, and her silver gown leading around the corner.

Like a punch to the gut, all the air leaves my lungs. Even if you put an ex in front of that word, she's got a hold on him I don't have. She's been the thing he so desperately needs. Goddamn. "No. I don't want to *wait* with you." *I don't want to be near you.*

"We haven't been formally introduced. I'm his wife, Victoria."

Wife. The more I hear that word, especially from her, I want to puke right here and now. "I... I'm Dylan. We did meet last night sort of. You might not remember."

"I think I know *exactly* who you are. I'll tell him you stopped by. Next time, call first, just in case."

My stomach rolls over. *Next time?* "There won't be a next time." As I awkwardly turn away from the door, I can feel her eyes stare into the back of my head until I'm halfway down the hall. I hear a small laugh until the door latches. I sprint for the elevator. I jam the button over and over, praying this one time it will make the car come quicker.

Once the doors close me in, I double over in hysterical tears. I grab the bar that wraps around the inside of the elevator. My grip turns first a pale pink then white. I find it harder and harder to breathe with each floor I descend. As a dancer, you look for the holes that rip you open and climb in. I know I've found the biggest hole of my life.

Chapter Twenty-Six

Elijah

I've been out running since six thirty in the morning. I don't usually power out a two-hour run on a Sunday morning, but I didn't want to be there when Tori woke up and left. Having her back in what used to be our apartment felt totally wrong. Not just because of it being a space I'd spent a lot of time reclaiming away from her. It was also because of Dylan.

It was Dylan's perfume I wanted to smell when I rolled to her side of the bed. It was her socks I wanted to complain about laying all around the couch. I wanted it to only have her mark. But I couldn't let Tori leave last night in the condition she was in.

The type of drinking she'd been doing; I didn't trust a cabbie to make sure she got home alright. Now this morning, mostly sober, she can take that cab or rideshare and it will be over. I slide my key in the lock and open the door. The smell of eggs and bacon hit me instantly.

She's got my dining table set for two, classical music playing softly on the speakers, and one of my flower pots as a centerpiece. "Hi," she says, setting my plate on the table. "I even had them send us a paper like we used to."

"What... what is all this?"

"It's breakfast, Eli. Our normal Sunday breakfast."

"Victoria, there's no more *our* normal anything. It's nice you wanted to make me breakfast as a thank-you for the inconvenience but..."

"Inconvenience? Is that what I am now?" she responds.

"Victoria, we're divorced. We've been apart for nearly three years. You've... moved on. I'm sorry things went south for you last night, but I've finally got my shit together after what you put me through."

"You're blaming me?" she screams.

"Tori, facts are facts. Blame won't help anyone. It took the help of several good friends, my family, and a beautiful woman to find me again. I don't want to go back in time. I don't."

Tori takes a couple steps back. "Does it matter what I want?"

"Of course, it matters. It should matter to you. I want happiness for you. It's just we will never be us again. I want more for myself."

Five words. Five simple words it's taken me years to say to her.

"Who is she?" Tori asks.

"It's really none of your concern. Dylan has nothing to do with you."

"Dylan. The tiny blonde from last night?"

"I don't want to discuss her with you."

"I don't think you'll need to discuss this with her either. She's seen it. She knows the score."

My heart roller coasters from my throat to my stomach and back up again. "What do you mean, Tori?" I allow my voice to rise. "Answer me."

"She was here about half an hour ago. She was looking for you. She got the hint."

I stalk toward Tori, praying I can keep calm. "What did you say?"

"I said that you were out for a run and..."

"And what?" I growl.

"I said I was your wife. Technically that's not a lie. She saw the remnants of last night in the front hall."

"Fucking Christ!" I tear off through the apartment, tossing all of her clothes from last night off the floor and into her arms. "I bet you were all too happy to let her think we fucked too. Goddammit. What must she think? You need to go *now*. I'm going to find her."

Tori stands there in the middle of my apartment as I blow past her to pull on my jeans and boots. She finally looks around at what was once where she lived. I can finally see her eyes register that everything is very different.

"Even after I came home to find *you* in this place, in our bed, with *him*, I never *once* said I hated you. I never *once* wished anything bad for you. How could you fuck me over again?"

"Oh my God." She drops the bundle in her arms lower. "You love her."

I stand before the woman I once loved, as I slide on my leather jacket and say it for the first time out loud clearly, "Yes. I love her."

My bike is the quickest mode of transport I can get to. I abandon Tori to shower, change, and close the door behind her. I ask my building security to lock the apartment after they see her leave. I am on a singular focus. I need to get to Dylan.

There's so much damn traffic for a Sunday morning. The sound system in my helmet is giving me a string of beats that's only making me more impatient. I weave from lane to lane, hoping to gain a few seconds.

If only I hadn't gone on my run, I would have been there to open that door. If only I'd just driven Tori home last night instead.

I pound on Dylan's door for a couple of minutes before I run over the other places she could possibly be in my mind. There was only one sure bet. The performance hall. I race across campus and violate several laws doing so. I ride up the wrong way on a one-way because it's faster. I park on the sidewalk because I don't want to waste time looking for a space.

The side door is propped open with a rock. No one would notice unless you really looked. Quietly, I pull the door open. The music is loud, louder than she ever plays it. She likes it loud enough to feel it in her soul but not shake it to the ground.

I recognize the artist immediately. It's Sara Bareilles. She's not an artist Dylan usually picks. She loves music that rides the border between playful and angst or a hard driving beat. This song feasts in the middle of sadness. It's minor chord after minor chord.

The side door leads to the right stage wing. I slide my sunglasses into the front of my T-shirt while I undo the chinstrap of my helmet. Finding an opening between the curtains, I peel back the heavy velvet while never taking my eyes off her. Her movement is pensive and broken. I've never seen her move without a slickness to it. She's usually smooth, like a hot knife through butter.

This is very different. Her hair is even more wild than usual as she slices through the air with her fists. She growls and starts the music over. The beginning of the song haunts with several chords before Sara's voice cuts through. The first lyric talks about the pull of the woman to another. It's about how it happens again and again. It's eventual. Like gravity.

She pushes herself from standing center stage off the soles of her feet, into the air with simple points of her toes. Dylan again doesn't land with the subtlety I'm used to seeing in her movement. It's heavy, like she has an anchor attached to her. She wraps her arms around herself but claws at her skin to move that touch away.

She's following the lyrics with her movement. Drowning in love is captured with a deep bend to her back that allows her hair to graze the floor. She trickles her fingers over her neck then takes a hold of her ripped crop top and pulls on it like the imaginary water is eating at her skin.

Dylan rotates in the air in a couple of leaping circles, landing in a deep knee bend. She clutches over her heart and her belly like she's in clear physical pain. I slide along the wall and down the stairs off the stage, so I can see her from the front. I need to see her eyes.

She turns quickly. I think she hears me. She doesn't. Dylan stands tall. Her hair shielding her face, she raises both arms over her head and accents the beat with fists to the sky. She shakes them to the lyric, defying the notion that she could be tamed and under someone's power.

I've never wanted to tame her. She is exactly who she should be. I wouldn't want her any other way. The same chorus echoes again. The sentiment of being set free is what echoes for me. What does she want to be set free from? The image of Tori? Expectation? The clear conflict and pain she's in? Me?

The music begins to build like a geyser just below the surface. She leaps so effortlessly into the air, before crashing to the ground in a calculated roll to her back, then to her knees. Her musicality and stature are nearly as captivating as her unequivocal raw emotion. She's dancing a diary entry. I shouldn't even be watching, but I can't tear my eyes from her. In fact, I lean in by wrapping my hands over the orchestra pit rail.

She pounds the floor of the stage from her knees with the side of her fist as well as the flat of her hand. Finally, Dylan flips her hair back, and I can see her eyes for the first time. The tears are flowing down her face.

Her chin rises, and that's when she sees me watching her. The tension in her jaw grows infinitely at the sight of me. The pure anguish she's been pouring out across the stage is now mixed with a fiery anger.

She keeps pounding the floor on her knees while she locks into me. Dylan is in a battle. She's fighting feelings. She's fighting herself. I think she's fighting me. Her finger points straight at me before her disjointed movement carries her in calculated kicks around the stage.

The higher Sara's voice soars, the deeper in despair Dylan appears. The words "keeping me down" roll like a wave from the stage, through me, and into the back of the auditorium. Is that what she thinks of me? The last lines repeat the first. It's about the pull of the woman to another. It's about how it happens again and again. It's eventual. Like gravity.

The last chord rings into silence. Her chest keeps heaving. She leans heavy on her right hand. I'd like to run to her. I don't think she wants me to. I want to say something. I don't know what the right thing is. I lead with the first thing that comes to mind, right or wrong. "Viper?"

"How did you know I was here?"

"I went to your apartment. When you didn't answer, this was the next logical place."

"I needed to think. I needed to escape." She finally flips her hair back off her face with her forearm. Her fingers slowly wipe away the tears still falling from her eyes.

"That was... intense."

"It's how I feel."

I don't want this figurative and literal distance between us. I walk back across the rows and up onto the stage. Dylan has since moved forward so her legs are dangling over the edge into the pit. Getting close enough, I want to touch her, hold her. I don't think I can take the sting of her rejecting me so I get as close as I can.

"Tell me with your words how you feel."

"Reality hit me hard today. The dance was about me swallowing the pill and acknowledging what is."

"What's the reality as you see it?" I ask.

"I'm a distraction for you, just as you are for me. I don't fit in your world. You don't fit in mine. You have your wife back. I know you struggled without her for so long. I'm happy for you that you can get your life back."

That knife she wields that's usually smooth just got jagged in a hurry. "What do you mean you're a distraction? Fuck that you don't fit. As far as Tori, nothing happened with her. She was drunk as hell. This is what I tried to explain, wanted to explain. She threatened to ruin everything for you, for us. She couldn't make it home in that condition. After you left, I had no choice for her safety. She slept on the couch. That was the end of it."

I don't know if she believes me or not. If she does, she doesn't say anything. She only shakes her head a little. "I've felt the reaction when we're out together. The looks we get at work functions. The crap you'll take for me because of my age. The half-truths you need to tell your family. You're trying to find something through me you missed the first time around. It's too much. It's all too much. Actually, meeting your wife officially today puts everything in perspective. Someone like her is what you need. Someone with a certain wisdom and who just knows how to not take away from you."

"Dylan, you've never *once* taken anything. You've only given to me time and time again. How can you think otherwise?"

"Elijah, I don't think we should see each other outside of the office anymore. If you want Skye to even take over my internship evaluation, I'll understand."

This is not just her having a reaction to Tori. This is about something much deeper. This is about what the song said regarding me holding her down. Or maybe, the dance was about me. She was dancing for me. I'm the one gravitating to her and she feels she holds me back.

"Dylan, how can I convince you that what we are is real and works?" She takes my hand in her lap. "You can't."

"Look at me," I beg her. "Look at me."

She doesn't let go of my hand and finally turns her head. "Don't let anyone dull who you are. Your soul is here in this room." I inhale deep. "I told you that if you weren't happy, I'd let you go. I came to find you because I need to tell you something. I want you to know, I still want you to know, I love you. I'm sorry it took me so long to say it out loud. I said it to you once while you slept. I'm sorry that it's not enough. I still want it to be the last words in this space between us."

I lean over, pressing my lips deep into her cheek. As I stand, our connection breaks, and I walk away slowly to the stage door. I can feel that hole begin to rip open in my chest again. I can't turn around to see if she's watching. I can't know if she's crying. I can't.

The sun that was out on my way to find Dylan has given way to a light rain. The drops cool my neck. I sit motionless on my motorcycle for a long time as the water begins to seep behind the collar of my jacket. I can feel it bleed into the cotton of my T-shirt. I back my bike off the sidewalk. Revving up, I take off down the street and decide to take the long way back, along the Hudson River.

My sunglasses still shield my eyes as I ride. The raindrops are coming faster and harder the longer I roam the parkway. My mind gets lost in my thoughts. I remember everything that happened with Tori and everything I shared with Dylan. It's now blending together in a blinding video, ending with the water cutting into my skin like razor blades.

The wind blows into me, pushing my bike toward the puddles pooling on the shoulder. I slow on the throttle as I exit on Seventy-ninth. The wheels catch in a hydroplane. Both lanes are blocked in front of me with cars at the light. If I brake, I'll flip. If I don't, I'll hit one of these cars head-on. I can't jump the curb. I don't have the room to lay it down. I can't…

Ariana Rose

Chapter Twenty-Seven

Dylan

I pull the sleeves of my sweatshirt down over my hands and curl up on the stage floor. I cry until I can't cry anymore. I don't have tears left. He said he loves me. I've been told I love you before. It never felt like that. It's the same feeling I have inside when I dance. It's a feeling of purity. Fuck, what have I done?

He'll be better in the long run. So will I, I try to convince myself. He wants a wife and kids. I'm not saying I don't want that. I do. Just not for a long time. We're just not at the same points. He says it's fine. I don't want just fine for him. He deserves everything he wants right now. He's waited long enough.

After I peel myself off the floor and pack my bag, the first thing I do is shut my phone off. I know him. He said what he said in the moment, but he always comes back to try and work it out. That's who he is. I can't hear that right now. If I have a hope of giving him his freedom, I have to be stronger than he is.

I stand outside my apartment for a long time, trying to find the courage to go up there and start to face the memories. He's still everywhere. I still want those memories, just not today, maybe not even tomorrow. A hotel for the night or two seems to be my only option. I walk to the Washington Square Hotel and get a room.

Closing the blackout shades is the first order of business. Next is sending two emails. One to Eli and copying Professor Stone, stating I won't be in class tomorrow due to illness. The second is to Skye telling her I won't be at the office after class for the same reason. A broken heart should be considered an illness.

The down duvet on the hotel bed calms my body enough, sometime around eight, so I can sleep some. I wake up at two to stare at the ceiling in silence until about five in the morning. After I cave and hit the mini bar, I sleep hard from eight until three in the afternoon.

I can't tell if my stomach is sick because all it's had in the last thirty-six hours is alcohol, or if it's the ache in my heart, or some true illness. Food delivery brings me chicken noodle soup, a baguette, and two liters of water. It's my recovery special.

I'm glad I don't have Tuesday classes to deal with, but it does mean I have to work ten to six at my internship. I'll have to see Eli tomorrow. I can't call out again. We have another presentation at the end of the week for the Roark Foundation. I know how much this means to Eli, Sam, and everyone involved. It still means everything to me. It must come out right.

The soup settles my stomach relatively quickly. I call the front desk for a wake-up call at seven so I can get back to my place, my life, to figure out how all this is going to work.

Even for how much I've slept, I don't move from one position all night. I haven't been this tired since the nights before my showcase. I've never felt emotions like this before. I can only assume one is a product of the other. After settling my bill with the hotel, I make the brisk walk back to my apartment.

I purposely make myself later than usual, so I only have enough time to think about a shower, clothes, hair, and makeup. I don't want time to look around or get in my head. Get in, get right, and get out is it. I cut it even closer than I intended to with traffic on the subway.

The meeting is right at ten. I wanted to get there thirty minutes early so I can be overly prepared but that didn't happen. I walk in off the elevator through the glass doors with only about five minutes to spare. I'll have to wing it as best I can.

I wave at our receptionist. She seems intense on a call. I know she wants me to stay and talk but I point to my watch, letting her know I'm late. I race to the boardroom, smoothing out my skirt and blouse before I give my ponytail one quick fluff. I open the heavy door to find the room empty. Did I get the day wrong? No. Even my calendar had reminders for today. Sam had the day off and was even flying in.

I circle back through the office suites and things are quiet. Too quiet. I don't get it. This is not how I want to start the day, but I need to find Elijah to figure out what's going on. All the blinds on the glass exterior of his office are drawn closed. His door is open a crack, however. The large desk chair is spun facing away from the door. I clear my throat to get his attention.

The chair slowly spins toward me but it's not Eli. His assistant, Anna, is sitting in his seat. I can tell she's been crying. "Hey. What's wrong?"

"Oh my God, Dylan. I've been trying to get a hold of you for almost two days."

"Yeah. I'm sorry. I had some personal things happen, so I went off-grid for a bit. Do you know what happened to our meeting this morning? Is it moved?"

"I need to tell you something, but I don't know how."

I slide into the chair in front of her. "It's okay. Just tell me."

"Dylan, Eli's in the hospital. There was a horrible accident. He was riding his motorcycle in the rain on Sunday. He hydroplaned. The police and witnesses said he tried to lay down his bike but ran out of room. His helmet saved his life initially, but he's in intensive care, in a coma. It doesn't look good."

I want to scream. I want to cry. I feel sick to my stomach. My whole body starts shaking. "Anna, what hospital?"

"He's at Bellevue. Andy and Jack are there with Evie and Lily. Hayley's been running back and forth with Wes between here, there, and the houses. I was getting the morning pickup ready when I just couldn't take it and sat in his chair."

"Get it all ready and tell Hayley not to come. I will go to them. I need to be with him."

I get up out of the chair and take a few steps before my knees start to shake. I reach out for the door frame to hold myself up. "Dylan?" Anna's voice calls to me. I hear it in a fog, nearly like I'm dreaming this whole thing.

"I'm going to get my sneakers on and my hoodie from my desk. I'll be right back."

I hold my left arm across my stomach and use my right hand to balance against the walls until I reach my cube. I slide the glass door open and little pieces of him greet me. There is the dried rose he took from the centerpiece from the holiday party and put in a tiny vase behind my keyboard. The antique Degas wall plaque he gave me for Christmas. The snow globe that reminds me of our trip to Vermont.

I don't want to make any of this about me, but I need a selfish moment. I sit down in my chair and find the tears again. He told me he loved me that day and I didn't believe him. I sit here and look at these things, and it was there if I'd only chosen to look past the surface.

I don't like to admit when I'm wrong or when I'm young or naïve. I was, and am, both. He never should have had to tell me. The proof was in every time he spoke. He came to find me, to tell me, and I sent him away. Those words he said could have been his last. They were given to me.

Ariana Rose

Chapter Twenty-Eight

Dylan

I clutch the tote Anna packed for me to my chest on the cab ride to Bellevue. I've only been in social settings with Eli's mother and grandmother a couple of times. His father and grandfather only know me as his intern. Hayley knows about us. Wes knows. How can I look any of them in the eye? I did this.

The cab drops me off outside the emergency department. I stand there looking at the automatic doors open and close, over and over again, as people file in and out around me. One man stops just in front of me to my right. He lifts up the brim of his baseball cap and turns back to look at me.

"Dylan?"

It's Wes. He's only ever seen me looking like a wild club dancer, dressed in a ball gown, or wrapped in one of Eli's sheets, not like a corporate executive. I didn't recognize him either. He's never got a hair out of place or lets the stubble on his face get too long. I can tell he hasn't slept, and maybe not even showered, in a couple days. "Wes. Hi."

"Fuck. I've been trying to call you."

I feel that shake coming back to my knees. "My phone was off."

"Come on, let's go. I'll take you up."

He tugs on my elbow to get me to follow. I don't move. My feet have become part of the concrete. "Wait." I take a firm hold on his forearm. "Just wait. How bad is it? I need to process that part here first."

Wes rubs the side of his face. "Let's go sit on that bench over there." He switches the duffel he was carrying to his other shoulder and guides me back to the bench. He sets his bag down and tries to take mine. I don't let him. There's a piece of Eli in here. I can't let it go.

I search his face for any glimmer of hope. I can't find it. "I'd like to be able to sugarcoat it for you, but there isn't enough sugar in the world."

"What happened?" I ask.

"No one knows why he was on the bike or why he was riding along the river, but he was. We got that downpour late in the morning. He was on his way back to his place, we think, when the exit and the water took him out. He never rides this early in the season." Wes holds his head in his hands. "Why was he fucking out there?"

I suck back a sob. "Me. He'd been with me. We'd been rehashing what happened on Saturday night. Thinking about it now, it was stupid. I went over to apologize Sunday morning. He wasn't there, but Tori was."

He sighs. "Fuck her. Dammit."

"She was in his T-shirt and had clearly stayed the night. I never really believed he'd been with her in any type of way. I know how he feels about cheating. He'd never do that to anyone. But…"

"But what?"

"The things she was saying. Seeing her in his place just amplified all the things I'm not and not ready for. He wants a wife and kids. I'm nowhere near ready for that."

"You fucking broke it off with him, didn't you?" His voice climbs.

"Don't yell at me. I did what I thought was right for *him*. He settled for years. I didn't want him to do that for me. Now it might cost him his life." I bury my face in the tote bag, wrapping my arms tighter around it.

Wes wraps his arm around my shoulder and pulls me to his chest. I feel his chin settle on the top of my head. "I'm sorry. Fuck. I just want to understand."

"He told me he loves me."

"I've known he has since summer. He walked into that club one person and walked out another. He was alive because of you."

"Was?"

"I mean is. Is."

"Now he might die because of me."

He sits me up and shakes my shoulders a bit. "Stop it. I'm not going to let you think like that. If you can't stay positive, then I won't take you up there. Blaming yourself isn't going to change shit, and the family doesn't need it."

I take a deep breath in and exhale out, while wiping my eyes with the back of my hand. "I need to talk about it, but now isn't the time. You're right. Tell me what I need to know."

"It will be a shock to see him. He's got cuts and bruises all down the left side of his body. His shoulder is pretty fucked up. He's not breathing on his own right now. The shoulder took the first hit, but his head took the second, third, and fourth."

"What does that mean?"

"The helmet saved his life. He's got a skull fracture. From the MRI and CT, it shows it from here to here." Wes draws an imaginary line on his own head. "There is a brain bleed causing some swelling."

"What are they doing about it?"

"Nothing right now. They're trying medication as a first intervention to see if the swelling goes down."

"If it doesn't?"

"Then they will have to relieve the pressure with surgery. None of this means Eli will be Eli again, even if we can get him through this part."

If. Two letters, one syllable. I hate it.

"Take me to him."

I walk a half a step behind Wes at first, until he reaches back for my hand. I take it for many reasons. One, I'm scared. Two, he's scared. Three, he's giving me something to focus on so I keep moving. But the most important one to me, I feel like he's forgiving me, which allows me to try to forgive myself.

Elevators. I'm growing to hate them. They haven't taken me anywhere good lately. The bell dings on the sixth floor and the doors open. We walk straight into this massive waiting area together. There are pods for each family who has a loved one on the floor. They have the comforts of deep leather seating, tables, a pitcher with cups around it, and a charging station.

I zero in on Andy right away. He's sitting on the short couch, staring off into nothing with his glasses resting on top of his head. Next to him is Eli's grandmother, Evie. They're holding hands like Jack and Rose at the end of *Titanic*. It's that don't let go grip. Her free hand is clutching a tissue that seems to have been well-worn by tears or just by holding it. Jack is pacing in front of the nearby window on his phone. He's rubbing his forehead back and forth as he speaks. I've never seen him untucked or sleeves rolled, ever. He's both today.

Eli's mother, Lily, is holding Hayley on the other long couch. Lily's hair is pulled back into a sleek ponytail. She's got an oversized cardigan sweater on which she's using to partially cover Hayley, who is curled into her mother's side with her legs tucked behind her. Hayley's eyes are closed. Wes still hasn't let go of me, and I haven't let go of him. "Hey, everyone. I found someone downstairs." He sets his duffel down and finally pries the tote from my hand to set down beside it.

Hayley startles, her eyes open to Wes's voice. "Dylan," she cries as she flies off the couch, wrapping her arms around my neck. I'm stunned a bit at first, but then bury my face in her neck and hold on. "I'm so glad you're here."

I whisper in her ear, "I didn't know. I'm sorry. I didn't know."

She sniffs. "I tried to call and call."

Jack, ending his phone conversation, comes over to address me. "Dylan. Anna said you'd be coming by. Thank you for doing that so Hayley could stay with us."

"You're welcome. Is there any news?"

"No," he replies. "Not yet."

"The tote has everything in it you asked for." I look down at the floor as I scratch the nail of my thumb deep into my hand. "Can he... Are they allowing visitors?"

"Just family and one at a time," Lily responds.

"Oh. I see." I don't know what else to say. My heart is pounding in my chest. The beast inside me is screaming at the top of her lungs. I want to see him. I need to see him. I don't care that they don't know about us. I don't care how bad it is, I want to be there at his side. I want to tell him I'm sorry. I want to beg him not to leave me.

"Mom. Dad," Hayley interjects as she holds my head to hers. "This is Viper."

"What?" Lily responds.

"Hayley. It's okay. Don't." I pull my hoodie tight around me.

"Don't what? Mom, Daddy... this is the woman Eli's been seeing. This is who's made him so happy. It's Dylan."

Jack slides his hand onto Lily's shoulder. "So you attending all the work functions as his escort wasn't about networking for you post-graduation?"

I stand up a little straighter but don't let go of the sides of my sweatshirt. "No, sir, it wasn't. I'm sorry we didn't tell you the whole truth. Eli and I talked about it and thought it was better to keep our personal lives out of the office. People had already been making comments about our working partnership, our obvious age difference, and playing favorites. We didn't want, or need, the added conversation for you, our clients, or for us."

Andy rings in from behind them. "You did a good job of keeping it that way, young lady."

"We weren't trying to be disrespectful. We met before I knew who he really was. He was just Goose to me."

Lily smiles at the reference. "He's only allowed Wesley to call him that."

"Yeah well, I let her in the club as a favor to Eli." He winks.

"I didn't know he was Elijah Sawyer until he filled in for Professor Stone. Things just went from there. I got the internship, and we started working on the account for the foundation for his friend together."

"You don't have to justify it to us, dear. Dylan may be a stranger to us, but Viper is not." Evie reaches her hand out to me. I step closer and take it. She squeezes my hand tightly. "You're shivering and your hands are like ice. Come sit next to me."

I settle in next to her and tuck the bit of hair that's fallen out of my hair tie behind my ear. This is not how I wanted them to find out Eli and I are together. Now that they do, the sky isn't falling. They aren't angry.

They don't look at me any differently. The woman I've heard called Gran a thousand times is here with her arm around me. Her tenderness reminds me of Eli.

"Daddy? Don't you think we can talk to the doctors and get Wes and Dylan on some list, so they can be with Eli? You know that's what he'd want."

Jack nods in agreement. "When we get our next update, I'll make sure of it."

"Thank you." I lower my head and focus on my hands. "Thank you very much."

"I don't know about everyone else, but I could do with some coffee. Anyone want to walk as well? Evie, be my date?" Wes asks.

"Mom, why don't you, Lil, and Hayley go with Wes and get some exercise? We'll take the next run."

Andy kisses Evie's hand in encouragement. "You can borrow my best girl, Wes. Sweetheart, make mine cowboy style."

She pats his hand. "I'll bring some sugar in case you change your mind. Do you want anything, Dylan?"

"No, but thank you, Mrs. Sawyer."

"You can call me Evie or Gran, dear."

I smile as she tilts my chin up with her fingers. Before they go for the elevator, Lily takes her sweater off and puts it around my shoulders. Hayley gives me one last wave as the doors close. It's only then I slide my arms in the sleeves of the sweater and wrap up. That's when I notice it. It's the unmistakable scent of Yves Saint Laurent. This is Eli's sweater. I pull the top of the threads to my nose and inhale deeply, until the scent reaches the bottom of my lungs. I'd give anything to smell this on him.

"Why Viper?" Andy asks.

I shrug. "I'm a fan of the movie too. Seemed right at the time. It just stuck, I guess. It gave me a way to just be me and for him to just be him. Made it easier."

"I know your father. I can see that."

"I figured you might. You both might."

Jack sits down to my left, so I'm sandwiched in between them. It feels nice and extremely nerve-wracking in the same breath. "Paul Cooper is hard to miss. I would have thought you'd intern for your father."

"It's complicated."

"Family and business can be, but it doesn't have to be so." Andy pats the top of my folded hands.

"I've noticed."

We sit there for a split second in silence, until it's quickly broken by the sound of footsteps coming toward us. I look up from the athletic-style shoes that enter my line of sight. Following the royal blue scrubs upward to a beautiful woman, who appears to be in her late thirties or early forties. The name on her white coat is Katie Collier, MD underscored with Neurosurgeon. She has flowing, dark black hair that's pulled back in a full bun at the base of her neck.

"Good morning, Mr. Sawyer."

"Dr. Collier. Good morning. Do we have an update?"

Eli's grandfather's hand clamps down a bit over mine. It's a physical sign of him holding his breath. "Well, we have good news and news that remains to be seen."

"Tell us something good first," Jack says.

"Elijah has been relatively stable since he was brought in. The vent has been keeping his oxygen levels up, which is helping us in the fight with any conditions that could arise other than his brain injury. However, the swelling in his head hasn't started to decrease yet, which could mean we will have to go in surgically. I'm only comfortable giving it a maximum of another four hours to see a marked decline in pressure. If not, I have an operating room and team on standby for tonight or sooner, should something emergent arise."

"Are you expecting that?" I ask.

"Dr. Collier, this is Dylan Cooper. She is Elijah's girlfriend."

I haven't heard it said like that before. He's never said it. I've never said it. His father just said it like he's done it a thousand times. It takes all the air from my chest. I quietly offer her my hand while I wait for her answer. "Hello, Dylan. The answer to your question is complicated." She sits down in the chair beside us. "We've kept Elijah in a coma so his brain will need less oxygen to function. I know it sounds counterintuitive but it's a good thing. We are also giving him medication to keep his overall pressure down. That's what I'm hoping will help."

"If it doesn't?" I ask.

"If it doesn't, we will do a burr hole procedure. I know that sounds scary and it is, but it's common. We drill small holes in the skull in the area that needs the blood taken away. If we have to, we can leave a drain in to assure all the fluid has been removed. These incisions can be closed with sutures or staples."

I feel a flutter in my belly and a heaviness in my head. I'm feeling completely flushed, but a shiver runs from my hands down my spine at the same time. "I need to see him. May I see him?"

I try to stand up and don't even make it before Jack slides a hand to my back and Dr. Collier takes both of my hands. "Sit down slowly, Dylan." She rotates her fingers over my pulse, glancing at the ticks of her watch. Andy hands me a small glass of water. "Your rate is a little elevated. Drink that cup slowly. Just sips and take a few deep breaths."

"Please. I need to see him," I beg.

Dr. Collier holds her hand over my knee, weighting it to the ground. "If the Sawyers sign off on it, and you won't pass out on us, then I think I can get you in."

Tilting the paper cup in my hand, I pull it to my lips and feel it shake. "I'll be alright." That's a lie. I won't be all right until Eli is.

Chapter Twenty-Nine

Dylan

I've never had to be in a hospital like this. No one close to me has ever been really sick, or worse, in my life. Both sets of my grandparents died when I was too young to remember. My mom and dad are healthy. I've only seen the inside of an emergency room with an occasional ankle or knee injury. Wes gave me the rundown outside. I acted like I knew what I was in for. I didn't.

Our waiting area is outside of the bays of rooms. There's a glass wall and these heavy security doors that separate the two. Jack comes with me to sign in and have the nurse allow us back. The buzz of the door alone makes me jump as the door begins to swing wide to let us pass.

Everything feels so different on the inside of the wall. It's like another world. There's one large central desk. This seems to be where all the doctors, nurses, and care staff meet. To each side is a wing of five rooms. They're all enclosed with more sliding glass doors and privacy curtains. Each room has its own story. Each room represents a family and someone they love.

"Eli is in room four." Jack points around the back of the desk. I'm taking in so many noises at once I don't even know where to begin.

There's the low hum of conversation at, and around, the main desk. There are beeps, buzzes, and alarms at the same desk but in varying volumes from every room. There is a whoosh every time a door opens or closes on one of the suites.

The smells I think are the worst. I feel like my head is in a bucket of sanitizer. As if I wasn't sick to my stomach enough, my nose nearly burns from the chemical smell. We stop outside of Eli's room. Jack motions toward an upside-down foam bottle on the wall. We both pull a pump into our hands before Jack opens Eli's door wider.

I look down at the track of the door on the floor. It's like the edge of a cliff. Once you go over, there's no coming back. Jack ventures inside past the curtain, sending it along its own separate track. I can see the foot of the bed. There's a blue woven blanket over him with a thinner white one on top of that. His legs are perfectly still.

I feel this large lump in my throat. I can do this. I have to be close and let him know I'm here. Jack turns to me. "Dylan? It's all right. Come in." He extends his hand across more than the simple few inches we're apart. He's offering to be a bridge through my fear to be with Eli. I reach for his hand to take my first step across that threshold.

The light is dim throughout the room. Even the shades on the two small windows are mostly drawn. All of the light is focused on Elijah's body. It's like it's lit with a spotlight. Wes, for the first time since I've known him, understated things when he said Eli was in rough shape. His gown is only attached at his right shoulder. His left arm is in a splint and tied across his chest in a sling. It looks like a bird's broken wing.

There are several different wires coming away from his body. There's a clip over his right index finger. There are five wires taped to different points on his chest, along with a maze of tubes coming from the IV on his arm. I can see a few ripples of his muscles peeking out from beneath.

There are too many cuts, bruises, and stitches to count on his skin before I even make it to his face.

Elijah's head is wrapped in white all the way around the crown. His left eye is so many shades of purple and black underneath and along that same side of his nose. There are deep scrapes to his left cheek that are now starting to be masked by his growing stubble. His father lays a steady hand on Eli's chest. I can see within an instant Jack's breathing sync with his son's.

That's the only thing that's not completely still. His chest. I can see it mechanically rise and fall with the hiss of the ventilator breathing for him. The life I've seen in Eli since that first moment in the club Labor Day weekend is gone.

"Dr. Collier says we should talk to him and touch him as much as we can. She feels it can make all the difference in his recovery." All Jack has done until this moment is be concerned about me. I know what my pain level is and can't imagine the amount he's in. I reach over to put my hand over his on Eli's chest. I close my eyes and pretend it's just Goose and Viper on a beach, in the shower in Vermont, or sneaking away to the Hamptons alone. I know better. I want the memory for just a second.

"You're his hero. You know that?" I tell Jack.

"I suppose that's the tale of a father and a son."

"It's more than that. My heroes are dancers, activists, and artists. His hero is you. We've had so many conversations about how you inspire him in life and in business. The way he talks about you and his mother is pretty special."

Jack's voice cracks. "That's nice to hear. So nice."

"I know I'm kind of here out of left field. Thank you for being good to me when you didn't have to."

"Like my mother said, we've known about Viper for a while. She put a smile back on my son's face. She brought light back into his heart. He's more himself now than he has been in years. My wife and I, our whole family, are grateful. Do I wish you hadn't felt the need to hide it? Of course, but I'm not angry."

"You could have been. We brought this into your business and our age difference could have been a concern. I didn't know what could happen."

"Does it feel right to you when you're together, Dylan?"

"At first, no. I didn't think of us like that. He was attractive and fun. I thought that's all it would be was fun. It was still fun, but..."

"Feelings got involved."

"If I'm being totally honest, my parents don't know about us either. My dad was pissed enough I was interning with AnSa, let alone if he knew I was seeing Eli. My dad has very specific ideas about my life. None of which have anything to do with what's important to me."

"Learn a lesson from this. Life is too short to be doing something or being with someone you're not passionate with, or about." Jack flexes his hand just enough so my fingers drop to wrap around his. He takes the tips of my fingers, squeezing them with his. "Would you like some time alone with him?"

"Yes, if that's alright with you."

"It's perfectly fine with me. I won't go far. I'll just be right outside."

He bends to kiss Eli on the forehead, just beneath his bandage, before laying a hand on my shoulder, giving it a gentle squeeze. I reach to touch his hand in return, but his fingers slide away just before I can. I hear his footsteps behind me until Jack glides the door open, then closing it even slower behind him.

I fold my hands in front of my lips. My thumbnails rest against them, and before I know it, I'm nibbling on them. My heart is still pounding hard. It has been since before we first came into the room. The sound was all I could hear initially so I wasn't able to really clue into the noises around me. I did hear the vent moving air in and out of his lungs. What I didn't notice were the other things I needed to pay attention to.

The blood pressure cuff high on his left arm powers on and off every five minutes or so. I can see the numbers register. I feel they're high for him. Too high. The symbol of O2 on the screen is his oxygen level. The wires on his chest are scanning the beat of his heart. That's the most important thing to me. Watching that line is like the pulse of a song. I run the tips of my fingers slowly over the tattoo on my neck, the pulse through the heart. As long as the line is still moving, he's still with me. If he's still with me, I'm still moving.

There is a tiny patch of his bed open under where his arm is folded across his chest. The deep V I know is there, under the sheets, gives me a small place to slide in next to him and be closer. I wish I could rest my head on his chest to feel his heartbeat under me.

Instead, I reach across for Elijah's right hand and hold it gently in mine. I press lightly across the tape holding the needle in place. The small birthmark at the base of his ring finger is nearly covered. From the moment we met, I was attracted to the strength of his hands.

The way he uses them to illustrate a point. He's sometimes overly animated. The way he held me as I danced. The way I was able to easily spin inside them and know I'd be able to stop. The way he pushed my wrist into the pillar. Every time he's held my back with them.

The thing I'm struck by now is how weak he feels. I hate it. More than anything, I hate how it didn't have to be this way. "Why did you get on your bike, huh? You shouldn't have been on it. What were you thinking?

It's too early to ride this season. I'm so grateful your helmet protected you. I couldn't get within ten feet of that bike and you'd ask where mine was."

I hold my temples between my thumb and middle finger and sigh. I can feel all my emotions blending inside me. "I'm sorry. I'm so sorry. I'm not usually a jealous person. You know that. But when I saw you dancing with Tori, it was something different. I should have just told you seeing you dancing with her, for me, was like watching you have sex with someone else. Often, it's more intimate to me. I should have just said that instead of not letting you explain then walking away.

"That's what I came to tell you Sunday morning. When she opened the door, it was a double knife. You know? She knew what to say and how to say it. Also, it was because I saw what you had with her. She was in our space. It became the space you shared together, not the one you had with me. Every insecurity I never let you see was magnified a thousand times.

"I wish I could go back and do it over. I would never have left. I would have gone home with you. We would have gone to bed together and done Sunday breakfast our way. You never would have been in a position to be on your bike."

I can't finish. I remember first what Wes said. Blaming myself isn't going to help him. The second thing is what Jack said. Talking to him, touching him... those are the ways to connect with and help him.

Music began our bond. We physically touched then let our own music follow. I reach into the pocket of my hoodie, underneath Eli's sweater that still blankets me. I surf into my music, diving into Eli's playlist. I hope he'll hear me at least through this.

Dialing through the different songs, I scroll back and forth. Each one has its own meaning or another way I can pull at him. I keep stopping on the same one. It's from one of his favorite albums. It's the song that brought us together in the first place. I slide my finger over the triangle to start the playback.

The first notes of the guitar fill the space between us. I turn up the volume just enough, so it blends with the beat of his heart. The lyrics. The lyrics have always been made for us. The thing that's different this time is I can't look into his eyes. I close my eyes and pretend I'm looking into his.

I remember every move from that first night. His fingers in my back. The way they slid into the grooves between my ribs. I'd spun like a wild ballerina in his hands, and he never lost hold. The song says so many times over and over again, I'll wait for you.

I am waiting, Eli. I'm right here.

Leaning in, I press my lips as close to his as I can get. The corner of his mouth and cheek begin to tremble beneath mine. Is he moving? Am I imagining it? I open my eyes to be sure. The movement is expanding to all parts of his body. The monitor starts beeping all over the place and so fast. His hand is twitching in mine. I slide off the bed as the door whooshes open.

Three nurses and Dr. Collier rush in. I can see Jack standing in the hallway. I'm so confused. One of the nurses blocks my view. "You'll need to leave."

"What's happening?" I try to get past her to see Eli.

"You'll need to leave now. Go in the hall."

She walks me backward while all I can see is chaos in front of me. Eli's body is twitching. His legs that were once still are twisting side to side. One nurse is lowering the head of his bed flat while trying to hold his head still without restricting his movements.

"Someone, please answer me," I cry.

I feel a tug on my biceps from behind. "Let them work."

Jack's pulling me out into the hallway, away from where I can see Eli. "No. I need to be with him. What happened? Why aren't they saying anything?"

"I don't know, Dylan. I don't know."

Jack doesn't let go of me. We both watch into the room terrified. Two nurses are on the far side of the bed. One seems intent on his vital signs. The other is putting some kind of medication into his IV. Dr. Collier and the nurse who forced me out are on this side. The doctor is checking things with Eli's head. I don't know quite what but she's doing what I was dreaming I could, checking his eyes.

In what feels like forever, Elijah slowly begins to settle. All four of them talk over his body before the two on the far side stay near Eli. The nurse who backed me out walks past us without a word to the main station. I turn and call out to her. "Isn't anybody going to talk to us?"

Dr. Collier comes out of Eli's room immediately foaming her hands. As she's rubbing them together, she watches all the disinfectant disappear before she answers my question. "Mr. Sawyer, Dylan... What you witnessed was a seizure. I was hoping Eli would avoid this, but he didn't."

Now I'm the one shaking in Jack's hands. "What does this mean?"

"We gave him medication to hopefully prevent any other seizure activity. Unfortunately, I think we've reached that point I was talking about earlier. I'm having my team assembled in the operating room. We need to remove the blood to relieve the pressure now. I'm going to get ready while they prep him. I'll come out and speak to all of you when the surgery is finished. Stay hopeful. Okay?"

I can't even begin to formulate a single question or response before she's gone through the heavy doors. I hear them click closed and shudder. In the few seconds we'd been talking to the doctor, Eli was already set for transport. The sliding glass door of his room was pulled wide to accommodate his bed being wheeled into the hallway.

The harsh fluorescent lights make the cuts and bruises on his body even more evident. "Wait," I beg. I lean in and kiss Eli's forehead, where his father's lips had been not so long ago, then move my lips toward his ear. "I know you heard those lyrics. Leave off the with, I can't live *without* you."

As the bed rolls farther and farther away, I realize my phone is gone. "Where's my phone? I was playing music for Eli on it when..."

"We'll find it."

Jack and I both go back into the empty suite. I thought it was eerie in here with all the alarms before. Now I hate the quiet they leave behind even worse. The only thing left is the muffled sound of music. At the base of Eli's bedside table, I see the back of my phone case.

The microphone and screen are facing the floor. Jack bends down to pick up the case to hand it to me. The song that's playing isn't one I've heard many times before. Eli must have added it. As I clue into the lyrics, it's what I wish he would wake up and tell me. *I love you 'cause I need to.*

I grip the phone and hide my eyes with both hands in a lame attempt to hide my sobs. Eli's father pulls me in for a hug. My hands and arms are pinned between us. I'm trapped. I'm in this nightmare I need him to wake from.

Ariana Rose

Chapter Thirty

Dylan

The way back to the waiting room seems so long. When I walked it the first time, I was hyper aware of every sight and sound. Coming out, I see and hear nothing. Eli's grandfather has dozed off in one of the chairs. Nothing would change by waking him, so we let him sleep until the rest of the family returns.

The look on my face left nothing to question when they did. Wes knew it instantly. I wanted so badly to comfort someone, to be that cheerleader saying everything would be okay. I'm usually that person. I'm that person for Eli. I couldn't form the words. I heard them all from Jack. I processed them. I didn't have any way to communicate that made sense.

I hold on to Eli's sweater wrapped around me, as each person who loves him wrestles with their fear in their own way. Wes takes off his ball cap and throws it against the wall. Hayley sets her coffee down in front of me, grabs her coat, and leaves for a while. Evie holds on to Andy and him to her. Eli's mother takes a seat by my side to hold my hand.

We both keep an eye on the surgical timer. One of the nurses came to explain this to us. On the wall in the corner is a large monitor. With this monitor, you can see where your loved one is and what stage they are in.

If they're being prepped, you'll see it. When they're brought to the operating room, the code will change, and the clock will start. When they finish, the board will update to recovery.

The instant the board switches Eli's status to the operating room, Jack comes over to rest his hands over Lily's shoulders. The clock begins its painfully slow tick upward. First by the second, then by the minute, and finally by the hour. After the hour mark, I can't sit still anymore.

I give a small smile to Lily before I gently slide my hand free to walk away over toward the windows. My instinct when I have nervous energy is always to dance. If I leap high enough, turn fast enough, slice through the air hard enough, nothing will win but me.

I hold on to the windowsill and stare out. Without thinking, I begin my warm-up routine as if I was on the ballet bar. I roll out my right ankle first, then the left. I bend and flex at the knee to loosen them up. I rise to pointe in my tennis shoes and back down again. Over and over. I center myself in fifth position, rolling my neck slowly counterclockwise.

"Is ballet where your heart is?"

My head comes to center position then I look to my left. Eli's grandmother, Evelyn, is standing next to me. "Not completely. I did years of it growing up. I prefer contemporary, hip-hop, and lyrical. Not necessarily in that order. I'm supposed to have an audition for a company at the end of the week."

"Congratulations. That's exciting. I took some ballet lessons in my younger days too. Andrew and I do some ballroom on occasion."

I smile. "Eli told me. He asked me to teach him a few things that I do. I assumed he'd never danced before. So, I showed him. I put on a little music one night in my loft and he took me in hold. I was in total shock, especially when he started doing reverse turns. He's really quite good."

Eli told me that between you and his mother, he could fox-trot and waltz by the age of eight. He was always surprising me."

"And he will again."

"I want to believe that."

"Then do. There is one inevitable truth about all Sawyer men."

"What's that?" I ask.

"They never give up."

Andy walks over to give Evie a kiss on her cheek. "They've just changed the board. Eli's in the recovery phase. Hopefully, we'll have an update soon."

She smiles so wide her eyes nearly disappear. "See what I mean?"

I nod, but when I'm alone, before I return to the leather pod, I take in two huge breaths and let them go. One is for me. *He made it.* The other is for him. *Keep breathing.*

I wind my neck back and forth in my hands as I take my seat next to Hayley. She reaches over with her right hand and takes mine. I feel something cold and hard against my skin. I flip our hands over to see the Sawyer crest on her thumb.

"When did you get that?"

"They mentioned to Dad it was in Eli's belongings. He asked to have it. My father was going to put it in his pocket. I wanted to wear it instead for luck and a connection to Eli."

"I get it."

The heavy doors open again as Dr. Collier emerges from behind them. She's tugging on the cap over her head that hid her hair. She's balling it up in her hand as she approaches us.

"Hello, everyone. Are we all here?"

Wes tries to keep it light. "Physically, yes."

"I'll take it. So, Elijah had one more small seizure just prior to us starting. It came and went quickly so we were able to proceed. For those who weren't here earlier, we drilled two small holes into Eli's skull. From those two holes we were able, with guidance from imagery, to drain the blood that was causing the pressure in his brain.

"We're cautiously optimistic we won't have to do anything more invasive. It might take him quite a while to wake up. Once we're convinced his vitals are stable, we'll move him out of recovery and back into the ICU."

"What are things we have to watch for?" I ask.

"That's a good question. We decided to remove his breathing tube after surgery. We'll continue to monitor his oxygen levels, blood pressure, and the pressure in his head. We've added an antibiotic to his IV as a precaution in case of infection."

"When will he wake up?" Lily questions.

"Eli will wake in his own way and in his own time. I wish I could set a timer for you. This is a trauma unlike anything he's experienced. He might have holes in his memory or lose time. He might not act or react like he used to. Try not to make too much of it for his sake or your own."

Eli remains in recovery for a couple of hours before he's transferred back to the Intensive Care Unit. As much as we all want to see him right away, we have to go in shifts. I don't mind going last. Everyone asked if I wanted to go first. I don't feel like I deserve to.

Andy and Evie need to go home to get some real sleep. They go in first. I offer to call Anna and give her an update, so she can let all the AnSa employees know what's going on. I find a secluded spot in the far corner of the waiting room. We're the only family left here.

My call didn't take long. I gave her enough information so an email could be sent, and a press release could go out. I pretended to be on the phone for much longer than I was so I could get a few minutes to myself. The minute the doctor left, the thing Wes told me not to do happened. I started the blame game in my head.

If I'd stayed and talked to him at the gala, we wouldn't be here. If I'd waited with Tori, we wouldn't be here. If I hadn't chosen to let him go, he'd never have been on that bike in the rain. The pain that's been in my heart for days, and the hours I've been here, radiates throughout my body.

My head is pounding. My eyes are raw from crying. My stomach feels like it's eating itself. I could be sick if the breeze blew just right. "Gran and Pops didn't want to disturb you. They're heading home until morning. You look like shit."

Wes slides into the chair next to me. I toss my phone down into my lap, praying that rubbing across my belly over and over will somehow help the situation. "Thanks. At least I showered today. It is still today, right?"

"Yeah. I'll go home and shower in a bit then come back. I mean it though. You don't look good."

"I'm not feeling particularly amazing in any way."

"What can I do? He's going to want to see Viper when he wakes up. You're about garter snake level."

"Jokes aren't going to fucking help," I snap.

"Oh, I see where we're at. Got it. Get up. We're getting you some coffee."

"I don't want coffee."

"Get up. It's not a request."

Wes is always happy-go-lucky with a smart-ass remark for everything. He's got a tone right now that pisses me off. I don't need to be ordered around. I just want to fucking wallow for a few minutes. Is that too much to ask?

"Fine. Where?"

"There's a little pantry down the hall. Follow me."

He spins his hat backward as he rises from his chair and storms ahead. I toss my phone into my purse as I follow. I'm not as steady on my feet as I was twenty minutes ago, but I'm not going to show him that. If he wants a fight, I'm going to give him one.

He condescendingly holds the door open. "After you."

"Don't act like you're some kind of gentleman all of a sudden."

"Oh, I know I'm not. You needed to go in first so I could do this."

Once I'm past him and inside, he locks the door. His back is to the little window so no one can see in. I charge at him. "What the fuck? Let me out of here."

"No. Not until this is settled. I told you before that you were not allowed to sit and blame yourself. I wasn't going to let you up here if that's what you were going to do because they don't need it, Eli doesn't need it. You suck it up and get in check.

"Pops and Gran are gone. Jack, Lil, and Hayles are not here. It's just you and me now. Give it to me. Let me see it so when Eli wakes up, it's just you and him in that room, not you, him, and the big ball of guilt I see on your face."

"Fuck you." I shove him back. He's nearly twice my size. There's no way he should move, but he does.

"Is that all you've got?"

"Fuck. You," I scream as I shove him again, but this time I bounce off and tumble into the seat behind me. The chair rocks back and forth. The sound of the metal legs on the floor echoes until it settles, blending with huffs, puffs, and pure anger along with Wes's words.

"Yeah, that's right. Fuck me. You think you're the only one who feels responsible? Do you? I could have stepped in and taken care of Tori for him. I could have steered her away from Eli. His sense of honor wouldn't allow it. He knew she would make a fucking scene, like the damn diva she is, if she didn't get what she wanted. Rather than embarrassing the guests, family, and having her figure out about you before you were both ready, he took the bullet.

"That was the start of this whole mess. We all could have made different choices *including* Eli. But none of us did. What happened to him on his bike was an accident. It wasn't because I did or didn't do something, or you, or him. It was a fucking accident that he *will* walk away from because I won't accept anything else. I won't."

"He told me he loves me, and I didn't say it back. I didn't fucking say it back. We always say I choose you. We do. We chose each other. Then I chose to walk away. I basically said his choice wasn't enough. Then he told me he still chose me, *and* he loves me."

"Do you want to say it back?"

"I need to go. Wes, let me out. Please."

"No. Answer the question. Have the fucking balls to say it."

"I'm not going to answer you when I haven't answered him. He gets to know before you." I drag my body out of the chair, reach around him, and pull on the door. I forget it's locked, and my fingers rip from the handle. My feet tangle up as I tumble back into Wes. His hands catch me just under my arms.

I feel like screaming, crying, punching him, but I've got nothing left. When my hand leaves that door handle, all the force that was holding me upright is now dragging me to the floor. I can feel myself sinking lower and lower. It's like my legs no longer work.

"No, you don't." His arm wraps at my waist and he lifts me back to the chair. "You've been here ten hours. When did you eat or drink last?"

"Ummm, coffee this morning. Soup last night."

"I'm no doctor, but damn. Lay your head on your arm. Until he wakes up, you're my wingman. I'm not leaving you. Hear me?"

"Yes." My nose buries into Eli's sweater sleeve. As I close my eyes, I hear several layers of swear words as Wes feeds dollars and coins into the vending machine.

"There's soup in here. I'm going to warm this up and you're going to fill the damn can with crackers and eat it all. Got it?"

I reach back for his hand, hoping like hell he'll take mine. "There's nobody here. It's just you and me. You're scared, aren't you?"

"He adopted me as a brother a long time ago. That's a story for another time." Wes's tone is so different as we talk about Eli. I get a real sense that these two have been to hell and back in ways I don't know about. "He's the smart one. He's the brave one. He's the glue. I'm not willing to think about a world he doesn't exist in."

"I wasn't ready to say it. I choose you was safe. It was true, and he knows what it means to me. Because I choose him, I can't let him give up his dreams. He's never asked me to give up mine. He deserves to be a husband and a father. I can't tell him right now, today, that I'll ever be ready."

"Instead of worrying about what you're not, think about what you are. You weren't here for the clean up after Tori walked out. It took him three years to take the damn ring off and took him an hour with you to feel alive. I thought it was the sex alone, but it was you. You'd move, he'd move. He's always given more than he gets. Not this time. You're his equal. He's not going to give that up. You shouldn't give up on him."

The microwave finally beeps. It's like the bell ending the round of a fight. This round is a draw. We both got things out that we needed to before it turned even uglier. I still need to answer his question, and I will. To Eli.

For about ten minutes, I drink the warmth down slowly while Wes rests his head on his arm and closes his eyes. His hand cups over the top of his hat. I may have even heard him snore once or twice. He jerks awake and looks around confused. I offer him my hand as a place of comfort, if he wants to take it. He does.

I take in about half my soup and most of a bottle of water before I'm even allowed up out of the chair. I answer his silent question of if I'm okay with a simple nod, and I motion with my head for the door. We wander like zombies back to the waiting room. My body is so tired it aches.

"Viper. Catch a few Z's. I'll wake you when Jack and Lil come back."

With the soup still in my hands for warmth, I curl up in one of the oversized chairs. Eli's sweater covers most of my body. My head rests deep in the crack of the cushion. After I close my eyes, I can hear Wes dial someone on his phone. I hear him say, "Hey, Mom." That's the last thing I hear.

Ariana Rose

Chapter Thirty-One

Dylan

I'm punching the air.

I'm so angry. I want to fight.

I leap into the air with my toes hooked to the sky. I land with such force that it vibrates up my body.

I hold my hands over my ears. I don't want to hear the music anymore.

Eli appears in front of me.

He's smiling, but his face is scratched, his jacket and T-shirt are torn, and there's a trail of blood running down his cheek.

Every time I reach out to wipe it away, he backs up.

"Don't," I tell him. "Stay," I say.

"Dylan."

I hear my name. He's calling me from the back of the auditorium.

"Dylan."

I feel a string of chills wave down my arm. When I look down, Eli's hand is over mine. His ring is shimmering blue.

"Dylan?" My chest bolts upright. The hand I thought was Eli's is really his father's. His fingers wrap around my wrist in an attempt to give me a little comfort. "I'm so sorry I startled you. You were talking in your sleep."

"It was a dream. Shit. I mean, I'm sorry." I push the heels of my hands into my eyes, while I try to pull air back into my lungs. "How long was I asleep?"

"A little more than an hour, perhaps. I found you in the chair here. Wes is still out cold behind you."

"Any change?" I ask.

"Not yet. Hayley is driving her mother home for a shower and change of clothes. They'll bring something back for me."

"Can I get you anything, Jack? Water? Coffee?"

"If you had brandy in that purse of yours, I'd take that. Odds are not."

"I switched bags yesterday, otherwise I would." He smiles at my lame attempt at humor. "How can I feel worse after a nap?"

"I think, in this case, it's two things. You didn't have enough time to recover, and reality came back. I came to ask if you want to go sit with him."

"Yes. I do. I want to talk to him. How does he look? Is it like before?" I've still got vivid images in my mind of all the wires and tubing attached to him. The look of his raw, dry lips forced around his ventilator.

"Well, he's missing a bunch of hair where they had to shave a portion of his head on the left side. There are more bandages than before, protecting his head wound. However, with the tube out of his airway, he looks more like my son. When you're ready, I left the chair pulled up next to him for you."

Jack sits down in the chair I just left. I observe, from a little distance, as he peers over behind him watching Wes for a second. Jack's normally the happiest person I know. You can hear his booming laugh up and down the halls at AnSa. I don't think there's ever been a time, until now, when I haven't seen him smiling.

This has taken a huge toll on him. His shoulders are rolled more forward. His eyes no longer shine bright behind his wire-framed glasses. His salt-and-pepper hair now seems more salt than pepper. He lays his glasses over his knee and rubs out over the bridge of his nose into the inner corners of his eyes. Eli does the same thing when he's tired.

I walk slowly back to him in his seat. "Mr. Sawyer? Jack?"

He looks up at me. His eyes are glazed over. I've caught him in something very private. "Yes, Dylan?"

"I know it's probably not proper but... do you need a hug?"

He smiles for the first time since we've been here, even if it's only for a fraction of a second. He slides his glasses back on and rises out of his seat. "You know, I really could."

I slide my hands under his arms, holding over his shoulder blades. The hug in the ICU before was to comfort me. This is about him. As he releases me, Jack gives me a squeeze over the caps of my shoulders and motions with his head for me to go.

I walk away again, but you'd think each step closer to Eli would be easier than the last. It's not. It's a level up in horror and anxiety with every step. I feel like I triggered him last time with the music. It's what I know. It's what brought us together. I have to trust it and figure out how to reach him.

I find myself spending a minute collecting my thoughts outside the entrance to Eli's room. I don't know quite why, but I run through the same checklist with my body as I do in a performance. I make sure every muscle group I have is relaxed. Nothing good comes from forcing it. My hands settle over my abdomen, and I take a deep breath in through my nose and out through my mouth. I repeat this to the count of three. From it, I can find my center but also my strength.

The nurse is just leaving his bedside when I finish. She tells me I can go in whenever I'm ready, and if I need her, the red cross button on the bed will alert her. I don't want to need her, but I'm glad I have the option after not knowing what to do before.

The glow over Eli's body is less this time. Instead of his whole body being in a spotlight, he's illuminated from mid-chest up. Jack was right. He does look more like Eli without the tube down his throat. I slide my purse off my shoulder, setting it on the floor beside the chair before I get close.

His chest is moving so shallow, but at least it's moving on its own. I get the strongest feeling of *here we go again*, as I nest in on the bed at his side. His left arm has been rebandaged and slung tighter across his chest. Eli's right hand is lying limp along his side.

They left his hospital gown off so I can see his chest, or most of it at least. Even though it's only been a couple of days, I've missed his body. For as much strength thoughts, words, and feelings can give you, his body is about action, protection, and adoration. He's so good at making me feel like the most important person in the world.

Pieces of his hair are pointing in every direction out of the top of his bandages. My fingers want to play in the tangled mess. It seems like the safest way I can touch him right now. I gently pull the strands carefully this way and that. He's starting to look like he does when he's sleeping normally.

When I was here the first time, the volume of the alerts from the machines was so high. It seems they've been turned down. It's very quiet now, but it's anything but peaceful.

"You'd hate this silence, Eli. I feel like you always need music in your space or the noise from the street. It's like that's what calms you the most. Things have changed a lot in a few days," I tell him. "Not just you taking a dive for attention either. Your family finally knows everything. Hayley told them.

"Eli, they've treated me so kind. Your grandmother is so sweet. She was asking me all about dancing, and she told me about how she and your pops do ballroom. Your granddad figured out about my father. He didn't question it or ask me why. It was nice."

I try to keep the sleeves of Eli's sweater up on my arms, but they keep falling. Instead of fighting it, I pull them down over my hands, putting them in a blanket of their own. They're frozen and trembling at this point. "Hayley has treated me like a true friend and more. She's okay. I'm taking care of her too. Wes, on the other hand. We got into a fight." I give those words a second to see if it registers any bit of movement or reaction from Eli. It doesn't.

Is any of this talking even reaching him? Can he hear me?

"Your mom is even nicer the more time I spend with her. We held hands for a long time. She thanked me for making you happy. It seems funny to thank someone for that. Did I, Eli? Do I really still make you happy?" *Please answer me.* I slide off the bed from his left side, shuffling over to the windows. It's nearly completely dark outside. There's still a sliver of light left on the horizon, but that's quickly fading to black.

"Your father has been the one holding me and everyone else together. I don't know how he does it. He has this strength and conviction about him. If he says something, I know it will be true. He keeps telling me you'll be all right. He encourages me to hope. You know that's not who I am, Eli. You know I'm the realist. What is real here, huh? Tell me.

"All I want is for you to talk to me. If you don't want me in your life, if you want to be done, I can handle that. What I can't handle is a world without you in it, and I know your family can't handle that either. What do you want?"

I watch his body from afar. His chest rises and falls. The beat of his heart still moves on the monitor. Don't expect him to be the same, the doctor basically said. Does she know what that means? Eli's spent so much time in recent years pleasing everyone around him.

He's happy to do it, and it's a major part of who he is and who he wants to be. But he's finally found himself again. He knows who he is outside of work and outside of pleasing people, including the woman he's attached to. He's feeling and growing and changing and you can see him stand taller.

Does that have anything to do with me? I don't know. "You promised me fun, Goose. This isn't fun. It isn't fun worrying if I'm good enough, strong enough for you. It isn't fun to have your heart ripped out by anything other than art. It isn't fun for you to tell me you love me then never give me the chance to see if I can say it back. If this is a dance, you left in the middle."

Fucking dance with me.

As much as Wes is his wingman, so am I. He let me learn how to be a part of a couple, without labeling it in a way that would scare me. He asked for my opinion constantly, instead of telling me what it should be.

Eli has given me so much. That first night, his hands gave me fire. In class, every challenge he dropped at my feet gave me a new way to look at things. His honesty about relationships built a new perspective. He gave me an additional safe space to explore my dreams without fear or having to hide.

Talk to me, Goose.

My fear of never saying what I told Wes I need to say to Eli is greater than the risk of a replay of before. I poke my finger through the knit of Eli's sweater to unlock my phone. Another thing he's given me is the poetic appreciation for the music of U2.

I'm going to try again. When I explain my love of dance, I tell people it's an outward expression of your scariest, rawest, inward emotions. It's the things you don't dare say because they're too real. I have something to say. It's as real as I can make it. I refuse to say it unless he can hear it.

There's one song I can't get out of my head. It's us.

The lyrics show a push and pull. It shows what one person wants and what the other person wants. Sometimes they meet and sometimes they don't, but at the end of the day all the other person wants is their other half.

All I want is you.

Eli's said that to me a million times. I feel like I've said it between the lines of I choose you, but I need to be sure he knows. I'll give him what he wants in time. I will. He just needs to be here for it.

I turn the sound up loud enough so it covers the little bit of noise from his machines. The beat vibrates next to my heart for a bit before I set my phone down on the table near his head. I want the lyrics to be clear and in his ear.

I've never wanted to dance more than I do right now, with his arms on and around me. I wait for Bono to really begin digging into the lyrics. Staring at Eli's lashes, I pull his right hand into mine. The tape has been changed from before. I can see more of the top of his hand.

I want a mental image of his palm. The imprint is in several places on my body and never leaves, but this time, I want the burn in my eyes instead of my skin. My fingers slide under his IV tubes and press his weak hand against my chest. The tips of his fingers rest over the smallest bit of skin on my collarbone. The usual warmth of them isn't there, but the feeling I get from his touch is.

I close my eyes to let the music fully into my system. I don't just hear it with my ears. I feel it vibrate between my body and Eli's. I let the visions of color the music always creates flow through the bright and dark hues. With my eyes closed, I can remember all the other dances. Just a simple sway with his hand on my chest is enough.

I begin whispering the lyrics to myself. Some words stand out to me more than others. You say. Promises. Love. Through the night. Talking about cradles to graves and begging for love not to grow cold.

His hand is cold, and I never got to say the words.

"Keep dancing with me, Eli. All... I want... is..."

"You..."

A low, dry throaty single word breaks inside me as the fingertips that were once tensionless are now slowly moving against my skin. I gasp as a single tear slides down my cheek. "Say it again. Tell me I heard it."

The pads of his fingers pulse and tug at my skin. "You. Vi...per."

He hears me. He knows me. "Eli. Oh my God. Keep talking." I don't know how many times I press the red cross button, but his nurse rushes into his room within a few seconds. "He spoke. He's awake." She tests a few of his vitals and makes a call out to the nurses' station. She's asked for Dr. Collier to come up right away. "Eli. Do you still hear us?"

"Shouting. Loud. Too loud."

"Okay. Okay. Shhh. Calm down," I whisper and quickly lower the volume of the music. "Are you hurting anywhere?"

"Every...where." His pathetic soft groan breaks my heart into a million more pieces.

"They'll take good care of you. The doctor is on her way. I don't want you to talk anymore. Just focus on my voice." He groans again as his eyes begin to flutter a bit. "That's it. I'm here. I'm right here."

"Never. Leave. Wing. Man." Each word for him was a struggle to find and get out. Those four words reach straight inside my chest, taking hold of my heart.

"No. I won't. I couldn't." Reaching inside the pitcher on Eli's bedside table, I pull an ice chip into my hand tracing the outline of his lips. He sounds so dry. I don't know what else to do for him. I want to do everything, anything I can.

His tongue reaches out for each little droplet that melts into his mouth. Once he's captured them all, he gives me two more words. "Kiss. Me."

"I need to tell you something first. I need to tell you I'm sorry. I need to tell you I'm a coward, and this is all my fault. I need to tell you that I not only choose you, but I love you too. Do you hear me, Sawyer? I love you."

"Knew. It," he sighs. "Kiss. Me."

The doctor and her staff begin filing in. I don't care. I'm not going to let this chance slip by me. I delicately put my hand on Elijah's chest and lean over him to grant his request. The kiss isn't long, but it's meaning is full. I love him and now we both know it.

Ariana Rose

Chapter Thirty-Two

Elijah

I'm having to be reminded of things, simple things, multiple times. Things like where I left my keys, my computer password, and the days of the week are still hard. I can remember everything from my childhood, all my loved ones, and what the forecast projections are for Quarter One next year. It's all so confusing.

My brain has to work so hard at some things and not at all on others. The hardest part is I've called Dylan Tori a couple of times. The words roll out so fast, and I can't take them back or process them quickly enough. It's not happened in the last week or so. I hope it doesn't happen again.

She's taken everything in such a great stride. I could see, even in my earliest fuzzy states, how physically drained she was. She never complained. She spent the first three nights sleeping in the chair next to me until I was pain free enough to insist she move to a cot at least. Dr. Collier helped to find her a fold-out lounge chair. She could at least lie down at night.

Dylan would only leave if someone was with me and was never gone more than two hours at a time. She studied while I slept. She ate when I did. She snuck me in a dessert or two, along with my laptop when I wasn't supposed to have it yet. I wanted so badly to be able to comfort her in ways we're used to. I'd hear her whimper in her sleep, and I'd still be too dizzy, or my head would pound enough that I couldn't get up, so I'd sing to her until she settled again.

By the end of week one, I was up taking short walks around the hospital corridors. By midweek two, I was told I could go home if someone would be staying with me. For her, it was never a matter of if she would, it was when she would be able to get the rest of her things.

My parents drive us back to Central Park West after my discharge. Mom wants to make sure I have a fully stocked refrigerator today, a grocery delivery scheduled for next week, and that I'm safe in my bed. My father has other things on his mind. While Mom forces Dylan to sit at the dining table while she brews some tea, my father sits on the end of my bed while I lie back against my headboard.

"I've spent two weeks in bed. I'd like a different view please."

"I know you're going to do as you please as soon as we leave, so don't make it hard for your mother. Just stay here for now and she'll be none the wiser later."

"Fine, Dad. I'll stay here."

"Son, we should talk about Dylan."

"I was wondering when this would happen. What do you want me to do? Make her quit? Is turning the interns over to Skye enough?"

"Calm down, Eli, it's nothing like that. You and she have been nothing but professional at the office that I've seen. We don't have a fraternization policy. I would like you to be somewhat transparent with the board at some point, but no, it's not about that.

"We adore her. She's your soulmate. Anyone with eyes can see it, which is why you should know this. I know your brain is still foggy at times. I came upon a piece of information. I'm sure she'd rather I said nothing, but Dylan missed her audition last week."

"Audition?" Then it clicks. My mind has been doing these race things since the accident. It's like fast rewinds of periods in time. Her performance piece. Her sadness. Her triumph. My pride. Her in my arms. Dylan sleeping against me on the drive to Vermont. Her two fingers up. Her dream audition. "She missed it. How could she miss it?"

"I think she made a choice, Eli."

"Screw that. She chose wrong. Dad, I need a couple of favors. Will you help me?"

"Eli, I still don't think this is a good idea. They said not to push yourself."

"Dylan, I'm not running. I'm not working. I'm not even doing what I'd like to be doing with you. I needed to get out. It feels like spring today. I just wanted to walk around campus. We can take a cab there and back. We can even stop by your loft to check on things and grab your dance bag."

"Why? I don't need it right now."

"I beg to differ."

After a little more subtle banter, I win. I wasn't going to lose this one. There's too much at stake. The car ride this time of day is about ten minutes. It is damn near impossible to hide the nerves I have coursing through my veins. She has no idea what I have waiting for her.

Our cab driver drops us off at Dylan's loft. It feels like a lifetime since I was here last. I asked her to get her dance bag, but she seems intent on leaving it behind. I'm going to have to take matters into my own hands. Tape. Her favorite rehearsal costume. Hair tie. Music.

I walk along the ballet bar in her home studio and have another one of those memory flashes of our waltz here. My left hand reaches up to touch the patch of peach fuzz on my head where my hair is growing back in slowly.

"Is your head hurting?" When I look up, the panic on her face is real.

"No, Viper. I'm fine. Do you have everything you need?"

"You're alive. Yes, I'm good."

Setting the dance bag strap on her shoulder, I seal it with a kiss. "I'm not leaving you alone. I promised."

She pulls the door open with a level of irritation. "People break promises all the time, Eli."

"That's very cynical, even for you."

Dylan is very quiet as we cross campus. There's a damp chill in the air that I can't ignore. I pull her closer to me as we walk. Her head goes on a swivel to see if anyone is around.

"Beautiful, we're not hiding anymore. I refuse. I thought you were gone. You thought I was gone. There's a lesson in there about wasted time. Don't you think? Dylan, I want you to come with me somewhere right now. No questions. No arguments."

"You expect me to not have questions?" She cackles. "You're kidding, right?"

"Fair enough. The answer to where we're going is the auditorium. The answer to why is because I want you to dance for me."

We march up the steps to the performance hall and enter from the side door, not the back of the house. The lights are fully up over the stage, so the audience is completely obscured. I ask her to get changed and meet me center stage as soon as she is. That should give me just enough time.

I hook up her music to the wireless system and hold her MP3 player in my pocket. Just as I get to the top of the stairs, stage left, she appears. She looks just as she did the first time I saw her dance on this stage. "Damn, you're stunning."

"Eli, you've seen me in this outfit a thousand times."

"Each time is better than the last. Are you warmed up?"

"I mean, as much as I'm going to be I guess. I'm not going to really go hard."

"Yes, you are. You haven't danced in nearly a month. I'm not alright with that. We made promises, Viper. You and me. You once told me any relationship you were to be in wouldn't allow the other person to sacrifice their dreams or compromise your own. Isn't that what you've been doing? Sacrificing yourself?"

"You could have died because I was selfish."

"No!" I shout. "I had an accident. Besides the lovely side effects, I'm glad it happened."

She shoves my chest. "Don't say that. Don't you ever say that to me again."

"That's it. Get passionate. Feel. That's what I want. I want to feel your spirit and fire inside me." I cue up Sara Bareilles. It's the same song she was fighting her way through the day of my accident.

"Shut it off."

"No, Viper. This is what I want to see you dance to. I'm not the gravity. Dance is. Move. Move through it. Move for me." I turn the volume up, so it rings and pings from every single corner of this vast space. "Move, Dylan!"

I start the music again. The first chords, she's frozen. As soon as the lyric starts, she faces me. She reaches out for me with open extended fingers in both hands. The more they reach, the more they shake. Just when she can't reach anymore, all the tension leaves them, and they fall in defeat at her sides.

Her head bows and rolls to the left as her body follows in a canon. Her hands wrap across her chest in a sheer statement of pain. She's clawing at the dance top she has on, and I can hear the fabric snap back on her skin as she lets go.

The cut of this music has a quick build. She takes the three steps in time with it and launches her body into the air. She lies completely out in midair before she tucks and rolls to her side. She ends on her knees; her toes are in full point behind her. Dylan arches her right side to the floor, extending her right leg to the sky. As she does, she pounds her fist into the floor over and over again.

She pushes off the floor through her feet, winding her body to spin and spot one, two, three, four, five quick times before she allows her body to go limp like she's injured. I know how much pain she's in. She's been in pain since the gala.

We haven't spoken about it. We haven't addressed it. She doesn't want to upset me. What she doesn't understand is I've felt it all. If I had the ability, I'd stand next to her and do what she's doing. I'd put it out there. Get it out there just like that. It's moments like these when I'm truly jealous of the instrument that is her body.

Her gorgeous shadow vaults, spins, leaps, and falls through every spotlight on the stage and weaves in, and through, every beat of the music. The song is coming to a two-beat swift close. As the lyric tells us, something always brings me, or her, back. It never takes too long.

Before I know it, the two-minute roller coaster is nearly over. It's two beats. She stops on the first to face me, and on the second she covers her face in gasping sobs, lowering to her knees. Now I can be in it with her. My feet carry me to her where I lower myself down to the floor and crawl a couple of feet to pull her into my arms.

The instant we connect, and she melts into my arms, her once silent audience erupts into appreciation and applause for what we all just witnessed, which is a triumphant return.

"Jesus, Eli. Someone's here."

"There are many people." Lining just behind the orchestra pit railing is Hayley flanked by Wes, my parents, and my grandparents. All six of them in a row. The seventh guest is making her way up the stairs before Dylan can comprehend what's happening.

"Mr. Sawyer. I'm Jill Wallace. Hello again, Dylan. I think we were supposed to meet the other day."

"Oh my God. Ms. Wallace, what are you doing here?"

"Giving you something I don't often give. A rain check. You have a very persuasive boyfriend, Ms. Cooper. This was your reintroduction to dance. I'm going to show the film of today, along with my analysis of your senior performance, to our committee. You'll be hearing from us after graduation, requesting a more formal audition. If all goes how I think it will, we just might be seeing a great deal of each other. Congratulations."

Wes hauls off with a whistle over and above all the claps and shouts of congratulations. Dylan sits stunned in my arms. If I were to breathe too hard, she would likely fall over. "Dylan? Hey. Did you hear what she said?"

"How did this happen?" It finally registers. "What did you do?"

"The day I came home from the hospital, my father told me you skipped your audition. I didn't remember you even had it. I wasn't going to let that go. You worked too long and too hard to just walk away from it. So after a few phone calls, I got a hold of Jill."

"But you're back, Eli. You need me. Your recovery is first."

"Viper, I'll still recover. I will. Do you see all of them? They're behind us. *Both* of us. We're not alone, you're not alone, and if I have a damn thing to say about it, you never will be again." I reach inside the pocket of my leather jacket to pull out a small black velvet pouch. "Hold out your hand."

Her fingers pull away from her lips and shakily lower near her lap. I rise to one knee and cup my hand under hers to help hold it still. Out of the pouch falls a vintage ring. It has a diamond-influenced, oval-shaped appearance with six small diamonds on each side in the channel. In the center is a one-carat round with matching half carats above and below. It's ornate, delicate, and extremely unique, just like Dylan.

"This ring belonged to my great-grandmother, Pops's mother. Gigi was an amazing lady. She was tenacious, fun-loving, stubborn, and had a spirit like no other. She would have loved you. I know I do."

"Get to the question, would ya?!" Wes hollers a millisecond before Hayley punches him in the chest.

Dylan is staring at the ring in her hand like if it moves it will burn her. She looks at it, then looks back at me, and starts shaking her head. "Tell me you don't love me, Dylan. Tell me you don't."

"I can't. But I also can't have everything."

"Why not? You're the one who taught me *I* can. I can be who I am in every part of my life. I'm living again *twice* because of you. You asked me once if I could get married again. I told you to the right person I could. That person is you. Look out there. Look at all of those faces. Those people are your family. They didn't come here today for me. Well, I mean they did, and they didn't.

"They knew what was going to happen, or I hope will happen, and they wanted to witness it. Do we have it all figured out right now? Not even close. That would be boring. All I know is I choose you. Viper, be my permanent wingman. Dylan Elizabeth Cooper, would you please do me the extraordinary honor of being my wife?"

"Are you sure?"

"I'm fucking positive. Be my wife." Her left hand shakes as she extends her fingers out to me. With what I'm sure is the smile of my life, I slide the ring on and over her knuckle. It's a perfect fit. "Say the word. I need to hear the word."

"Yes."

"Yes. So it's a yes, yes?" She nods quickly and wraps her arms around my neck. Without thinking, I stand up and whirl her around in circle after circle in my arms across the stage. Each time we spin, I see something different. A thumbs-up from Pops. A blown kiss from Gran. My parents hugging each other. Hayley jumping up and down applauding. Wes trying to hide a tear in his eye. *I fucking knew it. Marshmallow.*

"Stop. Eli, stop. I don't want you to hurt yourself."

I whirl a couple of times back in the other direction to right us again. "I can't hurt. Not anymore." I whisper in her ear a quote from my man Bono, *"The soul needs beauty for a soulmate. When the soul wants, the soul waits."*

I waited a long time to be this happy. She waited a long time to feel this loved. There *is* no more waiting.

The End

Ariana Rose

Also By Ariana Rose

The Stone Series

Turn to Stone (Book 1)

No Stone Unturned (Book 2)

Written in Stone (Book 3)

Heart of Stone (Book 4)

The Desire Series

Harbor in the Tempest (Desire #1)

All the Promises We Break (Desire #2)

All I Want Is You (Desire #3)

Susan Stoker Operation Alpha

Chasing Paige

Standalones

Surrender

Double Exposure

Guardian Angel

Of Lost Things

The Enigmatic Mr. Sinclair

Interference

February

About Ariana

Author and hopeful romantic, Ariana Rose, dabbles in all forms of contemporary romance. All of her novels do have one thing in common. Her heroes and heroines are as passionate about life and love as they are about each other.

Born and raised in the Minneapolis area, she is a proud mother of two. Ariana has always been a storyteller with a flair for the dramatic. When she's not writing, she can be found at the rink in a figure skating lesson, binge watching her favorite shows, screening an 80s movie she's seen hundreds of times, and exploring history or traveling to any of her current or new favorite places.

Ariana first published in August of 2018. You can find her exclusively in Kindle Unlimited. Also, sign up for her newsletter, watch her website or find her on all her socials to catch all the latest and greatest on upcoming projects.

Always remember that passion is never a bad thing, it's where dreams and reality collide.

Facebook: www.facebook.com/ArianaRoseAuthor

Instagram: @VariationsOnAriana

Ariana Rose

Website: www.arianarose.wixsite.com/arianarose

You can also find her on Goodreads, Pinterest, Amazon, BookBub and Twitter!

Milton Keynes UK
Ingram Content Group UK Ltd.
UKHW030626200924
448513UK00001B/144